Back to Birdsville

Drawing from her earlier life as a rural midwife, Fiona McArthur shares her love of working with women, families and health professionals in her books. In her compassionate, pacey fiction, her love of the Australian landscape meshes beautifully with warm, funny, multigenerational characters as she highlights challenges for rural and remote families, and the strength shared between women. Happy endings are a must.

Fiona is the author of the non-fiction book *Aussie Midwives*, and lives on a farm with her husband in northern New South Wales. She was awarded the NSW Excellence in Midwifery Award in 2015 and the Australian Ruby Award for Contemporary Romantic Fiction in 2020, and was short-listed for the same award in 2023.

Find her at FionaMcArthurAuthor.com

Also by the author

Red Sand Sunrise
The Homestead Girls
Heart of the Sky
The Baby Doctor
Mother's Day
The Desert Midwife
Aussie Midwives
The Bush Telegraph
The Farmer's Friend
The Opal Miner's Daughter
As the River Rises

FIONA McARTHUR

Back to Birdsville

MICHAEL JOSEPH
an imprint of
PENGUIN BOOKS

MICHAEL JOSEPH

UK | USA | Canada | Ireland | Australia
India | New Zealand | South Africa | China

Michael Joseph is part of the Penguin Random House group of companies
whose addresses can be found at global.penguinrandomhouse.com.

Penguin
Random House
Australia

First published by Michael Joseph, 2024

Copyright © Fiona McArthur, 2024

The moral right of the author has been asserted.

Cover photography by Australian Camera/Shutterstock and
Peopleimages.com Yuri A/Shutterstock
Cover design by Louisa Maggio Design © Penguin Random House Australia Pty Ltd
Typeset in Sabon LT Pro by Midland Typesetters, Australia

Printed and bound in Australia by Griffin Press, an accredited
ISO AS/NZS 14001 Environmental Management Systems printer

A catalogue record for this
book is available from the
National Library of Australia

ISBN 978 1 76104 799 2

penguin.com.au

MIX
Paper | Supporting
responsible forestry
FSC® C018684

*We at Penguin Random House Australia acknowledge that Aboriginal and Torres
Strait Islander peoples are the Traditional Custodians and the first storytellers of the
lands on which we live and work. We honour Aboriginal and Torres Strait Islander
peoples' continuous connection to Country, waters, skies and communities.
We celebrate Aboriginal and Torres Strait Islander stories, traditions and
living cultures; and we pay our respects to Elders past and present.*

For Birdsville, an amazing small town
with the biggest heart

Prologue

Phoebe

Eighteen years earlier

Phoebe McFadden, seventeen and wise to her dad's fondness for the horses, tilted her head to watch her only parent straighten the new sign on the front entrance of the racetrack. His strong, lithe frame stood silhouetted by the sun, and she knew his red fringe would be plastered to his forehead under the tattered Akubra. The rest of the hair under that hat would be wet curls.

She'd inherited those curly waves and glints of red from her dad, though hers were long, but sometimes she wished her hair was black like her mum's had been.

'Looks good, doesn't it?' her dad called down.

BIRDSVILLE RACE CLUB INC. ENTRANCE. The green letters stood out brilliantly against the cream corrugated iron and wooden frame.

'Yep.' The sign looked smashing, and pride swelled in Phoebe's chest. Her dad had made that sign. He could make anything. Except, of course, money. Clever, wonderful, exasperating, financially bereft Dad. Sometimes she felt like the parent.

But he'd been her hero since she was old enough to stand up and gawp at him and nothing would change that.

Dad, so tall with his big hat and his heeled boots, ruggedly handsome when he smiled that winning smile. They didn't have much in the way of extras at home – never had, Dad said, since Grandpa made that infamous bet on a long-gone Birdsville Cup and they'd lost the family station – but they had enough.

Dad said he'd inherited Grandpa's luck, which she believed, while she'd inherited her dad's hair. But despite relying on lady luck, Dad always made her feel special and loved. That said, Phoebe remained determined to save her own nest egg for a better life.

From when she was little Dad's blue eyes would crinkle when he crouched down to say, 'How's my princess? You're so clever. So pretty.' And always, 'Dream big, baby. You can do anything.' Yes, she could. And would. And she'd look after him.

Today, he called down from his high ladder next to the old crane arm, 'Is that straight, Phoebe?' Like he did every year when she watched him do repairs to the racecourse buildings.

She laughed because she knew he had his own spirit level up there and didn't need her input. Dad was a gifted carpenter, a sign writer, opal miner, sometime training jockey, barman and a bookie's assistant. On race day, when the tiny outback town could swell from around one hundred residents to thousands of tourists, he was an excited racegoer.

Dad was her world, her small world, since her mother had died when she was little. Otherwise there was only her cousin, Scarlet, Scarlet's parents, and her other aunt – and school in Charleville, of course.

The year before, she *had* made friends – despite their age difference – with a young kid when his family ran the pub for a while. Atticus had only been ten, so there were more than six years between them, but the things he'd come out with! He was fun. Yes, she missed the little jerk. He'd been like the younger brother she'd never had – not that they would have become friends for real, if she hadn't spectacularly stacked her bike in front of him the first time they met.

He'd almost made her forget the scrapes on her knees and hands when he picked her up, telling her stories of the sensational disasters he and his older brother, now in boarding school, had had. His dad had taught them both first aid – they needed it so often.

She'd laughed, shakily, while he offered his handkerchief for the blood, realigned her bent front wheel, and dried her tears with the back of his hand. So grown-up for a kid.

He'd walked beside her, pushing his own bike, when she'd been too sore to ride home, and handed her over to her dad.

After that, Atticus paused to chat whenever he ran into her, and she'd humoured him – she'd even shown him her wreck of a car she would fix one day, the Desert Lizard, in all its disastrous glory and wonderful potential.

He was almost as tall as her despite the difference in their ages, with a smile that could show how glad he was to see her from across the street. She often wondered what happened to Atticus after his family moved on.

She'd run into him a lot when she was at home from school for a weekend or holidays – Birdsville was a very small town – but if her cousin was with her, Scarlet told him to push off. She said the older brother, Dali, was hot, but Phoebe wasn't drawn to him at all, despite him being closer in age to her and Scarlet than Atticus was.

She'd been sad when he said his family were leaving. Sad for the loss of her little mate – almost cried, though she'd hidden it. She'd never told Scarlet that story. Her cheeks heated at the thought of what Scarlet would have said.

She never fancied any of the boys at high school; she was too busy at her aunt's Charleville truck-stop, where she boarded during term time. There, she and Scarlet had learned to cook fast, clean well, and save their money. Auntie Daph believed in women standing on their own two feet – *she* wasn't relying on Grandpa's luck – and Phoebe took those lessons to heart. Any boys at the truck-stop were either petrol heads or cowboys with no manners, and none were funny or kind like her dad, so her heart was never at risk. Besides, her dad was her hero.

Dad, Scarlet's parents, Auntie Bee and Uncle Rob and Scarlet were such a big part of her life that she couldn't imagine not living here in Birdsville when she wasn't at school. She'd be with them forever.

Any time she could, Phoebe hitched a lift home with the cattle transports coming through Charleville Friday night on their way to one of the big stations past Birdsville. Mrs McKay had made it possible. She owned five of the stations in the channel country and she'd told Dad she'd arrange it. And she had.

Phoebe would always choose the chance to sleep behind someone's seat compartment if she could go home – even if it meant ten hours trucking Friday night and the same back on Sunday night – waking with just enough time to shower and head to school Monday. She missed home too much. Seemed sensible to travel since she had to sleep anyway and waking up at home made it all worthwhile.

But schooldays were spent at Charleville High along with Scarlet, coming back to Birdsville for the holidays. Soon she'd have her driver's licence. She'd be able to come home any time, then, with only a year to go before she could get a proper job in their little town.

It was holidays now; she was back in Birdsville before her last term of year eleven, and she'd already worked at the bakery when they were short. Hopefully, she'd get a few days at the caravan park too, and maybe a shift or two at the fuel depot shop if they needed her.

She'd been saving to repair the Desert Lizard, a Land Cruiser, for what felt like forever.

'The paintwork is so beaten it looks like she has scales,' Dad had said, and yes, the outside was a bit rough, though he said he'd help her panel beat and repaint when it was ready to be registered.

The old beast had been a present from one of Dad's friends on her fifteenth birthday. Dad had been broke that year and his mate had stepped in. A throwaway gift that turned into a savings goal she focused on with the intensity of a hungry kookaburra watching a snack-sized snake. Phoebe's red 80 series needed the engine rebuilt. Her good luck that Dad's mate couldn't be bothered selling the rest of the vehicle for parts.

But, for a smile from her, the boys from the garage had promised to help Phoebe get it up and running when she had her licence and could afford the components needed. With her own calculations – and she hadn't counted the stash under her bed since she came home – she was almost there.

Two years of saving. Two years of loving the interior of the car while it sat in Dad's shed, her humming a country song as she polished the old leather seats and wiped away the dust that had accumulated in the weeks she'd been away. That was the saying – *The dust never settles in Birdsville* – and it was true.

She'd saved good money this year because she and Scarlet were both clever in the kitchen and at the cash register and worked hard doing jobs for people. Both stashed coins and small notes away with weekend work. And especially, this month, in the kitchens at the once-a-year Birdsville Races. There was great money to be made this weekend.

Since acquiring the Desert Lizard she'd even saved the present money Dad gave her, often well after the birthday or Christmas, whenever he finally had cash to spare. Sometimes the dosh might come two months late, but always, eventually, he'd give her something. And she'd save it. She could be determined like that.

'Not like her mother or father,' Dad said with pride. 'You're a saver.' He always laughed at the fact he seemed permanently broke. Told her if it wasn't for the horses, they'd be rich. Yet, he'd always covered their needs.

Yesterday had been a big day. Dad had taken her out into the desert again in his car and, after watching her manage the sand hills, had pronounced her capable to drive. She'd already booked an appointment with the police office to go for her test as soon as her birthday came. Couldn't come quick enough.

'You wool-gathering down there, Phoebe?'

She was.

'Hold the ladder, would you, love?'

She gripped it firmly as Rusty began his steady descent from the roof of the entry gate. He looked down and smiled his million-dollar smile.

Such a shame, his daughter thought fondly, we can't bank some of that charm.

Phoebe pushed the ladder firmly against the brown rail to steady it and let go as he landed. Her gaze travelled over the empty ticket lines. So hard to imagine right now, but several thousand tourists would be here for race day, buses dropping them off at the gate, guiding them towards the open yard before the covered public area, where they'd mill around the stalls selling mementos and drinks.

Dad stepped back to examine the sign and Phoebe grinned at him. 'Looks great.'

'That it does.' But his gaze drifted over the long rail stretching around the huge red-dust circuit. He said, 'Two thousand metres in circumference. Did you know Birdsville remains one of only four tracks in Queensland that operates in an anti-clockwise direction? Like the Melbourne Cup.'

'Yes. I did,' she said. 'You tell me every year when we check the ticket office is fine.'

'Do I? Must be a true story.' He grinned at her and she grinned back.

She wondered who he was going to blow his money on this year. No way would she bet hard-saved money. Excitement fizzed. Soon it would all pay off. 'This week I'm going to get my stash and ask the mechanics to fix my car. Get it ready for my P plates.'

Rusty's face froze, along with his body. His gaze pinged back to her and away. Dark brows furrowed, and his mouth pulled down even as he forced it back up with a smile. His eyes slid away again, not meeting her suddenly intent gaze.

She didn't know why, but Phoebe's stomach sank. Were they broke? Did he need her money? He'd promised he wouldn't be silly this year. And the race wasn't even here yet.

Her heart began to pound, and she felt that cold skitter of fear, scurrying like a tiny gecko had slipped into the neck of her shirt to run down her back, leaving a dew-damp trail.

Rusty cleared his throat. 'That's exciting. How about we go to the bakery for a celebration?'

Phoebe's skin chilled more despite the heat. The bakery? That's where he told her he didn't have money for her birthday. A tiny cake in front of her. An excuse on his lips.

As if she wouldn't cry while the staff watched. It worked. She never did.

She narrowed her eyes. 'How about you tell me what happened now? Here. In private.'

She watched him swallow, his Adam's apple bouncing up and down, and she could feel her mouth pull tight as the gecko inside turned cold and dark and stopped in her stomach. Coiled, ready to bite.

He blew out a breath and screwed up his eyes as if he couldn't watch her face. 'I'm sorry, love. I had to borrow it, Phoebe. Your money's gone. But I'll pay you back.' He looked stricken. And ashamed. And lost.

Phoebe opened and shut her mouth. Trying to understand. Trying not to understand.

Suddenly she was more hurt, more horrified, more humiliated than she'd ever been. He borrowed it. Took it? From under her bed? Without asking.

She couldn't grasp the concept.

No. He'd always lost his money but never had he taken hers.

She struggled to get the words out. Had to swallow twice. 'Did my money go on the races?' Had he actually gambled her hard-earned cash?

His face paled and he clenched his hands. Didn't meet her eyes. 'In a way, yes.'

'In what way?' It didn't even sound like her voice. More of a soft croak of horror. So hard to comprehend. Then, not waiting for the answer, she whispered, 'It's all gone? The money for the Desert Lizard repairs? You took it all?'

'Yes. I had to. But I can explain.'

Explain? The hurt closed her throat until she struggled to breathe. She dragged in a breath. 'How could you?' Her eyes stung but she wasn't going to let him see her cry. It wasn't even the money: it was the fact her own dad had stolen from her. He'd cared more for the excitement of a race tip than for his own daughter.

Heck. She'd just been proud of him! Had thought that would never change. What a joke. 'You know what?' She wished she could just walk home but it was too darn hot. She'd melt before she got there. 'I'll wait for you in the truck.' And she turned and walked back to the old truck and opened the door.

That weekend after the races, Phoebe left Birdsville for her aunt's house. For good. She was never coming back.

Chapter One

Phoebe

'Back to Birdsville.' Phoebe McFadden's voice chuffed inside the car with a dryness that matched the dust ball smudging the cloudless sky behind. 'Here be Phoebe McFadden, driving back after eighteen long years.' Where had the time gone?

She had said 'never'. Never coming back. Yet here she was.

But she wasn't going down that rabbit hole of woe. Nicht. Nyet.

Scarlet's wedding would be a joyful occasion. Even she knew she had to be there when her cousin, her best friend from childhood, the one person who understood her and who she could totally rely on, was getting married. There would be fun and – not so much fun – she'd see her dad. She was facing the past for sure.

But she was a scary woman now, or so the junior nurses said, so while she was there, Phoebe would smile if it killed her.

The big bonus would be seeing Scarlet, hair as red as her name, temper that went right along with that if Phoebe didn't arrive early. Scarlet had plans and wanted her there in time for her first Birdsville Races in almost twenty years. That was a week away.

Then she had to stay another week for the wedding, until the bride and groom flew out three days after the nuptial celebrations. So almost three weeks. She could do that. For Scarlet.

Scarlet the larrikin, who'd dragged Phoebe into *so* many hilarious and hair-raising scrapes when they were scrub-kneed devil kids: sometimes she winced at how many times it had been too close to not ending well.

Except for the hair, and the gaze if you caught it, Scarlet was someone you'd pass in the street and not notice. People had no idea how determined the woman was. What a driving force. A cyclone in tiny proportions. Which made Scarlet's new fiancé a very brave man.

Oh, my. Scarlet's wedding. Phoebe could not imagine that white dress on her wildly sensual, rule-breaker cousin. Couldn't imagine her married and settled down to a family of babies, terrible twos, fractious fours – though Phoebe could imagine Scarlet's future offspring turning out just like their mother – but apparently that was the plan.

Really, now she thought about it, it wasn't just Scarlet, but most of Phoebe's friends who were married. Her brow crinkled as she mentally scanned her acquaintances. The ones from nursing and midwifery at uni? Yep. All of them.

She furrowed her brow more deeply. Yes. The majority from work in ED and her post-grad time in maternity were also permanently paired off.

Even the supervisors in the admin office, where she kicked and screamed against being rostered to a desk job purely because she was so good at it, had grandchildren. Even the ones who weren't married were in long-term relationships.

Except her.

Phoebe wondered whether perhaps something inside her had broken when she left Birdsville at seventeen, and now, at thirty-five, she'd only just noticed the damage. Maybe that was why no man had lasted more than a few dates.

What would it be like to go back home? Pretend she fit in. Blend into Birdsville.

Nowhere to hide in a tiny town – that was the kicker.

Though, hopefully, the townsfolk wouldn't remember her. They'd have changed. Left. Arrived. Scarlet had said the average stay was around four years for most families, except for those born and bred or married into the born and bred.

Most left when their children had to go away to high school, other than the many-generational ones, like the McKay family, who ran the big stations and cared about the towns surrounded by their properties. Or the First Nation families, who had lived there for millennia and were a part of the land and the history.

And of course, the gambling McFaddens.

She'd heard the pub had gone from strength to strength and become even more of an icon than before when it changed hands again.

All the outlying families from the immense stations would appear in town while she was there and especially for the races. Upright. Solid. Hard-working and people-focused. She admired those people. No doubt she'd see stateswoman and matriarch Blanche McKay and her son Lex: she'd heard Lex had married and his wife had had a baby. Heard they'd established an organic beef consortium that thrived on overseas exports.

The Birdsville Race Committee were probably old hands too. She used to be so familiar with all those women and men.

So conscientious, community-minded and brilliantly innovative at promoting their town as well as running their business enterprises.

Well, she was a different girl from the one who tore out of the channel country as soon as she could escape. Hurt and bewildered by her dad's betrayal. Devastated by her hero's clay feet. Lost and anchorless, until after her final exams her aunt had suggested Adelaide, where she found her career in nursing and midwifery. Away from Birdsville.

Never to return.

Ha.

Eighteen years.

And yet, here she was, driving from her city home, her home always of course, to Birdsville.

Still, she had to admit it was nice to be in the open country.

Driving north, she could admire the cerise and lilac sunset of the jagged Flinders Ranges, and, strangely, feel the edges of her soul bathed and blessed in unexpected beauty.

Staring through the windshield ahead she found the outback land so welcoming, beautiful, and wonderfully vivid. So big. So brilliant. It was bringing a buoyancy to her spirit she'd forgotten existed.

A long way to drive yet. And so much that had hurt her younger self awaited her. Still. Maybe it was time to forgive.

Explorers Way flew past. Parachilna and Leigh Creek flowed onto Lyndhurst and Marree, and the still-familiar vistas kept her eyes wide and strangely wistful as she headed inland.

In Marree she stopped and stayed at the pub for the night, which gave her time to walk the streets where the famous Mailman of the Birdsville Track had lived. Someone her whole family had been in awe of.

That walk allowed her to revel in the wild west feel of the town and smile at the liquid wit of the larrikins in the bar, until finally she questioned if maybe there wasn't a little bit of homecoming here, a homecoming she hadn't expected and was actually enjoying, and she wasn't even home yet.

The next day, she hit the long, wide plains, those rugged, dry and desolate vistas that made her heart lift with their rocky terrain, until she even hummed a forgotten cocktail song she knew every single lyric to. She and Scarlet had changed the lyrics to 'Making love on the dunes of Big Red . . .' She grinned. Her young virgin self had fantasised about that. Oh, my goodness, she'd been young.

Once she reached the channel country her heart fluttered and swooped, just like the budgerigars behind her in a cloud, as if her internal system had been constrained for years and now clunked free from unseen chains.

Eighteen years. So long. Had she been living as half a person? Had she really been inhibited by Adelaide's tall buildings, the paved streets, the surging population of the city? Had she become introverted for the half of her life she'd been in the city? Had that restriction suddenly departed – slipped away – or was it she who had chained herself by her stubborn refusal to go back to Birdsville? Back home?

As she entered the gibber plains of her childhood, the road grew rougher, noisier, yet still Phoebe's vision expanded further, eyes drawn to the cloudless sky. She could see where slicks of water and past sludge had left the road chopped at the edges and thick with ruts and ready to turn again into a quagmire if the rain came back. But her eyes roamed and she reminisced and recognised the mirages and magic of the country as it stirred that deeply buried something that had been wandering lost and lamenting inside.

Still her tyres ground on over the roughness of the terrain. Despite having proclaimed she never wanted to leave the city again, Phoebe had bought a Land Cruiser 200 Series, with its four-wheel drive and two-hundred-kilowatt engine that were as capable as any off-road bullyboy's ride. Funny she'd bought this particular vehicle on a whim.

She'd lusted after that much older model when she was a kid, and this modern version, painted retro-red by a master spray company, had caught her eye when a rich urban cowboy she'd been loosely dating had scratched the paintwork on a rock shelf, had a conniption, and sold it cheap because he thought perfection had been lost. No, it hadn't. Idiot. And it was red!

Nobody could walk past that bargain. Could they? Maybe. Anyway, she'd kitted her vehicle out for this trip. UHF radio. The hired satellite phone. Two spare wheels and recovery gear in case she ended up bogged in the sand, dust or clay. She'd learned how to use a winch as a kid and Maxtrax recovery tracks as an adult when they came into vogue. Had even played four-wheel drive on the deserted beaches outside Adelaide when she could get away.

She brought enough food for a couple of days and water for a week as well as a thick blanket in case she found herself stranded in the desert overnight. Probably wouldn't need any of it but Phoebe was the kind of woman who liked to know it was there.

A flash of wings distracted her: two Inland dotterels flew out of a small stand of trees and she glanced in the rear-view to watch them. Usually lazy in the daytime, it was odd of them to leave their clever insect hunts beside the road when it wasn't dark, but these outback plovers were a tell-tale sign Phoebe had hit the arid lands.

Rat-tat-tat went the stones under her feet as another cluster of gibber rocks from the Birdsville Track flew up and clanged against the bottom of the car.

Maybe going home wouldn't kill her. A bruise or two as she faced the past. Nothing terminal.

More stones. More shuddering bumps. Lucky she'd worn a sports bra because the juddering corrugations of the road needed moveable support. She and Scarlet used to joke about that.

She spotted dust from another car in the mirror, way back, probably kilometres, but it hadn't been there before so he must be moving at a decent clip. Foot down on the accelerator like an idiot in a place where things change fast.

The stony gibber plains looked a barren habitat, but they teemed with birds and other wildlife. Emus, rabbits, kangaroos and camels came and went, especially at dusk and dawn. With the recent rains, the fauna would be stirring all along the track and it paid to be careful.

She glanced in the rear-view again. Yep, he was flying. Richard Cranium. Phoebe's favourite derogatory title – she used it at work for the idiots.

Disastrous accidents happened on these roads, and she didn't want Mr Head sitting behind her waiting to overtake, blinded by the obscuring dust cloud. That's when drivers lost sight of the road and swerved off the track or pulled out into the path of oncoming cars they hadn't seen.

Easier just to let Dick pass.

She studied the road in front of her, and yep, coming up was another tiny group of trees. She eased off the accelerator, slowed more, letting the dust settle behind her, and gently pulled the cruiser well off the road onto the beaten ground. Others before her had stopped in the packed dirt and maybe stretched their legs, so she waited there for the approaching car to pass.

She left her vehicle running with the air-con to keep it cool, climbed down and closed the door while she enjoyed the movement of her cramped limbs. Arched her back. Stretched her arms and breathed. Lifted and dropped her shoulders.

The silence was broken by the crackle of packaging as she peeled a muesli bar, and the crack of a new water bottle from the first twenty-pack. Phoebe sipped and watched the side horizon for signs of movement, birdlife, and the ground closer for snakes and lizards. Saw a daddy emu rounding up spotted chicks to her left, bless his long legs, and peace settled over her.

It had been a couple of hours since her last stop, and already she'd lost the constant need to rush, to be somewhere – do something. Years of work deadlines had trickled shifts like grains of desert sand through her fingers, eight to ten hours of crisis-fuelled haste. Had she been in such a frenzy for almost two decades?

Surely not. She'd spent four of those years at uni in Adelaide studying, doing practical placements, learning her nursing and midwifery while working evening shifts at the pub to pay her way.

Once she graduated, four frantic years in the emergency department at Adelaide Central had been one adrenalin-soaked moment after another. Then she'd worked maternity and birthing, and despite the mostly soothing nature of the work, there had been crazy times, too, with babies in every room and staff run off their feet.

This last year as after-hours hospital manager had required quick decisions and lots of fast walking, putting out nursing and patient spot fires and ensuring the wards had cover. Her experience in emergency response had upped the ante and honed her spot-the-idiot skills.

Yep, she'd been impersonating a daddy emu chasing chicks for far too long. It was nice to have a month off to do a leisurely trip back to see Scarlet. She blew out a breath. Yes. To see her dad and lay some ghosts to rest too.

A distant roar penetrated her thoughts. Ah, Mr Cranium, or it could be Ms Cranium, she supposed, now tearing up the road towards her. Phoebe's own dusty cloud had mostly settled, and she climbed back into the cool of the air-con and shut the door to keep out the grit.

A whirlwind of heavy metal music, an enormous stockman bull-bar with more spotlights than a fly's eye, aerials whipping like eyelashes, roared past, a yahooing-Richard yodelling out the rear window. Hopefully he had his seatbelt on. Idiot. Temporary Australians if they didn't slow down.

But you couldn't inject brains, so hopefully at least they wouldn't take any innocents out. Eventually the racket and dust and disturbance died down, peace seeped back, a bird flew by . . .

When the dust had drifted down to the road again she eased back out onto the ruts and for the first time in a long time she wanted to really belt out a tune. She turned on Sara Storer and began to sing the lyrics to a song about coming home because she was . . . coming home . . . and nobody would know she was happy about that because they couldn't hear her.

*

Phoebe came upon the crash site three kilometres down the road and turned off the music. The silence hit her abruptly as the sight of the crash made her belly clench. The last of the red cloud still circled from when the utility had rolled. Probably tumbling over and over more than a few times – and nobody had crawled out yet.

Phoebe eased her rented satellite phone from its holder as she closed the distance and glanced at her odometer to check how far she'd driven from Mungerannie Roadhouse, where she'd stopped for lunch. She'd zeroed the tripmeter there. Old habits. Two-fifty. Sixty-fiveish kilometres from Birdsville. Pressed the call button. Knew this scenario was bad.

The signal picked up. 'Birdsville Police station. Senior Constable Bow.' Something familiar about that name. The voice, deep, gravelly and calm, held quiet confidence and felt unexpectedly soothing, like the best paramedics she'd met over the years: long-distance reassurance. A gift for the spike of apprehension in her gut.

Bow? Not an outback name. Except . . . Then she remembered. The pub. The pushbike. The little kid with the kind eyes. Or his brother? Surely not?

Ha. Imagine if it was. The deep, layered tones had the composed cant of someone who couldn't be confounded. Despite the circumstances, she smiled.

Of course he was calm. Not totally unexpected. The police out here had seen things. Managed diverse emergencies. Had to be resilient.

She was used to dealing with police. Hours in the nursing supervisor office, running a major hospital, managing dramas and Richard Craniums.

'Phoebe McFadden. Driving from Mungerannie to Birdsville. Mungerannie is two-fifty back. Just coming up on a rollover – though it's back on its wheels. Bunch of yahoos overtook me ten minutes ago. Can't see anybody moving yet. I'm pulling up now.'

'You alone?' Still laconic. No comment on her name.

'Yes. I'm an emergency nurse, but not a magician. Asking for back-up, please.'

'I'll get right on that.' She heard the smile in response to her comment. 'Be there in less than an hour.' There was the sound of a screen door slamming in the background. 'Hang on, I might have a chopper so we can bring the nurse earlier and the ambulance can follow. I'd appreciate you leaving the call open as you assess the casualties. I'll organise as I listen.'

Made sense. Anything to speed help was a bonus. 'I can do that.'

'Stay safe and hydrated.'

She resisted saying, 'Yes, Dad,' which was probably the first time she'd thought of Rusty without bitterness. Felt a sand grain of comfort at the quiet concern for her in the constable's voice. In Senior Constable Bow's voice. Of course, even if he wasn't who she suspected he was, the Birdsville police officer, a man the whole town relied on in times of crisis, a man with no immediate back-up except his own resilience, would be a decent guy.

Chapter Two

Charli

Charlene Bryce followed Lazy Luke into the pub, smiling a little because she'd been a barmaid, and now, here in this pub, she was a customer.

She'd always wanted to come to Birdsville. Ever since Nana Kate, her last and most understanding foster mother two years back in Roma, had helped her figure out that Charli's mother might have come from here.

Charli considered the stools at one of the high round tables, and glanced around the room to check no one was watching before she tackled it.

The stool was higher than she thought, so she had to hide the fact that her belly stuck out and made her awkward climbing up, but she managed without incident; she dipped her head so her hair fell across the right side of her face, and didn't think anyone noticed her struggle to balance.

Lazy leaned on the bar, and the only server in the place, a tall man, a few years older than Charli, with a scarred face, twinkling kind eyes and a gentle smile, stood talking to him.

She'd made it. And she planned to stay at least two weeks before leaving, and, if all went well or possibly stupendously, she'd be coming back here permanently to settle.

Despite the fact she and Lazy were like stepbrother and stepsister, they were no relation; they had just shared their childhoods through foster care, with a bit of brotherly protection on his side and wry affection on hers. Nothing more, so she'd paid him to drive her the ten hours here on his weekend off from washing cars in a Charleville car yard: she'd owe him nothing after.

Lazy had probably agreed because he didn't like to work. He only stayed at the job he had because it was three hours a day and he could laze around after. Maybe he just hadn't found something he liked, yet. That was her ambition for him. To find a passion for something.

But not wanting to work? Weird. Charli had always enjoyed mucking in to get things done. People liked hard workers and Charli's world depended on people liking her.

Most orphans depended on that.

Lazy Luke depended on drifting, luck and recklessness, and she had her suspicions on how well that was working out for him. Not very, she'd wager, if she was a betting girl. Which she wasn't.

Charli didn't believe in luck. Before she came, she had looked up all the businesses in Birdsville, found four webpages, and had written four emails because someone had said snail mail could get delayed for weeks out here in the desert.

She'd wanted potential employers to know she was staying a fortnight over the race period and was looking for short-term work, and it had paid off, because she'd had one answer from a private caterer already and was meeting her tomorrow.

What she hadn't shared with any of her prospective employers was her promise to the midwives she'd return to Charleville four weeks before her baby's due date. She suspected she might not get work at all if they knew she was pregnant. Fingers crossed: her clothes were loose and luckily her bump was small, and she still had six weeks to go.

But she was here, just Lazy and the bartender and her in the bar; and it felt a darn sight cooler than in Lazy's old ute. The inside walls of the pub were thick sandstone blocks, and the fan spun the cooled air-con air in a gentle breeze.

She sighed with relief and gazed upwards at the cluttered paraphernalia that hung on the ceiling. Rows of hats had been fixed up there and trailed down the walls. Mostly cowboy hats, some peaked caps, and a row of little coloured runners of triangular flags with football teams on. A couple of stuffed animals supplied the quirky and a set of big bullock horns added to the lofty craziness. Lots of stuff.

But best of all – so many photographs on the walls. Framed in huge wood and glass frames. Photo next to photo. Mostly old ones. Many of them with the pub in the background, and people packed shoulder to shoulder, some adults and some kids, all from the past in odd fashions or with old-style cars or horses. She felt her excitement rise as she eyed the walls of forgotten faces hungrily. Somewhere to start looking. Thankfully.

Her heart had sunk when they drove in after such long and lonely roads – that last one hundred and eighty kilometres of dirt from Windorah had left her weary. She'd been taken aback by the few houses, the empty red-dirt horizons stretching away in every direction, the solid wall of heat she stepped into . . . Plus the flies.

But here, in the pub, this was a good place to start her search. Some of the tension eased out of her shoulders. Information should be easier to source seeing as everyone knew everyone else in a town this small. The races weren't on for another week, so most tourists wouldn't be around for at least a few days. She'd known it would be the easiest time to get work with a big event coming up, but she had to time her investigation for when the town was still mostly full of locals. If she had family here, she needed to find them before she went into labour.

Luke brought over a tall glass of lemon squash, the ice clinking, and her thoughts returned to the now while her mouth seemed to wither up in parched anticipation.

'You okay?' His voice was gruff.

'Perfect.' She stretched out her fingers and took the icy cold drink tight with both hands. Not wanting to spill a drop. 'Thanks.'

His mouth twitched and he nodded before he went back to talk to the barman.

Before she sipped, Charlene lifted the cold glass and put it against her cheek to cool her skin. The damp chill felt wonderful, but she lifted it quickly, needing to slurp. She caught the gaze of the barman on her and he smiled. She blushed. He did have nice eyes, but she wasn't looking.

Brown condensation dribbled down the glass. The wetness had mixed with the dust on her fingers, so she wiped her cheek again with the back of her hand. Guessed she'd have a dirty stripe on her face now.

She'd sort it after, because lemon sweetness chinked against her teeth as glorious cold filled her mouth and ran down her throat.

Refreshing. Wonderful. So wonderful she couldn't stop herself from glugging it all down until it was gone.

Fingers crossed she didn't get that indigestion she'd suffered since the baby started to take up more room in her belly. Guess she would need another antacid tab if the heartburn got worse.

When she put the empty glass down, she noticed Luke had bought another beer and hoped he'd get her another squash, because she shouldn't waste her money after the expensive petrol it had taken to get them here.

She'd also paid for the accommodation at the tourist park for a week, till the Thursday before the races, a twin room with no ensuite, and Lazy could only stay a night. She hoped to get another week there after she got a job. Maybe she'd even find somewhere cheaper to stay when Luke left.

He wasn't so happy about bringing her now, because they'd had a flat tyre which would probably cost him his profit to get fixed, but she'd go halves in that. She wasn't letting on about that until he was ready to leave, though, or he'd just drink the extra cash.

Sitting here, looking around the walls, she couldn't be anything but glad she'd come. It felt right somehow. As if she could belong here. Now that seemed queer, considering they'd only been here for about ten minutes. Her gaze travelled the doorways, looking for directions; she found a polar bear with 'Gents' under it, so the ladies would be somewhere there.

By the time she returned with her face clean and hands washed, Luke had another beer in front of him. Charli's brow furrowed.

Settled in, Luke wouldn't want her to interrupt his conversation, so she texted him.

Need to check into caravan park. Want to go there now and you can walk back here?

She saw his head come up when his phone dinged. He read her text, looked across at her, frowned and then reluctantly nodded.

She wanted to study every photograph on the walls, but they had to drive to their accommodation for the night and get settled before dark. Lazy didn't need to get breath-tested by the local copper.

Luke wasn't a bad bloke. Said he'd been dropped on his head when he was a kid. She believed that because he had a ding in his forehead, but he also said the ding made him smarter. She wasn't so sure about that one. Sometimes he didn't make sensible decisions, but he'd always been kind to Charli, and Charli looked after him when he did something stupid or ended up in a fight. She could be fierce enough to protect him if needed.

For the last three months, after they'd run into each other again in Charleville, Luke had hovered on the edges of her world, said he'd check on her more often now that she'd done something stupid instead of him for a change. Like get pregnant.

Everyone needed a friend. People thought he was the father of her baby. No way. Be like sleeping with a brother. Yuck. But if he didn't drink and start a fight with someone, he was safe, and he cared a little.

Yes, she'd been stupid. Her pregnancy had happened when she was working at the pub in Charleville, saving like mad to give herself a nest egg for Birdsville, and been sweet-talked by an American cowboy over the course of a week. Turned her head, he had. Looking back, the fact she'd been wearing a covid mask that had hidden half her face might have helped, because she'd felt beautiful. She'd fallen hard and fast and been more outgoing than usual.

Then, after he'd got her into bed and seen her face in the morning, he'd left. Luke said he would have left anyway, but she didn't believe him. That cowboy had been implacable with closure, his words and his dust hanging in the air as he drove out fast.

Her heart still felt a little cracked, but by the time she knew she was pregnant, she also knew her baby was all her responsibility. The bonus now though was she would have someone of her very own to love for the rest of her life.

Trouble was, as she began to show, she'd attracted unwelcome attention from the drifters. Which triggered problems as the locals, and Lazy, tended to stick up for her and then it caused a ruckus in the bar.

One morning her boss suggested she needed to think through her plans for when the baby was born. Adding, not unkindly but being practical, 'Do you have a Plan B? Worst case scenario, what if something happens to you?' He knew her own mum had died when she was born. 'Thing is, Charli, who would your baby have?' She had no answer to that, but his words chilled her to the bone.

From that moment on, Charlene Bryce's life direction changed. Her whole focus turned to her baby's back-up plan. Her child needed a family to call its own.

Now, more than ever, it was urgent for Charli to find her past, a distant family, or even a permanent position where she could settle in a small town and make real friends. She wasn't a city girl, most of her life spent in mid- to small-town rural fostering, and she'd never felt comfortable under the bright lights of a city.

Birdsville had been the first clue she'd had about her past apart from the watch-locket she was found with a short time after her birth. Her first chance to find family, or even gravestones, if she had any far-flung relatives at all. Or maybe just to lay that final hopeful ghost to rest and find a true home if she was alone.

That's why she was here, in the Birdsville Pub. She scrambled off the precarious stool in time to follow Lazy to the door, but she couldn't dampen her longing to spend time studying the history on the walls.

Then Charli's gaze caught. One frame held a small fading photograph tucked near the bottom corner of the wood and something glinted on the pictured woman's chest. Silver. Round. She froze. Charli's hand lifted to her own throat.

The face in the photo could have been hers. The woman had the same straight dark hair. Same pale blue eyes. And maybe even a smaller pregnancy bump. But most of all, she'd hung a silver watch around her neck, just like the one Charli wore under her shirt. A quiver of awareness held her feet like flypaper to the floor, glued on the spot, and she glanced at the door.

Lazy had left and he wouldn't wait, so she lifted her phone and took a quick snap of the photo, then hurried to catch up. Her heart pounded in her chest and her breath came fast and hard and not from the quick-paced waddle she was using to close the gap between her and Lazy.

She wouldn't draw attention to what she'd seen just yet. She'd learned years earlier about jumping to conclusions.

Conclusions that she'd found a friend.

Conclusions that a new foster parent would keep her.

Conclusions that one day someone would come for her. No.

No conclusion jumping.

But she'd be back. She needed to think about how to find out more. And who to ask.

Chapter Three

Phoebe

Phoebe pulled over to the other side of the road, far enough away from the wreck in case of fire, and well out of the way of oncoming traffic. The track seemed quiet but she knew up to forty vehicles a day could pass in the busy times. Her narrowed gaze rapidly assessed the scene, while her heart sank at the lack of movement in the cab. The rollover must have been horrific to experience.

The dust-coated panelling was pocked and crunched with evidence of multiple impacts from rolling more than once at high speed. Dust hung suspended in the air like tea leaves in a tall glass of water.

Phoebe slid her sat phone, still open-line, on speaker, into the top pocket of her shirt and clipped it there so it wouldn't fall out. Meant it was facing backwards but she didn't want to drop it when she bent. 'Can you still hear me?' She wound down the window for airflow.

'Copy that.' The calm male voice helped more than a little as she parked there in the vast wasteland with heat belting down and flies instantly in the corners of her eyes and mouth. It was her, alone, there to find and help anyone living inside that destroyed vehicle.

She swallowed and firmed her voice as a shimmy of adrenalin shot through her. 'As I said, the vehicle has finished up on its wheels, though the front driver side is slammed up against a broken Waddi Tree.'

An inconsequential thought drifted through her mind. Those so-rare trees were protected. As they should be when they could be up to a thousand years old. The old men of the desert, as one of her friends, the daughter of one of the Wangkangurru elders, had shared with her.

Phoebe mouthed silently, 'Thank you, old man Waddi, for your sacrifice.' An upright vehicle made everything much easier. Though this was never going to be easy. She sniffed. 'Can't smell diesel. Hopefully that means the fuel tank's still isolated.' One blessing for now.

She took a quick swallow of water, tied up her long hair out of the way, jammed her wide-brimmed hat on her head, and reached back for the well-stocked first aid kit she always carried. When she opened the driver's door, she could immediately hear the moans. And whimpers. Victims too shocked to scream. This was not going to be fun.

Packing cubes of gory mind pictures in her brain was not what she wanted to lug for the start of her holidays. All she could hope was that there was something she could do until help arrived. Pulling on a pair of strong blue nitrile gloves she slid from the cruiser and headed across the dirt to the wreck as the sun slammed down on her. Drew a deeper breath. Triage first.

'I'll do a quick recon then treat.' Counted the heads in the car. Said out loud so the copper could hear her, 'Three.' Even from a metre away she could tell the driver's face had impacted the steering wheel, his airbag either failed or removed, and he would never be pretty again, if he had been. Less blood than she expected but flattened facial bones and broken teeth.

She leaned in, touched his throat through the shattered window, waited, and felt the slow pound of his pulse, and lack of response. 'Driver. Deeply unconscious but breathing. Male. Early twenties. Facial injuries.' The Waddi hadn't taken kindly to being hit and that wood was strong. The mess of his face broke her heart. No time for that. He was breathing. Always hope.

His breathing was laboured, but his airway seemed unob-structed with the way his head leaned to the side. Thankfully he wasn't chin on chest, closing his throat, and she'd rather not inter-fere with his cervical spine unless she had to. He was upright in his seat belt and if he had a worsening head injury there was nothing she could do.

She scooted around behind the car to the other side and that's where the blood was. 'Rear, one passenger. Shocked.' Of course, the door wouldn't open when she tried it. 'Door stuck. Broken window.' She reached in carefully through the broken glass and touched his throat. 'Slow steady pulse, large red bruise on his forehead, multiple cuts from flying debris.' She leaned closer. 'Can't see major bleeding. Just lots of small trickles. Airway clear.'

The boy, that's what he looked like, maybe mid-teens, alter-nated between moans and quiet gulping sobs and she could see his legs were jammed at unnatural angles under the front seat, which had buckled up.

She leaned in to him. 'Hey, sweetheart. Help is coming. Stay as still as you can until they get here.'

She dipped her head to speak quietly into the phone, 'Left rear seat probable multiple lower limb fractures. Conscious. Critical.'

Broken and unbroken empty beer bottles lay around his feet and bruised body – they must have flown around inside the car when it rolled. She could imagine small brown bottles smashing heads and faces and causing mayhem. Blinked the image away: back to checking his legs. She couldn't see any white juts of bone through his jeans so hopefully he'd avoided compound fractures. He was crushed into a fixed spot by the seat in front. His face and neck had dozens of small trickling cuts, none spurting, and early red bruises.

Whimpers from the front passenger seat drew her eyes that way.

She touched the rear seat boy's cheek, and when she did, he blinked, opened his eyes and looked at her fuzzily. Obvious shock. 'I'm checking everyone then I'll be back,' she said to him.

Moved on. 'Front passenger. Severe trauma to left arm. Critical. Arterial bleeding. Too busy to talk now. Out.' She rolled the phone in her pocket and cut the call in case she needed the battery. The assessments had taken less than thirty seconds but it would have been nice to have found him first.

This one must have had his arm out the window, because the smashed mess of elbow and upper arm had obviously been rolled on several times. He'd be lucky to keep his hand, she guessed. Blood pumped from the pulp of destroyed bone, muscle and blood vessels and he was number one. Meaning she had to use one of the things she never liked to open. Tourniquet.

Chapter Four

Atticus

Atticus Bow listened to the woman's soft, calm voice . . . No – not 'the woman' – Phoebe. Phoebe McFadden. Could it possibly be *that* Phoebe? Could it be her? It had to be. The one he'd had the crush on all those years ago. He'd been so young, but they'd had a rapport he never found later with other girls, and she'd been kind to an annoying kid. Truth be told he didn't usually have time for women – he had always thought when he found the right woman that he'd know her, do away with the whole dating drama and just marry her. Stupid thoughts. Someone called Phoebe McFadden had come across an accident and needed his help.

He imagined the scene: he'd seen enough trauma and twisted metal in his time, and even, one unforgettable and horrible day, had watched his own brother . . . He pushed that away.

Remembered the calmness she'd portrayed. Nope. He hadn't heard nerves. Unbelievable. They were all extremely lucky someone calm was there. He texted the last person he needed to notify so they could leave and grabbed his sat phone. Headed for the door, thinking how tough it was being the person who found a bad accident. Even tougher, he imagined, if she was aware of all the things that should be done and knowing a lack of resources meant people died. Like his brother had died.

He jumped in his vehicle and headed for the tarmac across the paddock. Atticus would get there as fast as he could and thanks to Lex McKay and his chopper dropping his mother in for a meeting, he'd be sooner.

The chopper would leave as soon as the nurse was ready. He'd been lucky. Big, rangy Lex had popped into the police station as the call came in, and had gone to track down the current agency nurse who'd been at lunch so they could pack emergency supplies in.

Atticus wished Gloria was here. He'd only been back in town a month but his admiration for the older nurse ran off the chart, but she didn't land until this afternoon.

He phoned the health centre and passed on what he knew about the three casualties. Atticus could call in the retrieval chopper from the mine between them and Adelaide because there was no landing strip for the flying doctor close enough out there. This was more luck: the larger helicopter would come from the mining company, picking up an extra nurse from Moomba to help stabilise the crash victims and extricate them to Birdsville, where the flying doctor would land and further stabilise them before flying them to Adelaide.

He placed a call through to the nearest cattle station, and the manager there promised to send out a crew as well.

'Ready to go, Atticus?' Lex called out; he enjoyed bush informality – he'd missed it while in the city.

'Coming.' He stood, pulled the door shut behind him, and flipped the sign on it to say *Called out*. The emergency number for Bedourie Police Station was there – even if it was just over two hours away when the road was good.

As they flew in over the crash site Atticus could see the destroyed vehicle well off the road. Another vehicle, a startlingly red 200 series, sat parked to the side – also off the road. He noted the approaching ball of dust – the two cars coming in on the side track from the nearest station were almost here. Good.

His procedural mind saw the tracks where the skid started, where the car had rolled, flattening sparse vegetation, grinding over boulders, and finally settled against the broken tree. Imagined the speed needed to roll that many times. Shook his head.

Damn kids. They needed to learn from their mistakes, not ruin their lives. Maybe the first responders could keep them all alive. If they had seat belts on there was a good chance.

Heat shimmered off the red dirt track and he imagined Phoebe would be wilting by now under the afternoon sun, though if it was her she had experience with outback heat. Had to be thirty-five degrees if not more. Lex had said he'd set up shade when he had the aircraft shut down, which would give some relief.

Atticus hoped Phoebe had a hat on.

He grabbed a bottle of chilled water and was first out of the chopper to cross the clearing with his head tucked low, eyes squinting, as the rotors slowed. Clouds of dust whipped up in a whirlwind made him peer through his lashes to see, despite his sunglasses.

He saw the wide-brimmed hat first. It was sitting on top of the vehicle, teetering, about to blow off. He saw the slim calves of feminine legs and then thighs and studiously avoided looking at her very shapely backside in cut-off jeans as the rest of the torso backed out and straightened until he saw the woman who had only been a voice. And an elusive memory.

Atticus sucked in a dust-laden breath.

He hadn't really expected *his* Phoebe McFadden, but it was her, looking like a model in cut-off jeans. God, she'd been pretty twenty years ago, and look at her now. Glints of red in the escaped tendrils of her long hair. Petite. Looking smaller and younger than he knew her to be. On the phone he'd thought her confidence meant big and strong but that wasn't what her body said. Their gazes met.

She had a pert nose and a lovely mouth pulled tight with concentration. Big eyes coloured like crushed violet, with a directness that was just a little confronting. That's where her strength lay. Intelligence. Will power. A woman who didn't suffer fools or believe anything impossible. None of the uncertain teen he remembered in that face today.

Confidence. Calm. Composure. All things he liked. Oh my.

He reached out and caught the hat as it flew off the car roof, then offered it and the water and she took both. 'Thanks. So, it *was* you?' Still calm as she straightened.

He nodded, ridiculously pleased she'd recognised him. 'Phoebe. Long time no see.' Not the time, Atticus, he reminded himself. 'Our nurse Hallie is here and has supplies. Less than a minute.'

'Not Gloria?'

Of course she knew the senior nurse. But questions were for later. 'Flies in this afternoon. What do you want me to do first?'

'Alvan needs fluids ASAP. He's shutting down.' Her hand lifted to wave the approaching nurse closer. 'How long till retrieval?'

'Thirty minutes just as we landed.'

She sighed. Murmured, 'Pretty good, really.' Gestured to the boy in the back. 'Pete here needs major pain relief. I'm not keen to move him with his crush injuries, so I think we should wait for the team to do that. I need to check on Oliver – he's unconscious in the driver's seat – as soon as Alvan's line is in, and the nurse takes over here.'

Her eyes locked on someone behind him and he stepped aside to let Hallie through, listened to the brief technical medical discussion, didn't understand half of it, and then watched as emergency paper packs started opening.

She looked back at him. 'You can be the IV pole until we rig something.' He had his own job to do, of course, but he had no doubt that this took precedent. She went to work with the nurse, changed gloves, her movements swift and economical as she inserted the first huge (well it looked huge to Atticus) intravenous cannula needle and the nurse primed the line and held it ready. He was left holding the bag.

He'd start taking accident scene photos as soon as he could be relieved.

Two hours later the retrieval helicopter lifted off. They'd managed to keep all three trauma victims alive. He wasn't sure how except by luck and amazing management by Phoebe and Hallie prior to the full team's arrival. Now they were on the way to Birdsville then Adelaide. Phoebe had even known the Moomba nurse.

Atticus was just glad he didn't have a dead body or three to take back to the morgue at the council depot in town. He'd passed on the details to the control centre in Mount Isa and police headquarters would ensure all the victims' next of kin knew they were being transferred to care. Glad that wasn't his job, too – giving bad news to good people. He hated that part of his work, especially as it brought back the past.

'I'm heading off now.' He heard her voice and he turned from watching them load the injured. For the first time, she looked weary, and he crossed to her vehicle.

'The young men can't say it, so I will: thank you. Personally, I think you saved their lives.'

She smiled at that, but he could tell she didn't want praise. 'Thanks for your help, Atticus. I'll drop into the police station in Birdsville later.'

'Leave it until tomorrow. You've had a big day.' And he wouldn't be back for a while yet. She didn't need to be waiting around for him.

'Thanks. Sounds good. I'll be there early.'

She waved herself off as soon as they'd loaded the injured. Lex had left to ensure he got his mother home before dark, and Atticus had a lift back to Birdsville when he was ready.

He knew where Phoebe was headed, to that wild cousin of hers, Scarlet, so he guessed she was staying in Birdsville for the wedding he'd heard so much about. Two weeks.

Rusty's daughter. He'd heard they were estranged. He couldn't quite believe the quiet, reliable guy who drove the ambulance and often helped when they had to go out to a remote retrieval could fight with anyone.

But Phoebe. Funny how keen he was to find out more about this fascinating, so-capable woman version of a past acquaintance. A little voice inside his head whispered there was something about her that pushed his buttons and kept them full throttle since he'd landed and caught her hat. Something like he wasn't going to forget this girl from his past.

Nope. This was work. He needed to find out more about the accident from Phoebe. Just work.

Chapter Five

Gloria

Gloria Revere shifted in the plastic seat; the small commercial SAAB 340 aircraft was buffeted by the wind as it zoomed off the runway into the sky above Toowoomba, the first short stop on the five-flight hop between Brisbane and Birdsville. At least she was on the plane. Finally.

It must have been the bustle in Brisbane airport that had rattled her. The hordes of people, the handing in of her luggage at automatic kiosks without even one human to talk her through the check-in process.

The slow snaking lines of bag-wielding travellers waiting in zigzags to go through customs. She'd become more unsettled having to empty her pockets and take off her jacket and stand like a prisoner to be X-rayed.

Was she getting too old for this trip, the yearly pilgrimage to Brisbane for remote nurse professional development courses? Not for the first time, an insidious voice whispered maybe she was getting too old to be the central hub for health in her remote town clinic.

No. She was just tired from the requisite study before the upskilling weekends, the stress of the exams that didn't seem to bother the young ones around her who navigated the weekend of intense learning with ease. At least she'd passed with flying colours as always.

She had said she'd be carried out before she retired from remote nursing but . . . At sixty-five, she did now notice the cramped position of her legs this morning, squashed up against the back of the seat in front, and the noise in the aircraft that rattled her ears.

I'm tired had become a sly, insidious, barely heard chant in her head, and the frequency of its whispers was on the rise.

'You'll be fine,' she murmured to herself, 'once you step off the plane in another five hours. Just morning tea while they refuel in Charleville, land at Quilpie, lunch in Windorah while the pilots have their break, and then home.' Birdsville. Corner country to Queensland, South Australia and Northern Territory.

She couldn't retire.

For lots of reasons, but mostly because she didn't want to leave Rusty when her quaint little nurse's cottage was given to her successor.

The plane droned and rattled. She took the savoury snack pack of pretzels and nuts – what happened to sandwiches from the old days? Still, the wonderful dark-haired air hostess, or flight crew – whatever they were supposed to be called in these times – had the warmest smile Gloria had seen in a week. Gloria squinted to focus on the badge as the woman handed her coffee. Vanessa. Such a lovely young woman.

Sipped and ate. Handed back the rubbish. Put away her tray table. Again.

Retirement? What was she supposed to do if she retired? Where would she live if she gave up the homey accommodation that came with her job? It wasn't like she could set up a tent or a van when Birdsville temperatures in summer hit the late forties and eggs could fry on car bonnets.

In any case, they came up so infrequently for sale in Birdsville. Building material costs were astronomical delivered that far away from suppliers, let alone hiring a builder to leave his business and come all the way outback and set up camp. A pre-fab house – trucked out in pieces – was possible, but even those were so expensive this far inland.

The nest egg was smaller than she'd need, thanks to saving it late in life with all the travelling she'd done earlier: midwifery in Edinburgh, backpacking around Europe, tour guiding in Asia. But she didn't want to rent and have her home sold under her at any time. No, she'd have to buy a house somewhere and live on what was left if she retired.

Of course, she'd be bored silly without work, though perhaps not as tired. And she'd miss Birdsville. Most of all, she'd miss Rusty. Ridiculous how she'd loved that man for twenty years and never done a thing about it.

She pushed the tiny flutter of panic away. These were all thoughts for when she was in the quiet of her home.

The engine noise changed, and she realised she must have dozed, because they were coming down again into Charleville and Vanessa was telling everyone to check their seat belts were fastened.

*

Charleville had been and gone, Quilpie too, and now Windorah lay behind them – she stared out the window as the tiny square of streets and houses plonked in the middle of red earth flashed past and away.

Tiny microcosms of life, these towns. Towns isolated by distance and holding on by the strength of their far-flung families, parched land between and only the touchdowns from pilots and truck drivers who covered vast landscapes keeping them viable.

Out of sight now. No more signs of habitation. The ground so far beneath them showed the tracing branches of a tree-like channel system, dry but smudge-lined with some hardy scrubby growth where the water would trickle and then rush and run the next time heavy rains fell upstream.

Swirling circles of ochre and ruby soil, dotted in different-coloured patches thousands of metres below like some glorious First Nations painting, all with the grey-green branches of the channel country snaking between the circles.

Every now and then a thin red stripe of a road cut through the land like the slash of a knife. Straight as an arrow and disappearing into the distance.

Gloria loved it all. The outpost airports like Windorah, where you put a coin in the steel box on the wall and took a can of lemon squash from the small bar fridge. The smiling, rough-shaven man at the gate who checked your boarding pass and would now go off and work in the local fuel stop until the next plane came in.

She loved the view beneath the wings and the tiny excitement of going home every return. But yes. Exhaustion tugged where before she'd felt renewed after each weekend away.

Six and half hours after lifting off in Brisbane her flight bumped down in Birdsville and Gloria sighed with relief. 'Thanks, Vanessa.'

'You're welcome, Gloria. See you next time.'

I guess you will, she thought, then twisted her backpack over her wrist and took hold of the thin aluminium handrail to ease down the steep, ladder-like steps one at a time until her feet were firmly on the ground.

'Thank you, Captain.'

'See you next time, Sister Revere.'

Gloria lifted her face to the heat, a welcome from her favourite town. She heard the clunk from the side as two girls, probably also working at the pub, unloaded her bag into the back of the ute from the rear of the aircraft. Funny how she'd felt at home here the first time she arrived – a feeling that had never gone away.

By the time she walked through the tiny pocket of the air-conditioned Rex terminal and out the other side, her luggage would be waiting for her.

It wasn't far to the health clinic, or the house next door to it where she lived, but it was too far to drag bags. She hoped Rusty would be there, waiting for her, as usual.

He was.

She studied her dear friend as he appeared beside the gate. His hair was turning silver, but then again hers was totally white – at least he had some dull red left.

But Rusty. The awful loss if she left. She didn't want to leave him. Or lose him. Or her friends in town. If she retired what would happen to her so-dear friendship with Rusty?

His lined but still handsome face warmed her, yet there was something about the strained smile today that made her frown.

As she drew closer, she noticed extra lines deeply etched in his forehead and worry in his eyes. Something had happened.

'How was your flight?' His voice sounded quiet and welcoming as his hand reached out to take her pack. He already had the case beside his feet, so the girls unloading must have been slick this morning. There'd only been five others on the flight by the time they made it here and the two left behind in the aircraft had been going on to Mount Isa. Rusty knew her bags. She used the same case every time.

'Good flight, thanks.' She almost added, 'I think I'm getting too old,' but she didn't. 'You okay? Nothing wrong?' Here was something she wanted to talk about – not the flight or her uneasy thoughts.

'Fine, fine,' he said. 'It's all happening in town at the minute. Another rollover out on the track. But that's not your problem. You don't start until tomorrow.'

'As if it works like that.' It didn't, and Rusty knew that. She tried to suppress a sigh. 'Was hoping for a quiet couple of days but it will sort.'

She felt Rusty's gaze as he side-eyed her expression, but all he said was, 'Come on, let's get you out of the heat and home. Eat a meal before you get called in. All that tea and biscuits is gonna be sloshing around inside you.'

'Did they take the ambulance?'

'Atticus flew out with Hallie in Lex McKay's chopper. Lucky chance he was in town for the Organic Beef meeting. Hassett's taken the ambulance to meet them out there.'

Hassett was the reliable desert recovery mechanic and sometime ambulance driver the nurses used when they needed more hands if

Rusty wasn't available. Hassett could always get people out of road trouble but Gloria preferred Rusty's assistance with the ambulance when possible.

'Maybe I should get you to drive me out there, too?'

'Reckon it would be all over by the time we arrived. They left a couple of hours ago. They've got the flying doctor coming in here soon and the woman who called it in is a registered nurse with lots of experience.'

There was something odd in Rusty's voice, and as they reached his four-wheel drive she looked at him properly. So many emotions were crossing her dear friend's face she couldn't decipher any of them.

'Someone you know?'

He inclined his head. Said quietly, 'Phoebe.'

'Your Phoebe?'

Rusty's leathered face sagged. 'My Phoebe? I wish that was true. She's back early for Scarlet's wedding. Not to see me.'

So unfair. And it made Gloria as cross now as it had when she'd found out what Rusty had done all those years ago. 'And whose fault is that?' She spoke quietly, aware others were near. 'You didn't tell her the truth when you should have. Or since.'

'Now, don't.' Rusty shook his head. 'Don't start that again.'

'Well, if you won't tell her this time, I'll be making sure she knows the truth before she leaves.'

He tilted his head at her. 'You threatening me, Gloria?'

'My word I am, you fool man. You deserve your daughter's love and admiration. It's about time she gave it.'

Chapter Six

Phoebe

Phoebe drove away from the crash site with a dehydration headache and the aroma from the antiseptic she'd washed with a dozen times permeating her hands. The vehicle and her hair were thick with dust and the smell of old blood on her clothes had turned rank, while her skin felt sun-scorched and desiccated. Methodically she chugged another bottle of water. She hadn't needed to pee yet. Not a good sign.

She felt like she'd done a Friday night shift in the emergency department and, as after bad nights, the poor, damaged faces were there behind her eyes. She knew from experience the images would take a few days to fade and would never really disappear. Shocked eyes popped back to visit and stare in dreams and nightmares for years. She pushed the thought away with the positive outcome of not losing any lives today. Amazing . . . a miracle the far-flung team had pulled off.

The remote response from Birdsville had been great and the retrieval team from the mines top-notch, but she'd never been so glad to see anyone as when Atticus, Senior Constable Bow, had caught her hat and asked what she needed first.

She thought about that moment as she drove, following the red stony road towards Birdsville, and huffed. How ridiculous to remember his face so clearly. But it was better than remembering the damaged boys.

Atticus Bow – such a name and so not Birdsville – still had the kindest blue eyes she'd ever seen. He hadn't looked mean enough to be the sole officer in charge of an area the size of the state of Victoria but then . . . the boy she remembered had never been mean.

Physically, he looked big enough to be the law: he'd certainly grown. She snorted out loud and it was good to feel amused about something. Oh yes, with that wide chest straining the buttons on his blue shirt that was simultaneously loose at his narrow waist. Big, corded arms tanned by the sun – seemed she had a thing for a strong bloke's toned arms – a six-years-her-junior bloke, she reminded herself.

Now she was a cougar? Who knew? A smile she didn't know she had inside her warmed the part of her she'd shut down as she concentrated on saving lives.

She blinked and stared at the road ahead. His steady gaze on her. Those crinkled, laugh-lined, dark blue eyes watching her, assessing her needs, her wellbeing, quick to see problems. Those caring eyes had been the thing.

Thing? What thing? She had no idea what thing.

Different from what she expected. Not young like he should be. Gentle and knowing. Good humoured yet whip smart. Wise, as if he'd seen pain and wanted to protect the world. Not like the street-hardened eyes of most of the police she knew – and she'd met many coppers, old and young, while working emergency in Adelaide. Saved the lives of a few when they'd been shot or stabbed or beaten. Some of the nurses said they wouldn't marry police. Be like marrying a soldier who went to war and might never come back. She'd hate to think anything could happen to young Atticus. Thankfully, violent crime was rare this far away from the cities, so maybe he was enjoying the lull as well.

That voice. Not the scratchy high-pitched voice of his youth – oh no. Grown-up Atticus had a wonderful voice: gravelly tones, deep and thrumming like the sound of someone sliding the back of a shovel smoothly over tumbled gibber stones. Ooh poetic. She was going crazy from the heat. Must be that if she was fancying young Atticus. Dehydration psychosis.

Still. Shame he wasn't in Adelaide. For when she went home. Shame he wasn't older. Shame he was police.

But he was in the middle of Australia. Nowhere close to her world. A cop, so much younger, and not her plan. What was he doing back in Birdsville? Of course, it had been so many years since she'd been here she didn't know who belonged in Birdsville. Except, of course, she knew it wasn't her.

Maybe best she didn't think any more about the delightfully blue-eyed and delicious young Atticus. Delicious? Good grief. Was she sixteen? When she had been, he'd been ten. Remember that. Her next big birthday was forty. His would be thirty. The old lady and the young man. There. That settled it.

Scarlet would give her hell if she suspected Phoebe had salivated over the kid she'd befriended all those years ago.

Scarlet, her cousin, the scallywag. The wise woman.

Yes. Think about Scarlet. The incredible cook working with the ingredients she had to hand, who worked seasonally for one of the tour services, catering sunset nibbles and drinks and making hampers for day trips. Plus this week she'd be making huge amounts of desserts for the races.

Scarlet also ran a backyard hairdressing service for the locals, though she didn't advertise that for tourists. Didn't even like the hair trade, but was good at it, if scarily unreliable. Everyone who visited knew that if Scarlet was having a bad day it could take two weeks or more for their hairstyle to recover.

Apparently, Scarlet's fiancé, George, had suffered half-a-dozen bad haircuts before he'd worn her down. It sounded like he had the sort of resilience needed for a life with Phoebe's crazy cuz. The thought made her smile and she encouraged the new direction her thoughts had gone in.

Fiancé George had worked all over Australia as a stock and station hand, horse trainer, jockey and farrier, but settled with his last employer, Lex McKay of Diamond Lake Station. George was a part of the consortium in a racehorse, the one Scarlet and her father, of course *her* father, had bought broken down; they'd formed a syndicate with Lex McKay to help rehabilitate the stallion. Just Finish might even get a run in the Birdsville Cup.

Horses. Crikey. Scarlet's excitement more than Phoebe's, because of the gambling, which she hated with a passion. She did, however, look forward to meeting the jockey who'd made her cousin go mushy enough to marry. Even if she still couldn't quite believe Scarlet was in love.

It was evening by the time Phoebe pulled up at the house Scarlet's parents had owned when Phoebe left all those years earlier.

Trying hard to be nonchalant, she glanced across the road at a simple dwelling with a big shed. No fresh paint anywhere. Her old car wouldn't still be in there, surely. In fact, it didn't look like anyone was home.

Phoebe knew from Scarlet that Rusty still lived there, but she wasn't going over today. Not yet. But she'd have to, soon.

Instead, she turned back to her cousin's house. Scarlet's parents had moved to the Sunshine Coast when Uncle Neville retired from the Diamantina Shire Council. She'd thought her cuz would have gone too but Scarlet had elected to remain.

Which Phoebe still didn't understand.

Though, now with George in the picture, she guessed Scarlet was here for life.

The freshly painted blue door flew open and a thin, wild-haired, excited woman catapulted out as if let free from a chicken coop. Scarlet's pixie face looked leaner, but her eyes shone brilliant blue and her smile could light up the world. People in town said it was a family thing, that smile. The sight made Phoebe feel loved. Welcomed. And home.

'You made it. I can't believe you're here. I can't wait to show you George.' The words tumbled out in her excitement until she drew closer and slowed. Scarlet's expression changed: a crazed farmyard bird morphing into the wily outback woman she was.

Her eyes narrowed. She lifted her pointy chin and studied Phoebe from her dust-coated ankles to the blood smeared across the chest of her buttoned shirt.

'You okay? That's not your blood? Oh of course. You were at that accident.' It wasn't a question.

'Yep.' And even though Phoebe had driven sixty-five kilometres since the crash, she wasn't surprised everyone in Birdsville knew. The whole town would have been involved in some way to mobilise the rescue team.

'Then come in. Leave your stuff in the car. Shower.' Scarlet nodded as if agreeing with herself. 'We'll talk after.'

Her cuz had always been decisive. Thank goodness, because clean water was all Phoebe wanted and the solitude of the shower felt like a good place to hide – not that she knew entirely why she wanted to hide.

'Thanks,' Phoebe said; she leaned up and brushed Scarlet's cheek with dry lips and went past, stopping to take her sandals off at the door and then turning right towards the bathroom.

'Towels under the bench. Robe behind the door. I'll bring your case in and put it in my old room, which is yours now.'

Half an hour later, Phoebe sat on the new fabric lounge, freshly showered and dressed in shorts and a long sleeveless top, with her bare feet resting on the smooth wooden floor. It felt cool in the house thanks to the air-con and the heat outside. Yet September provided nothing like the summer heat, which could get close to fifty degrees Celsius.

Even now it was too hot for locals to wander around. Tourists would be out and about with the early arrivals for the Cup.

Phoebe pretended to look under the furniture. 'So where is he? This amazing man? This hero?'

Scarlet's face softened and her cheeks tinged pink.

Wow, Phoebe thought, just a little wistfully. She'd never felt like that about any of the few men she'd been briefly involved with.

'He's working back at Lex McKay's station with our horse for a week. Home next Thursday. Plenty of time before the races and the wedding.' She added thoughtfully, 'And best he's out from under my feet while I'm busy.'

'You decided to have the wedding reception at the community centre?'

'It's a great space.' Her eyes took on a wicked gleam. 'You and I are going to decorate. I've ordered all these paper daisies online to hang up and dress the tables. Kelvin from the pub has promised to cater for the things I don't prepare. He's a great chef.'

'Kelvin?' Phoebe shook her head. 'Don't remember him.'

'Well, you have been gone for half your life. Kelvin's a good bloke. He got caught in a kitchen fire – he's pretty scarred, inside and out I think, cause he doesn't make any moves towards women. But he's a great cook.'

Phoebe blinked but Scarlet went on. 'We thought about holding the reception at the pub, but the tourists will still be around.' She grimaced. 'Then we considered the racecourse, but everyone would have to drive home full of grog and the new copper's as bad as the old one – watch out for that. All the buses from the races would have gone back to where they came from.'

Phoebe thought briefly of the full and empty bottles of beer that had caused so much damage in the rolled vehicle. Tried for a lightness she didn't feel. 'Funny how drink driving is illegal in outback Queensland, just like everywhere else in Australia.'

'Bloody coppers,' Scarlet said with mock seriousness. 'He would have been out at the crash site. Did you recognise him? From when we were teens?'

Phoebe had a sudden vision of those eyes and the determined

chin of the law pulling her over, having her wind her window down. He could ask her to blow in a bag. Ooh yes. Or step into a cell with him. She couldn't help the smile.

Which was good. Nice to smile after the day she'd had . . . Atticus had had that day, too . . . and then of course she was thinking of the accident again. And the boys came back. She forced her mind sideways to Atticus for comfort. 'I remembered him.'

'He's grown.' Scarlet waggled her brows. 'Looks like the older brother now.' Her brows drew together as if she was trying to remember something. 'Didn't you spend time together back then? Atticus Bow?' She sniffed. 'He was way younger than we were. I always fancied the other brother. I hear he died in a car accident. They say Atticus found him.'

Phoebe sucked in a breath. Poor Atticus. He'd adored his brother. 'How horrible. How? When?'

Scarlet shrugged. 'No idea. And nobody has asked. They say the copper is good. But he won't come here for his haircut. Drove into Windorah to the Outback Scissors. I reckon he has a girl there.'

And that thought brought ridiculous disappointment and some self-flagellation. He was six years younger. Of course he'd have a nice young girlfriend in her twenties. Good grief. Instead of following that line of thought, Phoebe asked, 'Why would you care if he went elsewhere? You hate cutting hair.'

'Not on good-looking men.'

'You shouldn't be noticing.' Though he was that. And neither should she. She pretended to tsk. 'Two weeks away from your wedding.'

'Sixteen days. And counting.' Scarlet flashed the gorgeous smile she'd missed. 'I can look if I don't touch.'

There was that. 'So how long's he been here?' Oh so casual, and a real fight to keep her cheeks from heating. Good grief. She hadn't thought she could blush.

Scarlet's eyes opened wide. Teased, 'My gorgeous fiancé, George?' She blinked innocently, right before she laughed. 'Ohhhh.' More wide-eyed blinking. 'You mean Senior Constable Atticus Bow? Oh my goodness: my cousin's a cougar.'

Phoebe laughed too but inside she winced. It was as if she and Scarlet had sat like this yesterday. Joining the game, she lifted her shoulders nonchalantly. 'Just asking about newcomers in town.'

'Riiight. You wanna hear about anyone else?' Scarlet drew out the word with a deadpan expression on her face. Then caved because if anything she liked a good gossip. 'Not locals, then. The copper's been here a month. He's not married – Emily at the pub asked. Last posting was somewhere in Western Sydney. Jocelyn has a cousin down there and she said it's a wild place at night – not like here where most just go to bed. And his parents lived in Mount Isa, but they're both dead now. Lost his brother.' Then narrowed her eyes. 'And he's had his hair cut already, and not by me.'

That made Phoebe's smile kick up, despite the fact her brain was racing with more information than she thought she had wanted. Scarlet could make her laugh, no matter how bad her day had been. Which was why they'd kept up their phone calls at least once a month since she left. She went for the last comment. 'And you notice his hairstyle because?'

'It's my job.'

'And how's the other job going? Desserts. Appetisers. You busy? Lots of hampers?'

Scarlet waved her hand, a flash of light from her new sapphire ring catching the afternoon sun. 'I'm making a fortune. Was crazy around the Big Bash and will be again around the races. I had so many hampers going, plus charter flights, they practically had to fly in a special load for me with the food I needed. You have to help me make a ton of desserts for the races unless I can get a kitchen hand. Have a temp coming to see me tomorrow, so fingers crossed.'

Phoebe had thought they'd be working anyway. This wasn't news. 'I'm yours to command while I'm here. So, you're settled? In Birdsville, I mean?'

'All my life.' Scarlet crinkled her forehead. 'Where else would I live? For that matter, where else could we afford to live? I bought this house off Mum and Dad for less than the yearly average salary. Your father's place is worth even less than that.'

Phoebe winced. She did not want to go there. No way. Not the first day. 'Sorry. No offence. I wasn't judging.'

Scarlet tilted her head like the bird she sometimes resembled. 'Yes. You were. You've had it in for Birdsville since you left. Not our town's fault you think your dad took your money.'

And there it was. No dressing on it. It had been a strange way to say it, though – *hadn't* Rusty taken her money? But she guessed it was her cross to carry. 'You're absolutely right. It's not the town's fault. And I did put up a barrier to coming back. Sorry.' And she meant it. 'From this moment on,' until I leave, she clarified silently, 'Birdsville is the most wonderful town in Queensland because my bestie is getting married.' It didn't seem enough. 'You know I am thrilled to bits you've found happiness with your George. And that I get to be bridesmaid. Tell me again about the first time you met him.'

Scarlet didn't hold grudges. Not like Phoebe did. There was that. So, rapport returned as fast as it had left.

'The first time I met him?' Scarlet's face softened in a way Phoebe had never seen and she felt her eyes sting at the emotion pouring from her cousin. When she met this George, she'd hug him for giving such joy to her best friend in the world.

Scarlet touched her mouth. Snorted a laugh. 'It was in the pub. Working in the kitchen. Kelvin had to go off sick, even though they had a bunch of ringers in. I'd kicked most of the kitchen hands out because you know I don't play well with people who won't work hard.'

Scarlet didn't work at the pub. Or only under dire circumstances. Just her own place. But, in calamitous situations everyone in town would do things for other people no matter how much they hated it.

'George came in for breakfast with a couple of other men and our eyes met.' She stared sightlessly into the past. 'Out of all the people milling around our gazes sort of connected . . . and sizzled.' Shook her head as if she still didn't understand.

She nodded at Phoebe's teary gaze and dropped her voice reverently. 'And there was just something about his smile.' She drew a deep breath, looking dreamy. 'I fancied that man from the moment I saw him. Like a switch turned on inside me.'

Her cousin actually blinked back tears, which was so not like Scarlet. 'He said it was the same for him.' Scarlet, who'd said she'd never marry, had gone all romantic. 'Said he'd waited all his life to meet the best cook in the world so he could marry her.' She laughed softly at the memory.

Phoebe screwed up her face. 'He discerned that from breakfast? An ordinary pub breakfast?' Surely there was more. 'I don't get it.'

'Well, I might have added a few things and dressed it up a bit and when his food came out it looked nothing like everyone else's. Let's say he got a good deal.'

Phoebe started to laugh. She could so picture that. There had probably even been a fortune cookie with a risqué message under the egg. Scarlet was nothing if not forthright. 'Did you take a photo of the plate? Please say yes.'

Scarlet shook her head.

'Did he?'

'George doesn't own a phone. Refuses to pay for a sat phone. Though he has a tablet he can get emails on when he's in a town.'

'Damn.'

Scarlet ignored her. 'Then he kept turning up for haircuts even when he barely had any hair left and I had to laugh. He asked me out. Took me for a picnic up at Big Red. Got food from the bakery so I didn't have to cater. Food wasn't as flash as mine, but he felt good about it.'

'And that was it? Big Red? Then you were a couple?'

'Said he had to go back to work but that when he returned he'd like to ask me out again. Silly man wouldn't sleep with me. But somehow,' she shrugged, 'I didn't want to go out with anyone else. It just went on from there.'

She blushed. Scarlet actually blushed. 'And when we did end up in the sack, oh, my God, the man is a master.'

Phoebe burst out laughing. Yeah, right. 'You're kidding me.'

Scarlet waggled her eyebrows and Phoebe waved her away. 'No. Don't tell me. Please don't. Too much information.'

'Yes, well, maybe I won't. Let's just say snaffling the man and keeping him in my bed for the rest of my life is a very nice idea. And with the whole wedding thing . . . Life is good.'

Scarlet's eyes zoomed in, and Phoebe knew what was coming. 'And what about you? Is there a man on your horizon? Some doctor? Nurse? Ambulance guy?'

'No one special.' Except maybe a young police officer she'd met at the side of the road on the way here. The thought seemed to jam in her brain. Had she had a first-sight, flashing-light, sirens moment like Scarlet's with Senior Constable Atticus Bow? Nah. And it wasn't first sight anyway.

But she did remember his capable hands and strong, carved arms holding the IV flask. His broad-shouldered reliability when she needed something. The occasional nod on that powerful neck to reaffirm she was doing well when it looked like they were going to lose the struggle. And his eyes. Holding hers with a strength she could draw on.

Since when had she needed any support?

Chapter Seven

Charli

Charlene's belly rumbled. Lazy Luke had spent all his money last night in the pub and she had just enough cash to give him his hundred dollars when he left – hopefully later today. Plus, she had twenty dollars emergency money in her purse. Folded up in a tiny square and tucked at the back. The rest was safely away in the bank on her card.

She wasn't silly enough to pay Lazy before he had the tyre fixed or he'd be stuck here with a hangover again and she'd be pitching in more to get rid of him.

'You need to put that wheel in at the mechanics this morning and get it fixed.'

'I'll do it on the way to the bakery,' he said. 'Just give me enough for some bread and we can pick up the tyre later.'

Could she trust him? He looked to be in one of his moods but . . . The pub was shut still. 'You have to bring me back change,' she said. 'That's all I've got.'

'You got more in that card of yours.'

She hadn't realised he knew she had a debit card, and that meant he'd been snooping. Which was a bit of a worry. 'Only a little I've saved for the baby. Promise me you'll bring back the change.'

He sighed. 'I'll bring back the change.'

She handed over the money and he slipped out the door fast-fast-fast, like she was going to ask him to do some chores. Fast enough to make her smile and shake her head.

She turned the kettle back on for another cup of tea while she folded her blankets and made Lazy's bed.

Boiling water for tea was a sweet bonus of getting a cabin rather than a site to park the car in and sleeping rough. In the cheap ones, like hers, you didn't get a shower and toilet of your own, but they had the shared amenities, which were clean, and you got a microwave and kettle and little pots of milk in your room. And tea and coffee and sugar in sachets. She could keep those for emergencies.

It was expensive, much more expensive than sleeping in the car, though not as expensive as the pub, but she hadn't wanted to be crumpled and smelly when she went for job interviews. And she certainly didn't want to be crumpled and pongy if she found a relative in Birdsville.

She damped down the hope that sprang and bounced crazily as if she had an errant curl in her hair. Which she didn't. Thinking of the photo. The woman's straight hair. Imagine if her mother was from here.

She'd packed one of those soft food bags with the silver lining you get at the supermarket that sort of keep things cold. And she kept coffee and sugar and unopened long-life milk in there. There were plastic mugs and the Thermos she'd filled up at Windorah with hot water because Lazy liked hot coffee. The people had been nice at the Windorah service station even after they'd slept in the car outside, because they'd bought breakfast at the café. Personally, she could drink tea or coffee cold. Didn't matter. But Lazy was better company when he was happy, and he was happy when he was fed, so it suited her to get him coffee and breakfast.

At the thought of fresh bread and maybe some of the eggs in her food cache she could poach in the microwave, her belly rumbled again. She had a big jar of peanut butter that had gone runny with the heat, though they'd put the noisy air-conditioning on high when they got in here yesterday. The jar's contents had separated into oil and nuts but it would still be good for lunch. Then Lazy could leave.

The night before, she'd slept the best she had for ages even though she'd been in the single bed. Lazy got the double – he was bigger anyway. She kept sleeping distance, especially when he was full of drink, and she was a sensible girl. All her foster mothers had said that.

Sensible and helpful with the chores, but like the boys who wanted to have sex, like when she fell for that cowboy, the foster mothers hadn't wanted to keep her.

Charlene picked up a towel Lazy had dropped on the floor. She put it back on the hook beside hers and caught a glimpse of herself in the tiny mirror on the wall.

Dispassionately she studied the left side of her face and the scar line to her nose where the surgery had repaired the cleft lip. She turned to the unaffected side and her face looked almost normal. Nana Kate had said she was pretty, but she wasn't. The bad side wasn't noticeable when her hair fell forwards or someone was looking from the other direction, but it was enough to mean nobody wanted her, because of that scar. She knew that. Had accepted it and decided that was okay.

Things might have been different if it had healed well when she was kid, though Nana Kate had sat her down after some girls had been cruel at school and said, 'You're lucky. Though it isn't perfect, it is fine. You think it's bigger than it is.' She had added, 'What's on the inside is what matters. And aren't you lucky you have a big heart?'

Yes. She guessed she was lucky. But she'd liked covid and masks.

Nana Kate had said, 'Maybe one day you might decide to make your smile even more beautiful if you want to, but you're a woman, grown, and can do exactly what you want when you want. Just be sure it's for you, not because of other people.'

After that conversation Charli had thought about going to a doctor and asking if there was more they could do to make her lip look normal. But now she was pregnant, and her baby was much more important – vanity sat so far down the list of priorities she didn't even worry about it.

She turned away from the mirror. Her little baby wouldn't see anything wrong. Her little baby would love her mother's face, and the thought lightened the deep, silent pain accumulated from all the times people frowned without meaning to when they saw she wasn't perfect like them.

Her hand slid down and cupped her belly. 'We'll be happy, baby, don't you worry. Mummy will keep you safe and loved always. I'll never leave you.'

She could have stayed with Nana Kate in Roma, except she'd almost turned seventeen by the time they got to know each other and Charli had been waiting to spread her wings. She did say Charlene could come back any time. Nana Kate was Charli's Plan B after her baby was born if she still needed somewhere to stay for a month or two.

But right now, Charli was on Plan A. As soon as Lazy left she'd go to the pub and ask about other jobs in town. And then the photo.

Her phone dinged and she read the text from Lazy to say he was coming back and she put the kettle on. Fresh bread. Yum.

Chapter Eight

Atticus

The next morning, Atticus wrote down the details of his latest case. Must be the season for silliness.

One of the local kids had broken a window with a cricket ball and bolted. The owner of the house had seen who it was and wanted to make sure their parent knew, and thought it might have more impact if Atticus followed it up.

He'd have that discussion with the child and parent. Get the kid to apologise and see if the parent would pay for the damage. That was the thing about really small towns. You knew who to see when trouble came. He'd seen that little terror chucking rocks out the window yesterday just before he got the call from Phoebe McFadden, and he'd mention that too. Little goose.

But Phoebe. The thought of her made him smile. And shift.

The office phone broke the silence and he scooped it up and cradled it against his cheek while his fingers tapped at the computer keyboard and recorded something he remembered from yesterday's accident. 'Senior Constable Atticus Bow.'

'Good morning, Constable Bow. This is Phoebe McFadden.'

His mouth curved. Think of the woman and then she calls. 'What time suits you for me to drop in to sign my statement?'

'Phoebe.' A clear picture of her straightening out of the wreckage, taking the hat and the water bottle with her small capable hands, her eyes fierce with concentration, and he thought, You are welcome any time at all, but he didn't say it. 'Sooner the better. And please, call me Atticus.'

The cricket ball could certainly wait.

Her calm voice murmured, 'I'll see you in ten minutes, then, Atticus.' The line went dead.

He liked the way she said his name. Liked everything about her, always had, though his memories had faded until yesterday of course. Since then though she'd stuck like a burred leaf in his mind, never blowing away despite the puffs and pulls of police work in the last twenty-four hours. He glanced at the whiteboard. The grey nomads with the second flat tyre were due in soon. He'd asked them to confirm at the police station on their arrival. He'd driven out himself and taken a spare tyre to get them to Hassett at the garage.

Eight minutes till Phoebe arrived. He lifted his hand and blew into his palm. Sniffed. Coffee odour.

Could do with a mint, he thought, and rifled the desk drawer for his small tin of breath fresheners. Took one.

Crossed the room and turned the air-con up another notch.

Checked the level of water in the electric kettle. Turned it on in case she wanted a cup of tea, so they wouldn't have to wait long for the jug to boil.

Good grief, he was almost nervous. He couldn't remember the last time he'd felt that odd sensation. He tried to avoid thinking about why his fresh breath mattered – he certainly hadn't intended to clean his teeth before visiting the parents of the child, and that thought made him grin.

Atticus ran his hand through his hair and sat, just a little more upright, back at the desk, to review the file pertaining to yesterday's accident on the computer and type up today's date for when she arrived.

He'd filled in most of the details, uploaded the photographs, and almost finished the report. Just Phoebe's statement to add. Phoebe, who had captured his attention, though he wasn't sure he'd captured hers. At least she'd remembered him, or remembered the ten-year-old him, which wasn't *such* a good thing. She'd been busy and he'd just stood there holding an IV bottle. Watching her. Nobody looked at the law, which had suited him too well, for too long. He would have loved to have phoned Dali, if he'd still been alive. Guess who I ran into? Remember that older girl I had a crush on in Birdsville . . .? Nope. Couldn't happen. Sometimes when Atticus thought of his brother he felt he didn't deserve a happy ending. But he needed to get over not being able to save his brother from himself. Dali had been on self-destruct for too long.

So, what had changed? Why was he willing to risk this woman being exposed to his past? Did he think Phoebe McFadden might understand his guilt?

He hadn't been able to stop his brother going off the rails. Or protect his family. Or stop Dali from dying.

Did he want Phoebe McFadden to notice him? Was he willing to risk not being able to keep someone else safe?

Or maybe she'd tell him to go to hell, she'd keep herself safe, thanks very much. Which would be a surprise and a delight, and he almost laughed out loud at the thought. Phoebe was no pushover.

Maybe he was feeling a ray of hope he hadn't expected. Shouldn't expect now.

If she was unattached. If she liked him. If she didn't only think of him as ten years old . . .

All strange thoughts to have. He heard the door open, saw through the screen when she entered the outer office.

He opened the door to the office behind and invited her into the big work area with a wave of his hand, and Phoebe McFadden glided in, her step light, the faintest wisp of some summery scent carried on the hot dusty air following her in.

Felt his mouth tug up just looking at her, because the woman was certainly something to smile about. 'Less than ten minutes,' he murmured.

That elusive scent seemed to wrap around him and he knew he wouldn't forget it. Or possibly, wouldn't forget her. So strange . . . perfume had never been his thing – until now? He shoved the thought away for later, on his toes quickly as he stood waiting for her to sit.

She smiled back. A fast, polite lift of one side of her lovely mouth, and something inside him wanted more. She was so reserved, not a gushing person at all – she hadn't been in the past either, but without being cold. Funny how he remembered that.

She said, 'It never did take long to walk around Birdsville.'

Ah. More past there. 'We walked a few streets together here back then.' Not a question.

Waved one slim-fingered hand. 'I left when I was seventeen.'

A year after he left. 'And became a very efficient life-saving nurse, apparently.' He'd actually visited for the races one year and asked after her at the pub. They said she'd left years back.

Her brow wrinkled, making her look vaguely uncomfortable, but she nodded in agreement. Not used to compliments? He couldn't believe that.

He added, 'Hallie's still singing your praises all over town.'

A minuscule shake of her head. 'Team effort. She was great.'

'I might have done a bit of singing as well.'

He watched her shoulders relax, as if now she knew he was kidding. 'Really? Do you have a good voice? I don't remember that.'

He winced. Yep. She remembered him as a little kid. But he wasn't giving up. 'Baritone. Rich as chocolate. Would you like to hear?' And finally . . . There. He'd made her smile. It was worth waiting for. That smile was cheeky, gorgeous and generous with white teeth flashing. Her whole face bloomed until she stole his breath and tightened his chest. Oh yeah. She'd always been a looker. And there was no doubt he liked looking.

There was still amusement in her voice when she said, 'I'd pay to hear that.'

He grinned. Maybe one day he would croon along to her. Where no one could hear. When he'd scrubbed out her memories of his younger self. If he got the chance. Better behave like a man if he wanted her to think about him like that. 'Another time perhaps. Please take a seat and we'll get this statement out of the way.'

She studied him as if he puzzled her, but settled into the chair opposite and crossed her legs. Lovely legs in knee-length shorts in a darker shade of purple than her shirt. Shapely legs. Brown and smooth. And her eyes. He'd never seen anyone with eyes that particular shade of soft lilac since . . . her. Like budding violets before they deepened into dark velvet.

Down, boy.

He sat as soon as she'd relaxed back. 'Thanks for coming in today.'

'No problem.' She reached into her pocket and held out a sheet of folded paper. 'I wrote out my statement. I'm happy to read it out so you can type if that's what you'd prefer.'

Even better. 'That would be easy. Thank you.'

He typed as she recounted. Mentioned she'd noticed the car pass. The speed of the vehicle. Had no idea how fast they were going because she'd been parked so anything would appear fast, but they had caught up to her within five minutes of her noting their dust behind her. She'd been travelling between forty and sixty kilometres an hour.

She explained she'd known her position at the crash site because of her habit of clearing the tripmeter between towns when she travelled outback.

Atticus held up a hand as he thought about the simplicity of that. 'I wish more people would copy you.'

She shrugged. 'Maybe we could put up a sign suggesting it leaving each town.'

Since arriving here he'd spent a lot of his police time trying to find people lost somewhere in the vast road system, let alone those who had wandered off the roads. 'Now that's a great idea.'

He slid a pad of notepaper across the desk and jotted down, *Tripmeter leaving town.* They could put it next to *Phone to your next destination.* He finished and pushed the pad away again. 'Thank you. I'll work on that.'

She read the statement out, her voice precise and calm, about her first sighting of the accident and her initial observations, and what she'd done before they arrived. She finished with her leaving the crash scene three and half hours later.

It fitted with all his suppositions and observations, so he finished typing, read it through, changed a couple of typos, and printed it.

When she'd read it, she nodded, and signed it. She handed it back. 'You're a good typist.'

'I've had a lot of practice since I entered the police force.'

'When was that?'

'Ten years ago.'

She nodded. 'So where did you go after you left here?'

'Mount Isa.' And he did not want to talk about that so he sat back in his seat and gestured to the tiny kitchenette. 'Can I offer you a cup of tea?'

'Sure. Strong black. Thanks.'

'Sugar?'

'No.'

'Same as me.' That shouldn't feel so good, but it did. Now who was a goose? Didn't take long with the kettle already boiled. He offered her the best cup without the chip and sat again.

'I heard you're back for the wedding of Scarlet McFadden.'

'I'm back to be bridesmaid and then I'm gone.'

'And to see your father?'

'He and I have been estranged for years.'

He'd wondered about that. Rusty was reliable, quiet, a helpful guy. Atticus already knew everyone in town again – that hadn't taken long, what with the town only having a hundred or so residents. A little more than half that in the heat of summer, he'd been told. He did wonder where they all went. Maybe summer jobs?

He wondered about the cause of such a rift. He seemed to remember some tragedy with Rusty's wife from years earlier, but he rarely saw the man and had never heard a bad word. By all accounts, Rusty was handy with a lot of casual work, often did a great job driving the ambulance, and kept to himself.

'I'm sorry to hear that.' He wasn't sure if he was sorry that she was estranged from her father or the fact that after the wedding the town was excited about she'd be gone. From the look on her face, she was wondering what he meant, too. But her expression also said don't ask.

A prudent man would just leave it at that. He could be prudent, so he shelved those questions for another time.

They sat in companionable silence as they sipped their tea. Which was odd. And restful. Every now and then their gazes met, held, and drifted again. It had been like that in the past. Companionable. Easy. Sitting by the billabong or under a tree. Chatting or not. Each with their own thoughts.

When they'd downed half a cup, he asked, 'Have you an agenda for the week before the wedding?' He knew it was on the Saturday, a week after the races.

'Once the races are done? Some wedding arrangements. And a hen's night.'

He smiled. 'No driving after libation, I assume?'

'Not by me.'

He'd known that. Gut feeling. She knew the consequences first-hand. 'If you feel like going on a drive other than that? I have to check out the parking area near Big Red in the next couple of days,

74

ensure there's no issues or rubbish before the influx of visitors for race day. If you'd like to revisit out that way, I can be flexible on when.'

'Weeeelll,' she drew the word out as she stood, 'that depends on what the bridezilla wants.' And smiled. Didn't say no. Interested, then? He did enjoy that smile.

'I'd like the company,' he pressed just a bit. Your company, but he wasn't quite ready to say that. Instead, he stood. Savoured the curved lips and mouth that wasn't as full of humour as when they were kids, but still spectacular.

She said, 'Scarlet's away till tonight in Charleville. She flew out this morning for the final dress fitting to bring home "the gown". Seems it took longer than expected, but when I'm able, I'd enjoy that. Be nice to see the desert out there again. Let me know when you're going.'

He could accelerate plans. 'We could go this afternoon before she returns. I hear there's no Big Red Tour today. Sunset is always spectacular.'

She nodded, thoughtfully. 'I'm free.'

Pleasure expanded inside his chest. Excellent.

Her eyes met his and he enjoyed the amusement in them. 'I don't suppose you have a couple of folding chairs?'

'I certainly do. Sunset, then?'

Her eyes lit up. 'I love the desert at sunset.'

He could see she did. Her face fairly glowed at the thought. 'I'll pick you up at five-fifteen. Sunset is six-thirty.'

'You know the times in case you need it?'

'I know because I do the weather every day for the Bureau of Meteorology.'

'You'll know the temperature then,' she teased.

'Twenty-five degrees at six pm.'

'I'll bring a hat.' She turned and he watched her walk away. Her back straight, her step fluid and graceful, and yes, he was watching her backside – who wouldn't? – but with absolute respect.

She opened the door before he could get to it. Was it his imagination or had she left the room itself feeling strangely bereft, to him as if someone had turned out the lights? But he would see her tonight. If not before. It was a small town.

Atticus shook his head at the ridiculous thoughts. Good grief. He'd best go and see the delinquent. Get his mind away from purple shorts and shapely calves. Do some work.

Chapter Nine

Phoebe

Phoebe walked away from the police station with her head high and her cheeks warm.

If she'd thought visiting Atticus Bow would dampen any of her previous awareness of the man, then that expectation had evaporated like water in the desert. The last fifteen minutes of AB exposure made her glow all over and she could not remember that ever happening before. Not with any guy. And she had never fancied a younger man.

The good news was her cousin had to drive ten hours back from Charleville and wouldn't see Phoebe's blushing face until tomorrow. The drive to Charleville and back had been something Phoebe hadn't felt she needed to experience again, so Scarlet had elected to take one of the twice weekly flights there and get a lift back. Too many years of sleeping behind the driver's seat in a cattle truck for Phoebe to want to spend twenty hours in a car if she didn't need to.

Which brought the kicker into focus. Those weekends she'd come to see her dad.

She needed to see Rusty. Today. Now.

Scarlet had threatened to drag her over to her old home if she hadn't been to visit by the time she returned. Phoebe should have gone yesterday but had cried off, citing exhaustion so soon after the accident. Even Scarlet had understood that.

Now Phoebe headed for the bakery. She'd take a fresh loaf of bread and a chocolate slice, his favourite, with her when she went.

At the thought of the bakery and all the times Rusty had taken her there to break some bad news to her, sadness engulfed her like one of Birdsville's unexpected dust storms. Particles from the past gathered around her and dimmed her vision as if she stood in a cloud of sand, but actually, the low visibility was caused by the stinging in her eyes. Shook herself. Stop it. The past was in the past.

But they had lost so much. She and her dad. So many moments of missed sharing.

Birthdays. Though he sent a card every year, and, after that first year, she had sent one back on his birthday too. But she hadn't sent love.

Christmas. Again, with the cards. But no conversations. The times he'd tried to talk she hadn't helped. Cutting it short. Choosing to work all holidays. Telling herself she'd ring him when she felt the time was right.

Never found that time. And now she wondered if she'd been right. Or very, very wrong.

So, thanks to her own inability to forgive there had been no parent in the wings to share her accomplishments, though she suspected Scarlet had kept him apprised of her career.

Scarlet connecting them. Like the time she'd notified Phoebe about Rusty's admission to hospital for renal colic. Phoebe had phoned the ward and been told he was in no danger. Satisfactory and improving. And she'd said, 'Thank you.' And, 'No. I don't want to speak to him.'

Which in the bustle of work and her life in Adelaide she could brush off as not having time.

Today, walking to the bakery in the biting sun, in the sleepy town she'd grown up in, her boorish ignorance of her father's life glared at her, exposed as what it had always been. Immaturity. Stubbornness. Unkindness for something he'd done many years ago, that she still didn't understand. Reasonable enough for an impetuous seventeen-year-old to decide she'd never forgive him.

At almost thirty-five what was her excuse now?

None.

Phoebe blew out a breath and pushed the tension away with it. No use beating herself up ten minutes before seeing him.

He'd survived. She'd survived. That's what people in the bush did. They survived and went on. Maybe there was something they could salvage to start fresh. And it felt truly surprising how much that thought snuggled in and eased her guilt. And gave her hope.

Bakery first.

The bakery had changed. Dusty Miller was gone, sold up, retired, and sadly was now buried out of town at the Birdsville Cemetery, with his larrikin humour only a wonderful memory.

Phoebe had worked for Dusty in the holidays and busy times, eaten his famous camel pie, and helped in the rush leading up to the races, when they made more than ten thousand of the pastry delights.

Her dad must have been greatly upset that his mate had passed on. Something else she needed to say when she saw him.

At least the bakery was still here, smelling as good as ever. The new owners had excelled at keeping it going. Kept it available to the town and the visitors. An oasis across the dry field from the pub.

She was served by Emily, a smiling young backpacker with an English accent. Phoebe knew she was a backpacker because she overheard the girl's conversation with a tourist couple while she waited for service. Tourists were good for this isolated town. Kept it alive.

Phoebe was a tourist.

A stranger. It felt strange to be a stranger. A guest.

Fifteen minutes later Phoebe walked the path to her father's house: not a garden path because most of Birdsville had gravel or dirt front yards with the baking sun. Though she'd noticed the school committee had put in a lot of effort and gained the rewards with an oasis in the desert for their pupils.

Her dad didn't have an oasis. Her dad had very little, the last she knew. When she realised there was a pattern to their lack of finances, and finally guessed he was a gambler like the grandfather who had lost the family station as a young man, she understood why. Why they'd always been broke. Why he missed her birthdays. Why he'd taken her money that last, devastating time. The horses.

Except he did own his house now, recently purchased from Scarlet's father when he retired, after years of his brother renting it to him cheap. So said Scarlet. Which made her wonder how he'd come up with the cash. A big race win? Or a big debt? Or something else?

She swung the bag with the fresh loaf of white bread and two chocolate slices but before she reached the steps the door opened, and Rusty stood there.

Her father. Not quite as tall as she remembered. Slightly bowed. Older. His red curls heavily streaked with grey, still handsome in an old-cowboy kind of way, a tentative smile on his face that broke her heart and reminded her of her childhood and all those night-time hugs when he tucked her into her bed and made her feel safe. And loved. What the hell had she been thinking to lock him out of her life?

She moistened her dry lips. 'Hello, Dad.'

'Phoebe.' His voice deep and quiet, so achingly remembered. 'Love.' His voice cracked on the last word and he harrumphed.

Her own throat closed, and she put her head down as she climbed the steps, staring at the fissured concrete below her, hiding the stinging shine in her eyes. Damn it. She lifted her chin. 'I bought some bread. And a cake.'

'So did I.' He stood right there in front of her. Thinner. Older. She'd thought he was so tall.

After all these years. Up close he had deep sun-creases at the corners of his eyes and down the sides of his brown weathered face in profound grooves. His veined hand reached out and she gave him the bread bag before she understood he was reaching for a hug.

Awkwardly, with the bread between them, they sort of hugged, arms and hands patting and retreating, and then he stepped back and gestured her inside and she slipped past with relief and a strange, sad, disappointment in herself.

She was so useless at this stuff. Though, when in her life had she become so out of practice? She had no idea. She hadn't really hugged anyone much until Scarlet yesterday and Scarlet had initiated that.

She could barely remember her mother hugging her. Auntie Daph in Charleville had not been an affectionate woman and Phoebe had gravitated to non-demonstrative friends to combat her own awkwardness in the big world of the city.

At work she'd always been put in charge and that meant a certain distance from co-workers as well. No close workmates. Her excuse.

She looked away from her useless relationship skills to the room she remembered from all the years before. 'You've got wood flooring and a new lounge,' she murmured, remembering the split lino and the old white vinyl lounge that could crack in half and make a slippery bed with a strange fondness.

Her father snuffed a pained laugh. 'A few years ago. It was pretty bad.'

She didn't remember it as bad. Always clean. Just old and worn, like everything they had back then. But back then, she'd had her dad who loved her and she'd idolised him. She'd thought that was enough.

Rusty said quietly, as if he'd heard her thoughts, 'I was a pretty poor sort of dad.'

No. He hadn't been. Except for the lack of money from what turned out to be his vice. 'We had good times.'

And there on the mantelpiece where her mother's portrait used to be, next to hers, was a photo of a horse. Of course there was. She damped down the surge of irritation. Pushed it away.

'About the money . . .' Rusty's shoulders looked like he had the weight of maybe a whole sand dune as large as the famous Big Red on his shoulders. 'I need to explain —'

She held up a hand. 'Please. Can we not talk about it?' She'd had enough. Had punished him and her enough. This was stupid. What he did with his life now was his own business and she'd return to hers in a couple of weeks.

She stepped in, put her arms around him properly and inhaled the scent she suddenly remembered from all those years earlier. Discovered, in a shock of heart-cracking warmth, she'd never stopped loving her dad. Awkwardly hugged him tighter until there was nothing half-hearted about it.

She'd just been thinking she hadn't forgiven him. 'Oh, Dad,' she murmured almost inaudibly. 'I'm so sorry I stayed away. And it's so good to see you. Can I put the kettle on?' She stood back and studied his worn face.

'But . . .' he said.

She shook her head and he closed his mouth, his expression agonised for a second, and she wondered if she'd done something else wrong by stopping him getting it off his chest. She didn't want anything else to come between them now, to affect their relation-ship. She didn't want either of them to suffer any more.

Finally, he nodded. 'Sure.' Though he sighed. Then he gestured with his head for her to go ahead.

With relief Phoebe stepped over to the immaculate kitchen, which still sported the pink Laminex and black handles – the same, except for the newish microwave. Dad had always been meticulous about the house, sweeping daily, mopping at night before bed, and he'd taught her the same. She still liked things tidy, sparkly, clean. Which wasn't easy in Birdsville, with the dust blowing most of the time and tracking in on your shoes. A fact that explained why most houses in town didn't have carpets, which would only trap the dust.

Her dad said sternly, 'But after a cuppa I've got something to show you.'

'Okay. And I want to talk about what you've been doing all these years.'

'Yeah, well, pretty much the same thing,' he muttered and took down two chipped cups. She was pretty sure they were the ones they'd had when she was a kid.

After the tea, Bushells brand and brutally black, she followed him out the back door to the three-bay shed in the yard, his slightly stooped shoulders ahead of her as she followed. She noticed he'd put an air-con unit in the shed, which seemed odd because she didn't remember him as a shed man.

He unlocked the padlock: another strange thing because he'd never locked the door. Birdsville didn't have petty crime, or not much, because there weren't a lot of places people could hide if they did steal something. If they got away on the road the next town's police would be watching for them when they arrived many hours later.

He pulled across the big sliding tin doors and the outside light spilled into the dimness within. To the left of his old truck stood a red blocky shape she thought, blinking, she just might recognise. Though it had certainly changed. Her mouth formed an O of surprise.

'The Desert Lizard,' she breathed.

'It is.'

'How?'

An embarrassed shrug. 'Yeah, well, as soon as I saved your money back, I paid the fellas to rebuild the engine. It's old style now, of course, but has the two-one-two horsepower straight six four-point-five-litre motor and will take you anywhere. Tow anything. Best four by four they ever made.' He shrugged. 'Been working on the body. Slow but steady.' He glanced away from the car and out the door into the heat. 'Since you left.'

She blinked: her eyes stung, although it wasn't tears. It wasn't. Eighteen years. He'd been working on her car for that many years. And she'd been ignoring him for the same length of time.

The vehicle literally shone. New paint all over in the original 80 Series red, polished and shining. So funny it perfectly matched the colour the city cowboy had painted hers.

But oh, my, the old beast looked good. Toyota didn't do chrome in the nineties but the trim around the lights was pure and brilliant and the black grille immaculate. Black, unworn tyres, not the cheap brand, and the body all over in showroom condition. The silver rims were spotless and the doorhandles pristine. No racks or snorkel or bull-bar marred the simplicity. Just an unadorned original.

Warmth, a surge of awe and rising tightness in her chest made the words difficult to enunciate. 'Oh, Dad. She's beautiful.'

He ducked his head. A pleased look in his eyes. A twitch to his mouth. 'Yeah, well, she's had every system checked for leaks, a bit of rust cut out under the left front guard but the rest I fish-oiled and I've gone over it all underneath. Coiled springs and solid axles. Reckon she'll take you anywhere. Still only got two hundred thousand on the clock and don't doubt she could do a million.' He gestured to the floor of the shed and she saw he'd had a small hoist installed under it. 'Been a project in the down times from work.'

The uncluttered lines of the totally restored vehicle were nothing like the cracked skin of the wreck she remembered parked outside their house.

Phoebe leaned in and opened the driver's door. It swung open smoothly, with not even a squeak. The waft of cleaners and carpet shampoo hit her nose and her gaze roamed the interior cab, again spotless, comfortable looking and spacious.

'It's thirty years old but there's electric windows and central locking. Always liked the split tail gate and the sliding third-row windows. These babies are worth more now than they were new.' Dad slid his hand caressingly along the side panel as if stroking a pet. 'She's yours.'

'She's beautiful. Perfect. Thank you. But . . .'

He raked his hair. 'I know. You have a real car. I saw the one outside . . .' His voice trailed off. Shrugged a little helplessly. 'I didn't think it would take nearly two decades for you to come back.' His crooked grin went with the shrug. 'But that's my fault.'

No. No, it wasn't. It was hers. And she had no idea what she'd been thinking all this time.

Before she could even try to understand the ramifications of his bombshell a text came through from Atticus that distracted her.

Raincheck on Big Red. Someone off a bike at Poeppel Corner. I won't be back till late.

Her dad's phone rang. Phoebe, still staring at the text, heard him say, 'Yes. Of course. I'll meet you down at the clinic.' And she realised they were probably hearing about the same accident.

'Sorry, love,' her father said. 'I have to go. Gloria wants me to drive the ambulance out to Poeppel Corner for her. Someone's called in on a sat phone.'

Her mind still spinning, she said, 'I thought someone else went with the ambulance? What happened to Reg?'

'Gone. Passed away. I've been doing it for years.'

Had he? The thought stirred an unfamiliar emotion she hadn't felt for too long. Her chest tightened when she realised what it was. Pride. 'I could come with you? Be a second pair of hands for Gloria or at least help to lift the patient.'

Her dad looked more relieved than she'd expected. 'I'm sure she'd love that. We'll be going via Big Red with the inner track under water the last couple of years. Could be a long night.'

'Then I'll duck across to Scarlet's and grab a couple of water bottles and a cardigan for later.'

Going that way to Poeppel could take anything up to seven hours depending on the road. They wouldn't be travelling much more than thirty to forty kilometres an hour once they hit the sand. And the same back. Plus the time needed for stabilising the patient.

She squinted at the sun overhead. It was late morning now. So definitely dark before they got home. She knew how cold it could get in the desert. And suddenly all those camping trips Dad had taken her and Scarlet on came flooding back. He'd been a wonderful parent those times. She should tell him.

Rusty glanced at his watch. 'You want to meet me down at the clinic?'

And there goes an opportunity to say, 'You were a great dad.' Instead, she said, 'That works,' to his back.

Phoebe walked quickly around the side of the shed then dashed across the road as her brain whirled, and she stopped, shocked – it was as if she stood back in the darned boxing ring taking punches, something she'd imagined as a kid watching the shows. She'd cut her dad out of her life for more than half her life. Idiot.

Once in Scarlet's house she penned a quick note to explain where she was going – Scarlet might well beat her back.

The ambulance would have sat phones and radios, though. Grabbed her phone for photos – not for non-existent phone service – because even though this was an emergency there would be amazing desert vistas.

She slipped to the loo because there wouldn't be much chance to do that for a while. Not in privacy anyway. And when she'd washed her hands and cleaned her teeth, she grabbed the extra water, cardigan, and a box of muesli bars that she'd had in her car, locking the house as she left.

Phoebe walked fast down the road to the clinic, passing Rusty's car, parked outside.

Chapter Ten

Gloria

Gloria carried the extra emergency supplies outside and paused beside Rusty as he stood at the lifted bonnet of the ambulance for his pre-departure check.

'Did you tell her?'

Rusty had avoided her eyes since he'd arrived. He glanced up quickly now and then away. 'I tried. She didn't want to hear.'

Argh. Gloria wanted to poke his chest but restrained herself. 'So? If you didn't talk, what did you do?'

He shrugged and went back to checking the oil. 'I showed her the Desert Lizard.'

'But she still thinks —'

He nodded. 'It's harder than you think, Gloria. I mean, she stayed away for so long. It's not all my fault. She waited this long to give me a chance to explain.'

'Which you didn't take.'

He wasn't listening. 'I saw her today. She's thirty-five years old. Thirty-five. My teenage daughter is gone. The little baby I watched grow, Gloria . . . I missed it all.'

So much pain in his eyes and she wanted to pull him into her arms. Silly, silly man. 'Rusty. Did you even hug her hello?'

'Tried. Awkward it was. She gave me another one later but the pair of us are like strangers who don't know what to do with our hands.' He looked up, his eyes shining with unshed tears. 'I used to hug that girl every night. Tell her I love her. She believed the worst and just dropped me out of her life for twenty years.'

'Come on. You're exaggerating. It's eighteen, and you exchanged cards.'

'Eighteen years. Right. We haven't spoken much but I guess we will.' His chin lifted. He looked as stubborn as his daughter. 'Right now, we need to think about this retrieval.'

He was right. She turned to the open back door at the rear of the vehicle. 'I'm sorry today didn't turn out for you but . . .' She paused and glared back at him. 'I kid you not. You have two weeks until your daughter leaves. Tell her or I will.'

Gloria lifted a bag of medical supplies into the ambulance and shut the doors, then turned around and saw Phoebe peering through the kitchen window of the clinic. She waved her through and watched her step out onto the back ambulance bay.

'Phoebe McFadden!'

'Gloria.' Phoebe's face creased into a big smile that made Gloria's heart warm. Phoebe's arms eased around her and hugged her tentatively.

Gloria was having none of that and hugged her heartily back. 'So good to see you. It's been too long.' Too darn long, you silly girl, but she let Phoebe go and straightened.

'My word it has,' Phoebe said. 'You look just the same.'

'I feel older.'

Phoebe smiled and stepped back. 'We all do.' She glanced at her dad and back at Gloria. 'What can I do to help?'

'Nothing.' Gloria waved a hand. 'We're always packed and ready to go. Your dad's just checking there's no stowaways or problems under the bonnet. Are you coming with us in the ambulance or going with Atticus?'

She saw Phoebe blink. 'I thought I was coming with you.'

Gloria shrugged. 'The police car might be more comfortable.' She gestured at the ambulance. 'You'd have to sit in the back here. For hours.'

When she didn't answer Gloria laughed. 'I don't think Atticus will mind – pretty girl like you. Here he comes now.'

Before Phoebe could say anything, Gloria made it happen. 'Hey, Atticus, reckon you could take Phoebe with you? She's coming to give me a hand.'

Atticus Bow smiled. Such a lovely smile that boy had. All white teeth and chiselled lines. Then he raised one sympathetic dark brow at Phoebe's pink cheeks, and his eyes twinkled. 'Seen firsthand how helpful she can be. Be honoured to have you along, Phoebe.'

Phoebe glanced at her dad, and Rusty was watching the by-play with interest. Gloria supposed she could have swapped places, but she'd rather travel with Rusty. Phoebe was outgunned and by the looks of her she knew it. But really, did she want to ride in the back of an ambulance, bouncing around, or in reasonable comfort in the front seat of the police vehicle with Atticus? Silly girl. No dilemma there.

Atticus inclined his head. 'Rusty. Good to see you again. You driving the ambulance?'

Rusty nodded and Atticus said, 'Let's go then.'

Phoebe McFadden. Gloria had so many memories of young Phoebe. And now she was here looking like a movie star with her dark good looks and calm manner. Coming with them today, which, even if Gloria did not entirely want to admit it to herself, she was glad of.

Of course, there was a conversation she would have to have with Phoebe when her father eventually told her the truth. Would Phoebe forgive both of them when she realised Gloria had to have known all these years?

Luckily, they didn't have time for that right now.

Rusty held the passenger side door of the ambulance and she climbed in but still managed to watch Phoebe follow Atticus down the driveway into the street where the police car had been parked.

She watched them turn west towards the Big Red Sand Dune and the QAA line.

Their cavalcade picked up the recovery specialist, Hassett, who'd bring the bike back in on his truck. All three vehicles sported a four-metre white pole with the orange flag at the top: this was required for sandhill visuals between approaching cars. Not that they expected to meet cars unexpectedly, with radio monitoring for other vehicles approaching from the other direction across the desert. But that simple early warning system had prevented many accidents. Gloria had been to a few collisions when a driver had forgotten to use the flag and paid the price.

'How you feeling today, love?' Rusty's question took her by surprise because she hadn't thought he'd noticed her exhaustion yesterday.

'I'm fine, Rusty. Nice to be home. Had a good sleep in my own bed and that's always a bonus.'

He turned his head briefly and gave her one of his beautiful smiles. 'Hope you didn't mind me bringing Phoebe?'

'Last thing I'd mind.' Darn glad of it she was. 'So . . . What did she think of the car?'

Rusty dipped his head. Watching the road from under his brows. 'She liked the Desert Lizard.'

Silly man. He'd spent years fixing that wreck. 'I think she'd more than like it. It's a labour of love and anyone can see that.'

'Maybe.'

'Well. You both looked a little easier with each other than I thought you might be.'

'Maybe we've turned the corner. Even if I haven't told her about her mother. We'll see.'

'Should have years ago.'

One shoulder hunched. 'Wasn't easy.'

'You just have to say it. The sooner the better.'

'You'll talk to her about it after?'

'I will, after you're done. God help me, Rusty. I never liked the lies.'

He sighed. Lifted his chin. Nodded. 'Seemed right at the time and there's no going back. We gotta make the best of it now . . .'

'You will. You both will.'

Rusty shot her a look of gratitude. 'Enough about that. Did you see the way that copper looked at her? He's too young for her.'

Gloria smiled at the frown in Rusty's voice. Just like a protective dad. 'And why wouldn't he? She's a good-looking woman.

Can't be more than half-a-dozen years between them. And they were friends as kids.'

'She's my princess.' His voice held that soft tone he always used when he spoke about Phoebe. Too many years blamed for something he thought he was doing for the right reasons, and too guilty about the truths he didn't tell. Her heart ached for her dear friend. The poor man had only ever tried to do the right thing.

As if he'd followed her thoughts he said quietly, 'Except for you, these last years have been the hardest in my life.'

Gloria's heart felt as if it was breaking. She slid her hand across and patted his knee. 'Everything will turn out fine, Rusty. You wait and see.'

Chapter Eleven

Atticus

In the police car Atticus couldn't help his smile. Seemed he'd stepped out on the right side of bed this morning. It wasn't the sunset trip he planned but this would last longer. Normally, he didn't feel happy when he was heading out towards a recovery job with someone injured, but the woman next to him improved the whole situation big time. And not just because of her medical knowledge and skills.

He wasn't wasting the opportunity to catch up on the years since he'd seen his delightful passenger. 'Tell me about you.' He slanted a look her way. 'What happened after we left town and how did you get into nursing?'

He watched her brows furrow and for a few seconds there he didn't think she was going to answer. His stomach sank. Blown it already? Maybe that wasn't a great question.

Slowly she said, 'You asking as police or travel buddy?'

Geez. Had he sounded like he was interrogating her? 'Definitely travel partner. No problem if you don't want to answer.' He waved a hand at the windscreen. 'We can talk about the weather. Or the terrain? Or what you had for breakfast?'

95

He caught just a glimpse of a tiny smile. Phew. Relief skittered down his throat. Might have recovered by the skin of his teeth.

She shrugged those delicious shoulders. 'I had toast. The terrain makes me realise how much I've missed the place. Funny, when I thought I hated it. And the weather is exactly as I remember.'

'I'm still getting used to the heat again myself.' He waved vaguely behind him. 'One of my predecessors reckoned, "the land of plenty. Plenty of dust, plenty of heat, plenty of flies."'

'That it has. And more.' Then she added more quietly, so softly he had to strain to hear over the engine noise, 'Plenty of beauty.' There was real awe in her voice, as if she'd forgotten how the desert could capture your heart. He'd never forgotten that, though he wondered if the girl beside him had been a part of the love affair he'd had with this land. Early days.

He could wait. 'The desert has beauty in spades. Though you need to carry a spade for when you get bogged.'

She smiled. 'You do indeed.' The conversation stopped again.

He glanced out the window, where everything was still. Strangely relaxed and easy. 'Love the silence.' And he did, even enjoying the companionable silence between them. No hurry if she didn't want to talk about her life. He wanted her to decide if she wanted to talk to him about the past.

'I was seventeen.'

Seems he didn't have to wait too long after all and concentrated on her words.

'Old enough to have my learner's but I didn't have a roadworthy car. So, I left in a cattle truck to my aunt's in Charleville and never came back.'

96

Not what he expected to hear. He waited, and once again was rewarded with her explanation.

Musingly she added, 'Before that, I used to come home in the trucks from school some weekends.' She shook her head, but he had the feeling it was more at herself than at him. 'Something happened between my dad and me. A rift for a lot of years – too many. Waaayy too many.'

He thought about her words and the remorse in them. Imagined he could hear the pain of regret. Knew about guilt. 'I'm sorry. Rusty seems a good bloke. I've only been on one recovery with him since I got here but he knows what he's doing.'

She smiled at that. Lifted her chin. 'He's good at lots of things.'

Indeed. 'Well, he's got a good grasp on horses. Especially racehorses.'

The woman beside him stiffened and he turned to glance at her but her face showed nothing. 'Like horses, do you?'

For some reason he could feel he'd fallen out of the rapport they'd just had. 'Doesn't everyone?'

'Like a bet?'

'Maybe? On the Melbourne Cup? Sure? Again, doesn't everyone?'

'Not me. Never. I hate gambling.' And then she seemed to pull herself together. 'Sorry. That was intense. Long story I'm not sharing.'

Hmm. 'Okay. Subject change.' He needed to retrieve this mood that right now seriously sucked. 'You know your dad's great with helping Gloria and has excellent pointers on driving in the sand.'

Her shoulders sagged and long fingers loosened in her lap. 'Yes.' She blew out a breath and even smiled at him and he blinked at the wattage. Fast change. 'He knows the desert,' she said. 'One of his best friends from when they were kids, Rob, he's the park ranger here, a respected elder of the Wangkangurru people: he's the real expert, and they've spent a lot of time together.'

Atticus wholeheartedly agreed there. His backside had been saved by that same park ranger on his first trip out. 'Amen to Rob.' He glanced at her and then back at the narrow track in front of them. 'I didn't notice any tension between you and your dad at the health centre this morning.'

'We're resolving things.' She sounded surprised. And pleased. And relieved.

He was genuinely glad for her.

This woman he barely knew and wanted to know more of. 'That's good.' And because he was still feeling bad about the question she hadn't liked, he offered, 'My brother and I gave our parents a run for their money. Lucky I was underage so none of the law-breaking stopped me getting this job.'

His brother hadn't been so lucky. Familiar guilt chewed on him. But all the help he'd tried over the years had backfired – moving out of reach had been a last-ditch retreat to see if making Dali stand on his own would help for a change. And then he'd died. Wrong time to not offer help.

'I'm sorry about your brother. I remember how much you admired him.'

She remembered Dali – or at least she remembered Dali from back then. 'Yeah. He went off the rails. I think sometimes I could have helped him more.' A lot more, as it turned out.

'Did he like getting helped by you? How'd that go? The little brother policing him?'

She'd nailed it. But her voice was kind and maybe she understood he had issues over all this. 'It worked better for him when we were both in trouble.' The thought almost made him smile.

But funny he'd told Phoebe even that much. Earlier indiscretions were not something he'd expected to share with a woman in Birdsville when he was the upstanding police presence here.

She raised those intriguing brows. 'Oooh, what did you do?'

And he'd dumped himself in it. 'Not something I'm proud of.'

Her eyes sparkled. 'Tell me, Senior Constable.'

He pretended to zip his lips. 'Nope. No can do. Not if I'm a senior constable.'

She laughed again and he felt the warmth in his chest expand. 'Okay, tell me, Atticus, what evil deed did you do before you were a responsible adult?'

'My brother's idea, but I agreed. Should have stopped both of us.'

They had been idiots, though young blokes did stupid things, which was why he hated to see them lose the opportunity to learn. 'We borrowed our mother's car on Dali's high school muck-up night. Him over eighteen and me fifteen. We were dressed in balaclavas and we pointed a toy gun at a security officer. Thought it was hilarious. Of course, he pressed charges.'

She blinked. 'Impressively stupid.'

'Yup.'

'What did your mother think about that?'

'She was horrified. Especially since she had personalised number plates and everybody in our small town knew it was her car. Then she had to pick us up out of the Perspex holding cells at the police station and listen to the recorded statements.'

He shook his head. 'Not one of my brighter moments. But one of the officers on that night took me aside later and offered me odd jobs around the station. Washing cars. Windows. Weeding gardens and so on. I saw another side of policing.' He shrugged. 'And here I am.'

'And the repercussions for your brother?'

He'd just known she was going to ask that. Guilt crushed down on him and he blew out a breath. 'Not something I want to talk about today, but it ruined his chances for a lot of jobs with a criminal record. He never had a chance. I was young enough to get away with it, but it affected his life.'

She said gently, 'You still feel guilty?'

'For someone who's already complained about *my* questions . . .' he tilted his head at her and looked over the top of his sunglasses '. . . you're persistent.'

She shrugged. 'I'm interested. You were a nice kid.'

A nice kid? Excellent. She thought he was a nice kid. And that didn't make him wince much. Ouch. She was oblivious to the insult. Before he could think of something clever to say to disabuse her of the fact he was still a nice kid, she went on.

'Yes, you're right. I'm being intrusive.' She flicked her fingers at the windscreen. 'It's great weather. And I love this run out to Big Red.'

His chagrin slid away, because, well, there was a honey in the seat next to him, so he laughed. She made him laugh. It wasn't so much that what she said was very funny. It was, but there was also a curious kind of joy just sitting next to her. Like there was some bloke out here on a sand hill shooting reckless Cupid's arrows from a crossbow – it felt like he had about six stuck in the back of his head. And he didn't even believe in Cupid. Had assumed when the time came, if it came, he wouldn't need arrows to wake him up. Seems he didn't.

She asked, 'How many times have you driven out this way before?' Still back on innocuous topics, thank goodness.

'Probably half-a-dozen. Between your dad, Rob and Hassett, they all made sure I had it down pat. We've had a couple of blokes with flat tyres, well actually, both guys had two spares and it was their third flat tyre that stopped them.'

'Ouch,' she said. 'Tyres do suffer around here. I was lucky on the way in and managed to keep mine intact.'

'You probably drove sensibly.'

She smiled, he assumed at the compliment, and he smiled back. 'Anyway. They all gave me a few hints on the way to approach the sand hills. And Rob filled me in a bit on desert knowledge.'

She nodded. 'Best teacher. Lived here all his life.'

'It's been such a learning curve. Even the low pressures in the tyres needed – way further down than I thought – under twenty just seemed crazy.'

'Seen people put them under ten PSI.' She shrugged. 'It's sand. Deep, soft sand.'

He nodded. 'Along with not roaring up one side and down the other, which was what I always wanted to do.'

'We'll do that.' She pointed at the bright orange flag on the long pole in front. 'I hear the flags are compulsory now. It's great! When I was younger the locals just hoped people would use them.'

He nodded. 'And people are using the radios more.'

'The boys who overtook me on the track didn't have one. Still channel ten UHF for the desert?'

Before he could answer his radio squawked. 'Two vehicles coming east on . . .' The static took the last number. Still a way away.

'Someone else on the main track.'

Phoebe frowned and cocked her head in case it came through again. 'I didn't catch the Q-marker. Did you?'

Q-markers were placed every five kilometres from the Big Red Sand Dune and gave a point of reference to assist people coming the other way. A simple process of announcing on the radio 'Three vehicles travelling west Q-four' gave everyone on the desert channel an idea of who and where other vehicles were. Except when the end of the sentence dropped out.

'Yeah. Drivers are pretty good about reducing unnecessary radio chatter.'

They both smiled at that, and she guessed he knew people who couldn't resist a chat, too.

She whispered, as if imparting a secret, 'I could tell you my dad taught me to drive up and down the sand hills before I had a licence.' She shrugged. 'But . . . because you're a police officer, I can't tell you that.'

'Please don't.'

She grinned at him. 'Anyway, if you get stuck, I can help you out.'

'Not happening. Too embarrassing to get stuck with the ambulance and the recovery team behind us.'

They drove in silence for a while after that and it felt ridiculously companionable for him coming from a family where everyone had been big talkers. Never were that many silences. Even his brother, even in his last, deepest, darkest moments, had still talked a lot.

Atticus liked time to reflect. Soaking stuff in. Loved trekking the outdoors on his own, which was his time. Give him a beach to jog down, or a mountain to climb, maybe a rainforest to walk through listening to the creatures in the foliage. All fabulous places that gave him more thrills than a concert with thousands of people and a mosh pit. Which made him think of the concert he'd missed in Birdsville, the month before he started: he was quite definite there'd been no mosh pit at that one.

'You been to the concert out on Big Red?'

'The Big Bash?' Her face lit up at some distant memory. 'They held the first one the year I left. With John Williamson playing. They were raising money for diabetes after a marathon. I went to the concert but not the race.'

'Not a runner then?'

'To escape from someone boring? Sure. For fun? I don't get it.'

'See. There go my Lycra fantasies.' He smiled. 'I'm not a runner either.'

She snorted. 'Anyway, they sold a few tickets to the concert as well as inviting all the locals for free. Fabulous night. I left in September. I hear it's a huge event now.'

'Too right. I've only been here a month, but everyone's still talking about it. I'm interested to see how it runs next year.'

'You reckon you'll be around that long?'

He felt her astonishment. Not that surprising, given the high turn-over in the outback. 'Who knows? I have an affection for the town from before.' Didn't say it had to do with her. 'And Birdsville grows on you – there's something special you notice, the longer you stay. I'm having a good time. They're good people.'

She sighed and he thought there was regret in it. 'That it does. And yes, they are.' Her voice softened. 'It's actually good to be back, even though I'm only here for a couple of weeks.'

'Leaving straight after your cousin's wedding, then?'

'The Tuesday. Scarlet can't fly out for her honeymoon until then, with the twice weekly flights.' She sounded adamant and his mood flattened just a tad as she added, 'I'll help her with the catering at the races. Be bridesmaid and celebrate – then I'm gone.'

Chapter Twelve

Phoebe

Phoebe heard the words echo in the car, though maybe only because they were just pulling up at the old Adria Downs truck monument and the engine was quieter. Still, she had sounded a bit intense there.

Atticus gave her the side-eye. 'Everyone has their life. I'll just slip out and let the tyre pressure out before we get onto the sand properly.'

Yes. She did have her life. In Adelaide. But for some strange reason she didn't want to think about that right now.

Two curious cattle turned white faces to the car and others skittered away. Behind them, the ambulance and the recovery car came to a stop to lower their own tyre pressure and prepare for the terrain ahead.

Big Red sat thirty-five kilometres west of Birdsville on the edge of the Simpson Desert, on Adria Downs, and was the start of the QAA line. Munga-Thirri National Park started another forty kilometres west from there. All drivers needed high-clearance four-wheel drive vehicles and to know how to drive them.

They set off to Big Red, climbed up and over the biggest dune in the desert, its sides crisscrossed with the tyre marks from ambitious off-road drivers ticking the box for their driving prowess.

Atticus took the gentler side slope and carried on over the top and down the other side with no heroics, and she smiled.

'I thought you might have taken the middle track?'

'When I bring you out at sunset, maybe we'll have a play.'

Her mouth went dry and that shut her up. So he still wanted to do that. She felt her cheeks heat and turned her head to hide the blush. Come on. He was just being a flirt. Young guys did that. Why on earth would it make her shy?

Discreetly moistening her lips, she said, 'I look forward to that,' as if she were a cucumber straight from the fridge. 'Though are you allowed to play in the police vehicle?'

'No. I'd bring my own truck for that.' He smiled, his eyes laughing at her, and she felt her heart jump an extra beat. Unfair attraction zinged through her. *Too young, too young*, her inner voice chanted.

The person, not the age, another voice whispered back.

Before she could stop herself: 'We could bring the new car Dad restored for me. I think he'd like the idea of me bringing her out to have a bit of fun on the dunes. And I'd like to see how she goes.'

'She?'

'The Desert Lizard.'

'Your original Desert Lizard? The wreck you used to keep in your dad's garage?'

'Yes. The red 80 series Land Cruiser.'

'Nice.' His brows furrowed. 'Didn't you say you've been estranged from Rusty?'

'Long story but apparently he's been restoring that bone of contention between us since I left.' She stopped and mulled over those words. Found more. 'And I never got over myself long enough to talk to him.'

The admission hung in the air. It was true. She'd stuck her head in the sand and refused to pull it out. Suddenly she was so very grateful she hadn't lost the opportunity to talk with her father. Imagine if he'd died and she hadn't come back in time. Cold settled into her stomach and she stared out the window. What an idiot she'd been. Stubborn. Sad.

Atticus said quietly, 'You can't do anything about decisions made in the past.' Something in his voice said he understood regrets; she wouldn't mind knowing why. She agreed with the sentiment, of course, and maybe it did help. A little.

Silence fell between them and she guessed they were both privately contemplating things they might have changed if they'd foreseen the future.

Once inside the national park, the remaining one hundred and thirty kilometres to Poeppel Corner traversed loose sand dunes and their speed varied mostly between twenty and forty kilometres an hour.

The hours passed as they followed the QAA line, and they stopped for a ten-minute walk around three hours in, a quick break from the track made by surveyors searching for gas and oil during the 1960s and 1970s.

The one-way trip took five hours, a quick trip really with the track smoother than she remembered it. As they drew closer, not for the first time, she wondered how the motorbike rider was managing without medical help.

When they finally drove up to the scene of the accident they could see someone had rigged a tarpaulin between two bikes; six other riders stood around, and the injured man lay in the meagre shade.

They all climbed out. Phoebe stood back to let Gloria assess him without interruption; her dad carried gear from the ambulance; and she was ready to help when needed.

Atticus spoke to the other riders and began taking notes and names in his notepad but none of them had seen their sixtieth birthday in a while and they were looking strained and exhausted.

The injured man had lost traction in the sand, fired himself over the handlebars, and crashed. A sorry older bike-rider with brittle bones and a pain-filled face.

Gloria and Phoebe rigged a sling for his shoulder and strapped his ankle.

While Atticus had his back to them, Hassett, the desert recovery specialist, had moved on with organising assistance to get the bike into the back of the recovery ute. In retrospect he should have asked Atticus because the older man helping gasped, slid sideways and collapsed. The bike crashed back onto the ground and Hassett swore.

The bike wasn't the problem.

'Not good,' Phoebe muttered to herself as she hurriedly kneeled beside the man, pulling his body straight, opening his airway. She slid her fingers down the side of his throat to feel for the carotid pulse but knew she wouldn't find it. She'd seen this before too many times.

As expected, no pulse. They were a long way from an intensive care and his chances weren't great. 'Cardiac arrest,' she called crisply and repositioned his chin again to open his airway.

Within seconds Atticus had appeared beside her, dropped the resuscitation bag and mask into her hands, and handed the portable defibrillator to Gloria, who'd also appeared.

They positioned his torso and Phoebe placed the inflation mask over the patient's nose and mouth while Atticus began external cardiac massage. Gloria opened the Automated External Defibrillator or AED.

By the time Gloria had yanked open the man's shirt, groaned at the matted white hair covering his tattoos, and shaved some spots to attach the sticky pads of the defibrillator, Atticus and Phoebe were in a good rhythm of his thirty compressions to two of her breaths with the bag.

'Clear,' said Gloria and they both leaned back, removing their hands. The man's body jumped and a gasping breath later the patient coughed and shuddered a breath, though his face remained deathly pale.

Phoebe glanced at the screen and the erratic heart rhythm with a grimace, but erratic was better than nothing.

Rusty could be heard relaying instructions from Gloria on the phone to the flying doctor because everyone knew they now needed helicopter extraction. This patient was way too ill to be bounced over hours of uneven roads.

Hassett said, 'Lex McKay's still in town. He's waiting for a part to come in on the mail this afternoon and has booked dinner at the hotel.' He dug out his sat phone. 'I'll see if I can track him down.'

To the relief of all, Hassett found Lex at a house in town where he was having afternoon tea and of course he agreed to leave immediately to pick up the cardiac patient and Gloria.

Within forty minutes Lex landed and Gloria and the patient were flown back to Birdsville, where the RFDS aircraft and retrieval team would take about an hour and forty minutes to arrive from either Mount Isa or Charleville, depending where the aircraft happened to be that day.

Which left Phoebe riding back to Birdsville with the injured motorcyclist in the ambulance with her father driving. They hadn't made it away from the accident site until six pm and the slow drive back in the dark meant they wouldn't arrive until after midnight.

The patient, Trev, slept most of the way, thanks to the morphine Gloria had given him and which Phoebe kept topped up.

Phoebe glanced forwards at her dad and studied the familiar face with a new intense appreciation. His expression was calm as he steered them smoothly up and down the side of another sand dune. His shoulders were relaxed, his hands loose and sure on the wheel.

Finally he said, 'You're staring. What? Have I got a spot on my face?'

He had plenty. Fair skin didn't do so well in the desert. But she was looking at the strength she'd forgotten. 'You're a handy man to have at a medical emergency.'

He smiled and slanted a look her way in the rear-view, his eyes warm. 'So are you. I'm very impressed with my lost daughter.' Words murmured with a look of pride that made her flush unexpectedly and she stared at her hands in her lap, suddenly shy.

'Thanks.' She lifted her chin. 'Still, every time we needed something from the first aid kit you seemed to know what it was and where it sat.'

'Experience helping Gloria.' He shrugged. 'She's done a great job for a long time but sometimes there's too much for one person. So I try to help.'

'She must appreciate that very much.'

'She does. We've been very good friends for years.'

'I remember.' And she did remember how Gloria had been there for knee scrapes and sudden illnesses and immunisations over the last years before she left. In fact, Gloria had been there for a lot of her teens. 'She's not as young as she was.'

'We all age. Even you. You've been away a long time.'

Silence fell between them, and she checked the readouts on her patient. He still slept but occasionally he murmured in distress. His analgesia was wearing off again.

'Pull over when you have a good place to stop and I'll check him again. Maybe top up his pain relief.'

Rusty nodded and spoke into the two-way to let Atticus know they were stopping. The police vehicle had been driving ahead, hopefully to encourage any wildlife to get off the road before the ambulance came through.

When they moved off again after resettling Trev, Rusty said quietly, 'How was your trip out with Atticus?'

Negotiating another sand hill, he wasn't looking at her, and Phoebe shifted her eyes to the red taillights in front of them.

'Easy. He's a nice guy. Do you remember him?'

'Yes. Wasn't a bad kid. Now got a rep as a very fair copper.'

'So why bring it up?'

A small shrug. 'I'm still your dad. He's only been here a month. I don't really know him. You've probably had more conversation with him than I have. Just wondered.'

Just wondered? Or worried? She could feel the concern. It felt strange, because even though he tried to hide it she could see his protective mode. Her dad. Looking out for his daughter. She'd missed that. She'd missed a lot.

She guessed he was always making sure she was safe when she was a kid but she'd forgotten that feeling in the years since. It sat awkwardly. Yet sweetly. That spot inside her warmed more. 'I have spoken to him more than you would have. I spent five hours in the front seat with him today and a couple of hours yesterday at an accident scene.'

'So? What's your impressions? Do you like him?'

She laughed. 'What is this? You asking me about a boy and whether I like him? I'm not a teenager, Dad. And he's way younger than me.'

'Gloria's younger than me too, but we get on great. And I can ask about men who look at you like he does. I missed most of that father stuff, what with school. And then you leaving.' There was sadness and maybe just a tinge of bitterness. He hadn't deserved her absence. Even murderers only got ten years for killing someone if they had a good lawyer. He didn't slay anyone, and she'd locked him away for eighteen. The thought made her squirm.

He wasn't the only one she'd locked away. Driving herself so hard she hadn't had time to think about what she'd left behind. Because it hurt to think about all she'd left and lost.

Ohhhh . . . the thought illuminated the past like a flashlight down a dark alley. She'd totally blamed her dad for that loss when in fact half of it had been her running away instead of addressing the problem. Young and silly. That's what she'd been. Sad for both of them.

But she was here now. Couldn't change the past, as Atticus had said.

Rusty said, 'I guess I'm out of practice being a dad. Doesn't mean I don't care.'

She reached forwards and touched his shoulder. Very lightly. 'Thanks for caring. I'm out of practice being a daughter but I'm going to try and remember how.'

Rusty patted her hand back. 'So . . . do you like him?'

She laughed. 'I think Atticus is a very nice guy. But he's just a younger kid I knew when I was at school. I'm heading back to Adelaide after the wedding, so he can't become anything more than that.'

Even hearing the words she winced. Yes, it was disappointing, but it was the harsh reality. And she wasn't going into why it seemed harsh.

Instead, she said, turning the conversation away from herself, 'I've only just remembered how strong your friendship with Gloria is. Tell me. Was there ever a romance?'

Her dad huffed out a breath. 'Should have been. I'm the fool. But no, we're just good mates.' He looked back at her, worry on his face. 'She came home from Brisbane yesterday. Trips to the capital always make her tired. Lately, she's been running on very little sleep.'

'Then I'm not the only one who thinks she doesn't look as well as she should?'

'You think?' He shook his head. 'Thanks to too many idiots keeping her up all night while she saves their lives.'

Phoebe thought about that. Today, even. A six-hour trip across the desert managing an emergency situation. A helicopter flight.

Transfers at speed. And then turning up again for the clinic tomorrow at eight-thirty. Gloria had been doing it for a lot of years. 'What's her roster like?'

'Sixteen days on and ten off.'

Phoebe sucked in a breath. 'That's sixteen days on call twenty-four hours a day?' she clarified. And she'd thought her roster was bad.

'Yep.'

Phoebe shuddered. Yuck. 'Has to take its toll.' There would be quiet days, but Phoebe was thirty years younger than Gloria and busy weeks like that would exhaust anyone.

Rusty said, 'Maybe you could talk to her. About cutting down her hours. Or even retirement.'

Phoebe drew her brows together. 'Why would she listen to me?'

'She doesn't listen to me.'

Chapter Thirteen

Charli

On her second morning in Birdsville Charli woke alone. Luke had gone yesterday. The flat tyre had been fixed, he didn't drink too much, and he didn't ask for more money. A relief. Plus, he'd got her here safely. She valued him, but he could be chaotic or turn up at the least opportune times. She wanted this to be a fresh start, and that probably meant not relying on Luke.

Charli touched the photograph on the screen of her phone with one gentle fingertip and wondered if she was dreaming – or wishful thinking. Then she frowned and slid her phone back into the worn pocket of her cotton swing dress. She should be thinking about the job interview. But as soon as the phone was tucked away she wanted to pull the screen out to study the face again.

She'd looked at the background, stretched the photo as big as she could get it, examining the cars and clothes in that photo and the ones around it, and it all seemed to date from about thirty or more years ago. The woman could be her mother?

What she needed to do was figure out how she could get the original photo unstuck from the wall of the Birdsville Hotel and out from the glass frame to see if there was anything written on the back.

Could this be her mother? Her real mother? And if it was her, had she been visiting, living in the area on her own, or were there more family around here?

She needed to stop now. Time was passing and she had to get a job.

Charli looked at the small mirror on the wall and smoothed the floating hem of her dress. She didn't look pregnant, just like a plump girl with a scarred lip, which she'd always been anyway. Hopefully the job would be hers.

It was right up her alley. She liked to work hard, which is what the advertisement said, and she liked to cook and see a kitchen sparkle after she was done. Always so satisfying when something looked as good as it could get.

The ad said only two weeks. Suited her. It was a start and Charlene knew that two weeks was enough to earn a reputation for hard work. Especially in a small town like this. More employment would come her way in the future if she worked hard, and she had a history of that.

She was a night owl. Read for hours lost in other worlds in her e-books from the library. Hardly slept more than five hours at night anyway. Went to bed late. Woke early. Could do long hours no problem.

Despite her nerves at presenting for employment, at the back of her mind she couldn't stop thinking about how she'd felt so hopeful when she'd found that photograph yesterday.

She needed to calm down. She'd waited this long for any news of her family. Soon she'd get to know people enough that she could ask them to lift the whole frame down off the wall and let her look.

She had to be patient.

Scarlet McFadden's house looked freshly painted and very tidy. Charlene's prospective boss could be one scary lady, though. Short and quick moving. Sharp-eyed, with red hair that said she had a temper, yet there was something about her that Charlene really liked.

She was small, and fierce, unlike placid Charli, who showed her meek side ninety-eight per cent of the time – that only changed if someone else was being picked on. Then people realised she was there.

Charlene and Scarlet. It worked. They went together like hard and work. Or good and will.

'I've worked in lots of kitchens. I like them clean,' Charli said. 'I'm careful with knives and I don't mind stirring things for a long time.'

The sharp eyes narrowed, and a small smile tilted the boss's face. It changed her whole look to one of almost warmth. 'Well, I've never had anyone say that before in a job interview, but the last girl I hired changed her mind and now the races are coming. You can't leave until after that. Can you give me that guarantee?'

Now there was a dilemma. But only one answer. 'Yes.' She wasn't gonna leave, unless, of course, something happened with the baby. But nothing had happened with the baby yet. She had six weeks before labour. Why would it happen now? She thought about that. Nodded again. 'I'll stay until after the races. Definitely. Longer if you'll have me. I'm thinking about moving here. Permanently.' The words surprised the other woman and even Charlene a little.

'Why would you think you want to move here permanently?' Scarlet furrowed her brows. 'Especially when you've only been here two days.'

Charli didn't want to share too much. But she might have to if she wanted this job. 'Just saying it feels good.' She'd never had a permanent home, and now she'd only been here two sleeps and already she'd said the P word. 'I'm looking for a home of my own.'

'Well, there's no houses in Birdsville. And rentals don't exist. Where will you stay?'

Something would work out. It had to. 'I could board. With a person who lives by themselves, if they have a spare room? I could do cleaning or cooking for someone old – something like that.'

'You've thought about it, then? Where you from? Where's your family?'

And this was the part she hated reciting. Underlining the loss all over again. 'They said my mum died when I was born. Don't know my dad. Been fostered all my life.' She wanted to say, 'And my last foster mother said my mum might have come from Birdsville.' But she didn't want everyone in town to know that yet, just in case her mum *didn't* come from here and then she'd look stupid. And she might just decide to stay here anyway.

Scarlet frowned again. 'True story?'

Charlene met her eyes. Hoped Scarlet could see the truth through them. 'Yes.'

'Okay. You got the job. I'll ask around to see if anyone wants a lodger, but I don't like your chances. How long you got at the caravan park?'

'A week from yesterday.'

'Okay. Come back here the day after tomorrow at eight am. Work eight till four pm. You might get a short evening shift at the pub after, if you want more work.'

Now that was a good idea. And she couldn't help thinking of the photo. 'Can't I start today?'

'No. My cousin's staying for a visit. She's a high-powered nurse in Adelaide. I need to catch up with her.'

Chapter Fourteen

Phoebe

Phoebe let herself into Scarlet's house just before one am. The front door clicked behind her at the same time as she saw the light under the kitchen door and heard the kettle begin to boil.

Scarlet appeared, sent her a searching look and then, as if satisfied, nodded. 'Nobody died, then. You hungry? Did you get to eat?'

'I had some muesli bars.'

'I'll make you an omelette. You'll sleep better with some protein in your stomach.'

Phoebe raised her brows. 'Haven't seen the scientific studies on that one.'

'A law according to Scarlet McFadden. It's in a book somewhere.'

Phoebe snorted. 'I've missed you sorely, cousin.'

'Yes, well, you,' Scarlet said, accompanied by a pointing finger, 'should've come back sooner.'

And that there was the kicker. 'I'm starting to see that.'

Scarlet sent her another searching look. 'Are you?' Her hands whipped eggs and milk deftly and on the stove a frypan sizzled with butter. When her cousin tossed shallots and mushrooms in to brown, Phoebe's stomach growled at the scent.

She sat heavily at the already set place at the kitchen table and poured herself a cup of tea from the teapot that appeared in front of her. 'I'm that tired . . .' Which made her think of the town nurse. 'Gloria must be exhausted.'

'Did she just get back, too? I thought she'd have been on the chopper. Lex McKay's, right?'

'She was. And yes, it was Lex who helped extract the patient.'

'I heard the chopper come back. Lex brought his mother into town for the race club meeting, I heard? Lucky he was around.'

She thought about the odds. 'Probably saved the man's life – if he survives overnight. Him and Gloria.'

'Gloria's great. She's called out too often. It's better with the admin there now, so she has less paperwork in the day, but she needs another nurse. We had a great post-grad girl here for three months.' She poured in the egg mixture and swirled the pan. 'Something about the funding meant she couldn't stay longer, but the grad made all the difference – she could do the clinic if Gloria had been out all night and needed a sleep. Not sure how much longer our G can keep it up.'

Neither was Phoebe. 'I said that to Dad tonight.'

Dad. She hadn't called him Dad out loud for years. Always Rusty. And she was still in shock from the revelations about the car he'd spent so much time restoring, but she felt too tired to go there, now, with Scarlet.

Scarlet turned, one hand holding the frypan, and raised a brow. But, unusually, her cuz didn't say anything. Which was good, in the circumstances, wasn't it?

Phoebe sipped her tea. Put the cup down. 'Anyway, I think Gloria's a champion, but she's not young.'

'Nope. You want her job?'

'Good grief, no.'

'Why not?'

'Because I have a life in Adelaide. A house. Friends. And a career.'

'Gloria has a career, too. A good career. You saying your career's better than hers?'

A typical Scarlet attack. If she wasn't so tired, Phoebe might have been amused. 'No. What I am saying is that one am is not the time to fight about it.'

'I'll give you that,' said Scarlet, her bristles falling as she slipped the omelette onto the plate in front of Phoebe. 'Eat. Sleep. And I'll see you in the morning.'

The next morning Phoebe knew she had to walk, to think, to ease the agitation of knowing everything wasn't as cut and dried in Birdsville as she'd thought it to be for more than half her life.

Guilt had kept her tossing and turning all night until she slipped out of Scarlet's house with her phone and strode off towards Pelican Point before the sun rose.

Birdsville had a billabong, a natural lagoon. And right at this moment, after eighteen years, she missed the peace she knew it could give: now was the time she needed that peace the most. She could picture it in her mind – had done so many times over the years when she'd been distressed – a beautiful place permanently filled with cooled water from the artesian bore. To top it perfectly, serene pelicans glided around the tree-lined edges, and noisy birds called.

As she passed the Birdsville Primary Health Centre, the last structure on the corner of town, she looked it over. It was new. A clean-lined building next to the old hospital, with a steel fence and gate leading up the fresh concrete path to the porch. Native trees had been planted in the dirt of the front yard. No grass but plenty of leaves and mulch.

It had a high gabled porch roof with two ochre-coloured columns. Nice. But then, this building and the people inside were an important part of the community and deserved distinction. She'd bet Blanche McKay had something to do with lobbying for the funding.

She followed the path to the open road. Past the new corrugated-iron horse riders permanently galloping at the edge of town to welcome the tourists. New? They looked slightly beaten. Well, new since she'd left, like the corrugated camels on the other road to Bedourie.

On the left she glanced across at another unfamiliar sign that read *Thutirla Pula Aboriginal story place*. That hadn't been there when she left all those years ago, either. Although, no doubt the actual place was there, just not the sign. Now a fenced area held a new bush-made shelter leading to the winding native garden paths at the back. An intriguing wander for another day.

Today she needed the billabong.

She'd pushbiked this track so many times in the past with Scarlet, and even with the young Atticus, two and a half kilometres each way, flat and dotted with scrub and trees.

At this time of morning before the sun came up, the peaceful sound of the birds and the crunch of gravelly dirt under her shoes were the only company she had as she turned off the main road and let herself through the gate. The gums along the edge of the gravel track to the billabong shone with life and moisture, so not long since the last rain. Soon dust would be everywhere again as people drove down here during race time.

She couldn't believe the races were so soon. It was as if she'd dived into the life of the town in the first twenty-four hours with everything that was happening. Emergencies, rescues and a seismic shift in her relationship with her dad. All that on top of Scarlet's wedding and her concerns about Gloria. But Phoebe cautioned herself to take Birdsville slowly, let things happen, salvage what she could and accept what couldn't be changed.

That was how she'd decided to play it when she woke up this morning and, strangely, despite all the emotion, she felt lighter in spirit than she had in years.

She turned her head, seeking and drinking in the scuttle of bush creatures, the swoop of birds and the watching owls, there even as the sun rose. Yes. She'd missed this.

In the past, she and Scarlet would race their bikes to the end of the road at Pelican Point. They'd laugh and chuck rocks into the water, slip into the cool depths and backstroke across the billabong in a race.

They were good times. There had been so many good times, and all of them lost in the bitterness of a betrayal that had too many levels to comprehend – and which she now had too many reasons to regret. With the benefit of hindsight, she would have come back sooner.

Before she could begin to beat herself up again, the whisper of wheels on the track behind her made her turn to see a pushbike, and the consistently remarkable Atticus Bow pedalling with leisurely speed towards her. Strong thighs were exposed: his blue footy shorts hid nothing of the long muscles sprinkled with dark hair. Waywardly, her brain took itself off to imagine the view from the back when he rode past.

He stopped beside her. 'You want conversation or to finish your thoughts in peace?'

'Impressive observation, Senior Constable. Were you thinking of having a swim at the billabong?'

'I was, actually.'

'Then how about I meet you there?'

He nodded and without another word pedalled off.

Phoebe blew out a soft whistle. Yep, the view from the back was as stirring as she thought it would be. Cougar, she whispered to herself. Nah, just enjoying the view.

Shook her head. Good grief. But great view.

Also, good on Atticus for picking up that she had something weighty on her mind and needed peace.

By the time she strode all the way to the end of the bush track where the spit of land at Pelican Point sat bounded by water on three sides, her thoughts had calmed. Until her gaze found the man sitting beside the round inflatable pontoon someone had dragged to the end of the track.

That was new, too. One of those inflatable rubber circles with ropes that would hang towards the water for catching and a small ladder to climb all the way up on. She wanted to push it out and sit suspended over the water on the net platform in the centre. 'Very cool. Where'd that come from?'

'Donated by the McKays to make it easier on social nights when people swim.'

'Fabulous. I remember barbecues here and swimming in the summer. They still have those nights?'

'They do. Went to my first one last week after a phone call. Never been summoned to a swim before. They told me everyone was meeting down at the Pelican Point for a barbecue and I was to present myself.'

She smiled. 'Nice.'

'It surely was. Great night and I didn't even get called out.'

The sun had risen higher and already prickled her neck with its rays. The air grew more heated and the idea of slipping into the cool water of the billabong beckoned. 'Race you to the water,' she said and began to strip off her shoes and socks.

Atticus, already barefoot, reached up and yanked off his shirt, and she blinked at the unexpected inkwork. He had an amazing eagle tattoo on his left pec. Widespread wings and arched claws out. Not usually a fan of tattoos, she might just have changed her mind, because this was one of the most beautiful ink drawings she'd ever seen. Or maybe it was just the canvas underneath.

Not something she could unsee. 'Nice eagle.'

He glanced down and back to her face. 'Long story. Not even a great story. Maybe one day.'

'Still a great tattoo.' She smiled. He had issues, too. She could reciprocate the privacy he'd left her in on her walk. Dropped her shorts and top and headed for the water fast. 'Beat you in!'

Phoebe took off to the left, knowing exactly where she was entering the water after years of experience, while he took a shorter route and ended up tiptoeing over sharp gravel, which made her laugh from her vantage point backstroking away from the edge.

Once he finally got to the water and swam over to her he groused, 'I'd forgotten about that better path.'

'Seems so.'

'You could have reminded me.'

She laughed. 'Could've, but I wanted to win.'

The sound of their quiet amusement floated across the water. Gentle. Peaceful. Just like the place. And she could feel the healing of the water and the reflections as the sun rose in the cloudless sky overhead. The golden rays were shining through the trees and to their right a stately pelican drifted calmly along beside the far bank.

She said lazily, 'Did you know they had a crocodile in Birdsville once?'

He shook his head. 'Thought we were too far inland for crocs.'

'A freshie. The locals still believe someone brought him down for a joke and let him go.'

'Imagine. A joke.' He widened his eyes in mock surprise. 'Idiots aplenty.'

'He was here for a while and then some trappers came and relocated him to Dreamworld or somewhere. Quite the tourist attraction.'

They floated. Companionably, not too close in the cool water, but close enough to chat when they felt like it.

The sun rose higher, and Atticus glanced at his watch. 'I'd better go.'

He stood where it was shallow, and she couldn't help watching the water sluice off the eagle on his chest. And maybe she watched the rest of him as well. Taut, defined shoulders, miles of tanned chest with a sprinkle of dark hair and washboard abs that went down to . . .

She jerked a little back to reality when he said, 'The station opens at eight.'

'Oh, right.'

'Did you want to try that run out to Big Red one morning? Do a sunrise and be back in town for seven-thirty?'

That would work. Scarlet rose later than Phoebe. 'Love to. I could walk down to the station before half-five so we have plenty of time to get there before we lose that special light.'

'Done,' he said and climbed out while she floated on her back and pretended not to look. There were worse ways to start the day than watching the tattooed Sergeant Bow get dressed and pedal off.

Equilibrium restored, Phoebe returned to Scarlet's house much more serene than when she'd left. Her cousin, tousled and sleepy, looked not long out of bed with wild hair and creases on her cheek from the pillow.

'I'd forgotten you don't sleep in,' she grumbled and then her attention jagged on Phoebe's wet hair. 'Where you been?'

'Pelican Point. Went for a walk.' She waved an arm towards the other end of town. 'I ran into Atticus Bow on his pushbike.'

'Soooo . . . You went for a swim with him?'

'He was there. Yes.' Phoebe hadn't been going to say that. Just that she'd seen him, but why lie when in fact, she didn't need to? She was a free woman. 'The water felt amazing,' she said instead.

Fat chance her cuz would be diverted by water reports. 'So,

what's he look like without a shirt?' Scarlet leaned in, eyes wide. Mouth just slightly open as if she couldn't wait.

'Tsk, engaged woman. Broaden your mind.' Phoebe couldn't help her smile. 'But, for the record, very, very nice.' And that was all she'd say. Although she could see that eagle oh so clearly imprinted on her mind. 'What is it you'd like to do today, cousin? I'm at your disposal. And how was Charleville? Sorry I wasn't here when you came back.'

Scarlet huffed. 'A mission to get there and back, as always. Glad I only drove one way. The dress fits perfectly now. I can stop worrying about that.' She looked happy. Content.

Maybe Scarlet wasn't going to be a bridezilla. 'That's wonderful news.'

'It is. But, at the moment, I'm thinking more about the gala night in six days and the desserts I need for the OBE tent at the races. I'll make and freeze most of them this week, and just dress them up on the day with fresh cream and berries.'

Phoebe remembered doing that with her aunt in Charleville. 'So, would you like a hand with that today?'

'Nope. I managed to jag a new offsider yesterday when I got back while you were out playing nurse. Young girl, new to town. Charli. Starts tomorrow at eight am.'

'Wow. Employee out here. That was quick.'

'Yes. I'm hoping she works out well. There's something about her that appeals to me.'

Scarlet didn't praise many. Especially people she didn't know. Interesting. 'Appeals? In what way?'

Scarlet shrugged. 'Not sure. She's a shy thing but I think there might be steel underneath. Except she hides one side of her face.

Got some piddly scar I can see she's blown out of proportion in her head. Wish she wouldn't do that. Looks like she might have had a cleft lip as a baby and it pulls her mouth up a bit, but it's barely there.'

All sentiments Scarlet wouldn't usually mention, so this girl had made a big impression. 'Esteem issues?'

'For sure, but that's not it.' Her cousin ruminated a moment before continuing. 'Says she was in foster care all her life and is looking for a place to settle. Apparently, she likes Birdsville.'

Phoebe laughed. 'So do you.'

'True.' Scarlet flashed her a grin. 'And so would you if you let yourself.'

Phoebe held up her hands in surrender, which surprisingly mollified her cuz.

'Charli reckons she likes to work and I think she's telling the truth. She's knowledgeable about kitchens and I like her old-fashioned ways. I think we'll do well together.'

'High praise from you.' Which meant Phoebe had less time in the kitchen than she'd expected. Not a bad thing, but she'd have to find something to amuse herself or she'd go mad.

Scarlet's brow creased. 'As I said, there's just something I like about her.'

'Well, great. So, if we're not cooking, what are we doing today?'

'This morning, before we party, I need to confirm all the orders for my catering.'

Phoebe had expected to help Scarlet with most of the sweets for the big VIP tent, but order confirmation worked too. She was nothing if not adaptable. 'We'll do the orders together. You talk and I'll write everything down for you as you go.'

'Great. Then after that I'm taking the day off and spending it with you. It's too long since we just chilled and chatted. Reckon after today it'll be full on.' She grinned. 'I thought we'd be really radical, take ourselves out to lunch at the pub, crack a bottle of wine and catch up on all the gossip.'

'Sounds good to me.' In fact it sounded like exactly what Phoebe needed, too, because she wanted to hear Scarlet's thoughts on her dad's life and Gloria's health.

Scarlet hadn't finished. Of course. She'd only mentioned one bottle of wine. 'Then maybe come back here. Watch a couple of chick flicks, crack another bottle of wine or two, and eat soft cheese and chocolate until we go to bed.'

'Tough day.' Phoebe laughed. 'Hope your dress still fits after all that. Thankfully, mine will stretch.'

'It'll fit.' Said as if the garment wouldn't dare misbehave again. Phoebe felt almost scared for that poor piece of material.

Chapter Fifteen

Gloria

Gloria pulled the comb through her undyed white hair and stared at the lines on the face in the mirror. Rusty said her hair looked lovely. She wasn't so sure about the bags under her eyes. She'd caught a couple of hours' catnap between when the RFDS took off with the critical cardiac patient and when she'd set the alarm to expect Rusty and Phoebe back with the injured motorcyclist. She'd had to be ready for the next transfer out.

She'd hit it spot on. By the time she'd had a cup of tea Rusty and his daughter had arrived, the flying doctor flew in, they'd transferred the second patient onto the plane, and all in Birdsville had gone to their respective beds.

She'd had some sleep, but she just didn't bounce back as well from late nights as she used to. She needed a holiday.

It was Wednesday today, so the RFDS would be in for the fly-in doctor's clinic, checking up on all those patients Gloria had flagged for medical assessment and following up on referrals and results. They'd be busy, but she always enjoyed the RFDS days.

Though she could have done with a slow one, she thought.

Well, that wasn't going to happen. Not this time of year with the races coming. Her busiest time. Although the swollen tourist season of the races had been superseded in numbers by the Big Red Bash in July.

Who would have thought a desert concert would attract ten thousand people wanting to camp in front of a sand hill? With the way that event was growing it looked like having twice as many people as the races next year. Birdsville had certainly put itself on the map.

'Come on, woman, time for work,' she told herself. She pursed her lips and painted a soft pink lipstick on. 'Okay then. Let's do this.' She stepped away from the sink and marched to the front door.

And Rusty needed to tell his daughter the truth. She couldn't believe he'd driven home with her and still not said anything or even arranged to meet to do so. She was so sick of that man making himself a martyr.

An odd thought struck her. Was she also making herself a martyr because she wasn't happy with her life and she wasn't doing anything about changing it?

Chapter Sixteen

Charli

Charli spent the morning walking around town, waiting for the pub to open, looking at the houses, stepping inside the businesses to see if anyone wanted a lodger for a couple of hours' cleaning. She knew she'd have to access the parenting payment after the baby was born, but she was looking for work with people who might just let her bring her baby with her. The only place she hadn't tried was the bakery.

'A lodger? And when will you have time for cleaning with a full-time job?'

'I like being busy.'

'Seems so.' He shook his head. 'Sorry. I'll ask around but don't know of anyone off hand.'

She nodded. 'That's fine. Something will turn up and I have a roof until Thursday morning.' She could sleep rough, but she didn't say that.

By the time Charli had left the bakery, she had a fair idea of every business in town and couldn't do any more about her immediate future, so she took herself back to the tourist park to eat and make herself a cup of tea. So far all had gone well.

The pub didn't open till ten so she did a small hand wash and hung her clothes on the caravan park's communal clothesline. Loads of new arrivals were setting up around her, more today than yesterday.

The demographic was older than she'd expected: it was mostly grey nomads in a fun mood. And there didn't seem to be any loud, obnoxious people, which happened sometimes with a younger crowd. Even when there were loud people, though, she loved the vibe of caravan parks.

People were on holiday, and they were happy to be there. She was happy to be there. She sat out on her little porch with her coffee and her egg roll, waving at people and watching a caravan and big four-wheel drive covered in dust turn into the park and drive past.

The driver sported a big white bushy beard and looked like Santa Claus. The thought made her smile. The woman next to him didn't look anything like Mrs Claus, with her bright purple hair and big red-lipped smile.

Charlene was glad to see them pull up only a couple of sites down from her and she did a little bit of dreaming as she sipped her tea. When her baby had his or her first Christmas, she would read stories of Santa Claus and Mrs Claus because she'd always wanted to see him. She might even give Mrs Claus purple hair.

She wished she could stay here at the caravan park, with all these happy people, but the five hundred dollars for the week had hurt her bank account. On her phone yesterday she'd booked a one-way ticket on a flight to Charleville for just under a month before her baby was due. The Tuesday after the races, on the first available flight.

She made sure she had it booked to Charleville, and would visit Nana Kate in Roma after, because she didn't have a place to live yet, but she was sure something would turn up.

When she'd finished her tea, Charli set off up Frew Street past the fuel station towards the pub.

She'd left it until ten-thirty, then she pushed at the wooden door midway down the white external brick wall and felt the chill hit her face. It was so much cooler inside. She knew from last time that the dining room sat behind the door to the right, and she pushed the door to the left into the bar where she'd gone with Lazy Luke.

The familiar hoppy aroma of beer tickled her nose, but her eyes were drawn immediately to the frames with the photos. Couldn't stop herself from drifting over there to stand staring at the frame with 'her' photo.

She forced herself to look around but there was no one at the bar to see, so she turned back and stared at it some more.

The woman in the photo stood on her own. No clues about a man in her life. But there was something in her eyes that said she was looking at someone she cared about. Though, even from this snapshot, Charlene suspected she might be a restless soul. Something about her made Charlene feel sorry for her. And there was her locket.

The clink of glass made her turn back and an older guy stood at the bar watching her as he wiped a schooner glass. Sadly, it wasn't the nice scarred man who'd been here when she arrived. This one looked like he had the worries of the world on his shoulders.

'Hello,' she said, and crossed the space between them. Tilted her face so he saw the unscarred side. 'I'm Charlene Bryce.

I emailed to say I was looking for work in town for the next couple of weeks.'

'Josh Barnes. Manager. Ever worked in a pub?'

'In Charleville. Got my RSA.' Responsible Service of Alcohol was the first certificate Charlene went for when she turned eighteen so she could work in bars, bottle shops and restaurants. 'Bar work. Kitchen work. Cleaning. I'm good at it all.'

The man's brows went up.

'I have a job with Scarlet McFadden from eight till four and was looking for evening shifts.'

'Glutton for punishment?' He seemed amused.

'Seems a good time to save money, doesn't it?'

His gaze drifted over her; he shifted his position, and studied her full face. She winced as he looked at her lip. 'Start you in the kitchen washing up. I can give you five pm to nine.'

Yes! She had two jobs. She forgot about his stare. 'That would be perfect. When can I start?'

'Start tomorrow night. Give you a bit of a chance before the hordes come in. The proper chef's not on until tomorrow. Tourists rolling in already for the weekend.'

Even better. 'That would be great, thanks. What would you like me to wear?'

'Black shirt. We have all sizes out the back. Slip round the back and I'll give you one now to take home. There'll be an apron to put over your clothes when you come in. Dark trousers if you have them.'

'Thank you. I'm a bit plump so I like a big shirt – is that okay?'

'Come round through the dining room. Take your pick. Don't you let that Scarlet work you too hard before you get here.'

She smiled. Repeated, 'I like to work.'

Chapter Seventeen

Atticus

Atticus woke early and lay, hands behind his head, staring at the still-dark ceiling. Yep, he decided, since Phoebe McFadden arrived in town the place had been filled with drama. Not all that drama had been external.

Some, maybe a lot, had to do with the seismic emotional rumblings he was having over Phoebe. Who thought of him as ten years old. He was a goose. Not only that, she was leaving in less than two weeks. He huffed out a breath. Sadly, he couldn't seem to shake her out of his mind.

He'd watched her closely when they went out to Poeppel Corner. Loved the way that, even though he knew she had a handle on everything medical, she stood back and deferred to Gloria as the nurse in charge. Worst part about that whole rescue had been Gloria flying off and Phoebe going home with the other patient and her father, instead of in the police vehicle with him.

Still. He'd been lucky with that swim but apart from early morning he'd only caught glimpses of her yesterday, with no further chance to talk. But today, they had that run back out to

Big Red this morning, and that would be interesting. If she wasn't too seedy.

He'd seen her at lunch time at the pub when he went over to have a word with one of the workers about complaints of speeding, and she'd been out the back at the big wooden tables with her cousin and two empty bottles of wine.

He'd become aware since coming to town that Scarlet McFadden could quite easily drink two bottles of wine on her own, but he suspected Phoebe had drunk her share at the girls' lunch. She'd actually sent him a come-hither look that hit him like a scrub bull, and damn that had been hot, before she pulled herself together, blushed and put up her hand with a laugh.

He'd grinned at her and chased down the bloke he wanted.

Oh yes. This morning would be interesting. Which reminded him: he needed to get organised for when she pulled up in that car her father had done up for her. Easiest get-out-of-bed he'd had for ages.

He wasn't sure if they should go in her vehicle, but he guessed she knew what she was doing. She grew up here.

He'd gone across to the shop after seeing her at the pub with her cousin and bought ginger ale in case she needed a pick-me-up. Funny how he did honestly trust her to not be over the limit this morning.

He'd also thrown in a can of Red Bull for each of them. The bakery didn't open till seven-thirty, so there was no fresh food coming that way, but he stuck some fruit in with the rest in the small soft cool bag with a freezer pack and set it at the front door.

By the time he'd showered, dressed and yanked his RMs on, she was pulling up in the . . . what did she call it? The Desert Lizard.

He'd not seen it out of the shed and indeed, wow, the vehicle was a winner. A real piece of retro beauty.

He pulled the house door shut behind him and opened the passenger side of the car. 'Nice ride.'

Her expression softened from the unreadable one she'd been wearing when she pulled up. She patted the dash. 'She is, isn't she? Let's see what she can do.'

'No speeding,' he said, and she laughed.

She didn't appear too hungover. Couldn't help himself checking. 'Should I have breathalysed you before we decided who was driving?'

'No, officer. I stopped drinking at six last night.'

'Good to see you're not too dusty, then.'

'Cast-iron stomach,' she said. 'Had one since I was a kid. Scarlet thinks she can draw me into her shenanigans, but I've been protecting myself from her for years.'

His turn to laugh. 'Love it. But it must be good to catch up.'

They drew away smoothly and turned out onto the road towards Big Red. 'It's great. Found out a few things that made me wish I'd caught up many years ago.'

'What sort of things?'

She looked at him with those raised brows.

Geez. He was doing it again; he held up his hand in apology. 'Only if you want to tell me.'

She shook her head but it was a tease. 'Told you I was estranged from my dad. Well, we're working it out and that feels good.'

'Want to tell me what he did?'

'No.' Her voice changed, went quieter as if she was thinking of the moment everything changed.

Seemed there was a lot of emotion under there. 'You're having a big week, aren't you?'

She turned her head and looked at him, a small, rueful smile on her beautiful face. Made him think he could watch her all day. 'Yes, I am. I'm having a very big week. But you are a bright light in that week, so thank you.'

He was? Thank the stars, because she was definitely the brightness in his world at the moment. Even that tiny bit of encouragement made him want to yank the handbrake on and pull her into his arms. 'Don't suppose you could stop so I could kiss you?'

She laughed. Blinked. And blushed. 'No.' Pink cheeks looked good on her.

'You got a reason?'

Primly, she stuck her nose in the air while still watching the road. 'We're not at that stage of our friendship. And you're too young for me.'

He smiled. 'Not friendship. It's more. Could be more, anyway. How about fledgling relationship?'

She shook her head, but the skin around her eyes crinkled with amusement. 'Rekindled friendship.'

'Nope. And I may be younger but I'm old enough to know who I fancy.' He said it matter-of-factly as if he'd been cued. 'Hope we get to that rekindling soon.'

This was pushy for him. But the too-young had stung. Who was this guy putting words in his mouth? It was as if someone else held the remote control. Thankfully she didn't seem to take offence.

She laughed again. 'You *are* a menace. We are going out to watch the sunrise. Be friends. And drive up and down Big Red.'

'Let's do that, then. Sunrise first.' He'd only just stopped his mouth saying, How about we both watch it from my bed tomorrow? Gawd. She scrambled his brains.

She didn't laugh, but as she stared ahead, concentrating on the rutted road, he could see the amused tilt in that beautiful mouth.

He slid his hand across and patted the seat next to her leg. 'I might even sing you a song if you're nice.' Then pulled his hand back and looked out the passenger window.

Smiled. He'd known it was going to be an interesting morning.

Chapter Eighteen

Phoebe

They stopped to let the pressure down in the tyres before they reached the sand, Atticus out one side of the vehicle and her the other, and Phoebe unobtrusively fanned her face.

In the pre-dawn light, here at the edge of the desert, the air lay cool against her skin, but she'd gained a little heat with the way Senior Constable Atticus Bow had been sliding sideways smiles at her.

The man was a menace all right, but she hadn't felt this tingling, rampant attraction for years. Ever? Plenty of good-looking men out there but she'd never taken much notice until now. Why now? Something about when this outback cop looked at her that made it a compliment, as if he couldn't quite believe that he was lucky enough to be in the vehicle with her . . . which was ridiculous.

Despite their age disparity, which apparently he didn't care about, the man was an absolute hunk. Plenty of women would consider a fling, even her, so should she stop overthinking this? She was returning to Adelaide regardless after the wedding, and they had to get the catering for the races done yet. No time for flings, but . . . if he was so relaxed about it all, why couldn't she be? It was just a little time of fun.

They climbed back in at the same time and apparently both internal monologues had gone well because they grinned at each other.

'A draw,' he said.

'Was it a race?'

'I had the feeling you were competitive.'

'You remember.' She steered the Desert Lizard over the top of Little Red sand dune and down the other side. Easy. 'She handles like a dream.'

Atticus raised his brows in comical disbelief.

She grinned. 'Well, okay, she handles like a strong, sturdy, reliable work beast that could tackle any terrain with quiet assurance.'

A bit like Atticus. The thought tacked itself onto the sentence, luckily unspoken. But true. He made her think he could manage any situation quietly and competently, and yet was capable of controlled force if needed. All while looking hot.

But safe to be with. That was it. He made her feel safe. Safe despite the prickle of electricity that zapped between them. Safe when she'd never needed anyone to make her feel safe – not since her dad and childhood anyway. She was a big girl. She did her own version of safe. Yet . . . How weird.

She changed the subject in her mind. 'So you reckon you can sing? How about you sing me something?' She so wanted to catch him out on this.

He looked anything but fazed. 'You got a request?'

Hmm. Too confident. Maybe this could backfire. 'Scarlet and I always sang "The Piña Colada Song" when we came out here, but we changed the words to "sand on Big Red".'

She could almost see him run through the lyrics in his mind until he grinned. Teeth white as he glanced at her. 'I can do improv.' He cleared his throat, then without any further hesitation started, his voice baritone and teasing, slower and deeper than the original, and the hairs rose on her arms. Confident much? Good grief the guy was a proper crooner. Every word perfect. All with deep velvet tones that brushed every nerve in her body. Oh my . . .

When he got to the part she'd mentioned, he crooned, 'Makin' love in the dunes on Big Red . . .'

She grinned at him. *Okay. Points.*

But he wasn't finished. 'Come to me and my bed.'

Phoebe laughed. Took one hand off the wheel and pretended to clap with one hand on her thigh. 'Again, I underestimated you.'

'Dangerous, Sister McFadden. Very dangerous.'

'I'm beginning to see that.'

'Only beginning?' An amused silence sat between them as they approached Big Red, now blooming orange as the eastern glow painted the dunes in pre-dawn colour. Sweeps of orange rust lightened at the tops and darkened at the base with pockets of deep shadow where the pre-dawn light hadn't touched.

Atticus picked up the radio and broadcast their position over the desert channel. No replies followed, so he hung up the mic again; and she could see the wide expanse of open ground where, only a couple of months ago, thousands of people had camped for the Big Red Bash music festival.

There, that was the place where rows of audience had watched the band on the stage. Where, delightfully, the world record for dancing the Nutbush had occurred. Five thousand, eight hundred people dancing in the desert, which had made her check out the rest of the wonderful photos when she read that. There may have been a twinge of FOMO then.

Atticus must have been thinking about the event as well, because he said, 'Amazing a town like Birdsville, with fewer than a hundred all-year residents, can host such an event.'

On the surface perhaps, but when she thought about it . . . 'Not really. There's a core group of town leaders who cover all the bases. The Bash has its own organisers, but there's still that pillar of townspeople, as well as your police department, who keep everything smooth. My dad said it reminded him of Woodstock, but way more organised.'

Atticus grinned. 'Except this and the races are mostly attended by camping grey nomads instead of young fans . . . or as one of my predecessors said, it's like schoolies for retirees.'

Phoebe laughed. 'It is. Right. Which is great, as retirees deserve the fun, having worked hard all their lives.'

'True.'

'Right now,' Phoebe mused, her gaze sweeping the dunes and the sandy vista, 'I wish I hadn't missed the Bash this year.'

'Any particular reason?'

She glanced at him mock seriously. 'I could have been in the Guinness Book of Records.'

'Ah,' he said, nodding. 'Nutbush. Missed your seat on that particular bus. You'll have to come back next year.'

'Meet you here.' She said it as a joke, but his face held unspoken intent when she turned to smile at him.

He captured her gaze. 'You're on.'

And for some stupid reason she blushed again.

She stopped the vehicle at the base of Big Red. Allowed the

ramifications of the last conversation to drift away as she looked at the glowing red sand dune and the three main wheel-marked routes to the top and over. 'I'll do the little one, the easy one to get us to the top, we'll watch sunrise then have a play. What do you reckon?'

'Sounds like a plan.'

'Gives me a chance to get used to the car.'

He said, 'I knew you were a sensible woman.'

She huffed at him as if offended. 'Sensible.' Not flattering but true. 'Yes, I am. You'll think I'm boring when you get to know me.'

He shook his head. 'Phoebe McFadden and boring do not go in the same sentence.' His beautiful mouth tilted and there was heat there in those blue bedroom eyes of his. 'Not the same thing at all.' And there it was again, a slow heat sliding down her body like a hot wave, all the way to her toes on the Desert Lizard's pedals.

She hurried on. 'After sunrise we'll do the mid-level grade then the big one.'

'Sure.'

She grinned. 'If you don't squeal, I might let you drive a few times after that.'

'Squeal.' His laugh reverberated around the cabin. Deep and rumbling, smoothing over her skin like warm hands in smooth gloves. 'I'm up for anything legal.'

She snorted. 'Stickler.'

The Desert Lizard chugged serenely up the easier slope of Big Red, Phoebe pushing the accelerator lightly, no excessive speed required.

They reached the rippled expanse at the top of the tall dune and Phoebe turned the vehicle around so they could see the sun crack the horizon in the east.

147

They climbed out to stand and watch and both sighed at the sight.

Below them the shimmer of salt and desert spread out to the horizon, brushed pink and silver, shifting stripes of muted colour.

Then the sun broke free from the far horizon, hit them first as an orange sliver, blinding as it grew to a ball of fire and light that spread across the desert and down the dune, capturing the shadows and swallowing them.

Phoebe sighed at the simple joy of being there at that exact moment. 'Wow.'

'Wow,' he repeated, his voice quiet, and she turned to share the joy, but he wasn't looking at the sunrise. 'You look incredibly beautiful in this light.' The words were sincere in that gravelly tone of his. 'Any light.' His gaze prickled her skin and she turned her face to where the sun had painted his frame red, his body agile and tough and yet gentle and quiet. A strong man with a peaceful centre.

'Thank you,' she said just as softly, a smile tilting her lips. 'And you look like a man I could cross the desert with one day.'

'You should. I'd like that. Very much.' His gaze held hers. 'And we'll take it slow.'

Darn. Her mouth quirked up. Just when she was thinking they could speed things up a bit.

He reached out and pulled her gently to him, leaned down and brushed her lips with his, a slow taste, peppermint and man, a firm pressure and then a teasing retreat. His big arms circled her body and he tugged her until she was back facing the sunrise, her spine to his chest. Apparently, he *was* taking it slow. Lucky one of them was being sensible.

*

The Desert Lizard thundered up the most difficult ascent without a pause and Phoebe couldn't hold back a little gasp of delight. She patted the dash again. 'You champion, girl!'

They sped down the slope again and she pulled over to the side. 'Your turn.'

They played, speeding up and down the dunes for the next half an hour, Atticus checking the desert channel twice more, and then headed back to town in time for him to open the station at eight.

Phoebe had probably had one of the best mornings of her life. With her younger man. Including that one gentle kiss. 'That was fun.' More than fun, actually. 'Thank you, Atticus.'

'My pleasure, Sister McFadden. There's a great view of the sunset from the back verandah of my house if you'd like to try that one afternoon.'

'I'll see what the bridezilla's doing. When I have a free night, I'll let you know.'

'Sounds good.'

She dropped him off and drove back down the road to pull in outside her dad's garage. He came down the steps and opened the doors before she could get out, so she drove straight inside and parked. Switched off the vehicle, patted the dash and listened to it run down as she met her dad at the garage door.

Rusty's face radiated delight. 'How'd she go?'

'Wonderful. Absolute machine. Love her.'

'And the copper?'

'Atticus? He's a pretty good sand driver, too.'

Her dad gave her the look that said he knew she was avoiding the question. 'Knew that. Didn't need too many pointers.' Inclined his head towards the house. Waited as if she would say more. She didn't. 'Tea?'

'Love some.' And the day became even brighter as she hooked her arm through his.

Once they were settled at the old table with tea in front of them her dad pushed his cup away. 'Phoebe. We need to talk.' He blew out a big, whistling breath and raked his hair. Though his face had creased with distress there was a certain grim determination to him as well.

And strangely, suddenly, she could remember that trait. The squaring of his shoulders. The jut of his chin. He may have been a gambler but as far as she knew he hadn't lied to her even that one time he confessed.

'I shoulda said this years ago, but it wasn't a conversation you and me could do over the phone. So, I haven't broached it until now. I should have. I'm sorry.'

She glanced once at the photo of the horse on the mantel. Had he lost the house? Done something more he was ashamed of? Her stomach sank but inside she shored up the worry. He was still her dad. She still loved him. She wasn't cutting him out of her life again no matter what he'd done. Not again. 'Tell me.'

Shockingly, he said, 'I didn't bet your money.'

The odd words fell into the room like a handful of coins falling into a metal laundry sink. No warning. Bizarre. Spinning and reverberating until they slowed and stopped like the lost pennies they were from the distant past.

'What?' She must have misheard. Or her father was talking about something else. She could still visualise the empty bag. Her face crumpling as she sat beside her bed on the floor when she checked after he'd told her the money was gone. On the horses. He'd admitted it. Said it was lost on a race. 'What do you mean you didn't bet it? You're a gambler.'

'No. I'm not.' He shrugged. 'I don't gamble at all. Just love the horses.'

'But my money was gone.'

'Not gambled by me – you just . . . presumed that. Not blaming you!' he hastened to add. 'I did take it. But I paid someone else's debt.'

'You gave it away?' Confusion pulled her face into a squint. What? To whom? she thought. How could he give away his own daughter's hard-earned money?

As if he'd heard the unspoken question he said, 'To someone who needed it more than you – though I intended to have it back under the bed before you found out. Except you said you were going to take it that day and I couldn't return it in time.'

'But . . .' She trailed off.

'So I let you think I'd gambled it.' His eyes pleaded with her to believe him and in the face of such obvious truth, well, what else could she do?

'Go on.'

'It wasn't the first time I left us short giving her money. I still believe she needed it more than you did . . .' He added very quietly, 'But perhaps not more than I needed your trust. I didn't know then it would cost so much.'

Her? A woman? Dad never had a girlfriend. Except maybe . . . Gloria?

He shrugged and seemed to shrink into himself, suddenly even smaller and very much older. 'But . . .' He sighed. 'I probably still would have done it. Though,' he said again, 'I meant to have it saved back before you found out.'

Enough. 'Who?' She didn't understand. Couldn't fathom . . . No. Let him explain. No more jumping to conclusions.

The silence stretched. Her dad blinking at her and breathing fast until finally he sagged. Gearing up to let it out? And unexpectedly she was scared, abruptly wanted to tell him not to say something she suspected very much that she didn't want to know. Again.

'Your mother . . . Celine.'

The shaft of shock froze her lungs, but he hurried on. 'I sent it to your mother. She was in a bind. I'd sent her money before. Kept us broke, she did. I asked every time if I could tell you she was alive – she always said no.'

The words fell into some hollow vacuum of space inside Phoebe; her ears tinged and pinged as if she had tinnitus.

This new information floated, made boo noises like tangible ghosts bumping her. Ghosts with fat gloves, like in Brophy's Boxing Tent in Birdsville Race week, puffy fists that kept socking her. Stealing her breath. Punching her in the heart, each time causing an oof of mental pain and dawning horror.

She drew a tight lungful of much-needed air. Said slowly and carefully, 'You told me my mother died when I was five.'

'I know.' He sighed. 'Your mother left us then. Took off with a truck driver and made me promise to tell you she'd died.' He lifted his head and met her shocked eyes. Her dad blew out a puffed breath and his face drew in until he looked old, too old. 'She was a bit of a lost soul, your mother. She was a twin, and her sister died when she was born. Was as if she was always looking for someone she'd lost.'

Phoebe tried to take it in while her father went on. 'So, I did. I lied. Lots of times. It was her wish, but I couldn't tell a five-year-old her mother had just ridden a truck away without a word. Celine often said she never wanted to be a mother. That I should have our child because I always wanted to be your father.'

Phoebe's hand had risen to her mouth, pushed her lips together to stop words pouring out. The child inside wailed. Long and loud like a train whistle. But the external woman said nothing. Showed nothing. She'd practised that face for years.

People didn't pretend to die. Hard to hide. Phoebe tried to work out how no one else had told her different. A whole town of silence. For a dozen years. Who else knew? Gloria? Scarlet? Everyone? A rabbit hole for later.

Rusty wasn't finished. His chin lifted and his eyes grew gentle. Apologetic. As if to warn her there was more. Good grief. More?

Before she could put her hand up to stop him, he went on. 'Your mother passed away the day you left. Her and her baby. Right after I sent her the money. She and her baby died. I didn't find out until the funeral was long gone. Then you were gone.'

Okay. That was more. Her mother had really died when Phoebe was seventeen. Her mother had left Dad and her, not died, and possibly everyone in town had hidden that from her.

But the one blameless person, her dad, she'd blamed for something that wasn't true. She'd vilified him for eighteen freakin' years. More than half her life and a goodly portion of his.

'Oh,' she said. It wasn't much but it was all she could manage at that moment. 'Oh,' she said again, and then it all rushed in. Implications. 'Oh, Dad. You poor thing. I'm so sorry.' And she went around the table to where he'd stood too, and she put her arms around his waist and sort of hugged him.

Her dad tightened his own arms and hugged her fiercely. 'I've wanted to tell you since it started.'

She tentatively patted his shoulder and squeezed tighter. Maybe it wasn't too hard, this hugging thing? She was getting better at this, until a thought zinged.

What did Gloria think about her giving her father the cold shoulder for all these years? If anyone knew the truth about her mother, Gloria did.

Phoebe felt spent, but strangely settled and calm as she talked with her dad, both sitting on kitchen chairs on the front verandah before the heat began, watching the tourists come back into town: some from the campgrounds to the showers; others to buy a coffee from the bakery. Still four days to go, but the town common between the edge of the houses and the racecourse three kilometres away was dotted with vans and campsites.

Gloria pulled up in her car and the older woman's face lit when she saw Phoebe. 'Such a wonderful sight. So lovely to see you here with your dad.'

Phoebe smiled and stood to give the woman a hug. 'How are you, Gloria?' The woman still looked far too tired. 'You've had a big week too.'

'It's about to get bigger, I'm sad to say. My poor temporary admin broke her collarbone and one ankle: she'll be out for the next month at least.'

'I thought I heard the flying doctor come and go.'

'Yes, they took her into Charleville, where they'll set her ankle. We're not sure if she'll need surgery yet. It was a nasty break. Poor Julie.'

'Painful for her. And for you. Couldn't have happened at a worse time.'

'Yeah. It's always a mad house at race time with the tourists, as well as the usual illnesses.' Gloria lifted her chin and pinned on a determined smile. 'I'll manage. But Rusty . . .' She looked at Phoebe's dad. 'I was thinking I won't be able to get away when the plane comes in today. Could you pick up my supplies, please?'

He nodded. 'Sure, Gloria, no worries.' He touched her arm. 'I'll drop them down as soon as they come in.'

'Wonderful. Can't stay. Need to get a few things done before we open this morning.' She flashed them a smile and turned to go. Waved her hand over her shoulder as she walked briskly to her car. 'Have a great day, you two.'

They watched Gloria go and once she was out of sight exchanged a look. Her dad's face creased with more than concern. 'I'm worried about her,' he said.

Phoebe was too. 'I'll have a chat with Scarlet. I am supposed to help her with as much of the cooking as we can do before the races, but she's found a new girl to work for her and she may not need me all the time. I can help Gloria when I'm free.'

'How? You're not registered in Queensland. Never worked in the clinic.'

'I can do the admin stuff.' She raised her brows, slightly offended. 'I've been supervising a city hospital at night, so your little clinic in Birdsville won't be a problem.'

She saw his amusement and had the grace to flush. Probably shouldn't have said 'little clinic'.

He let her off the hook. 'What about your holiday?'

'I wouldn't enjoy myself knowing Gloria is under the pump. I can help. Easy.'

'You're a darling.' He patted her shoulder. 'Proud of my girl.'

And she didn't deserve that, but she knew he wouldn't agree. Instead, she said, 'Proud of my dad. Gloria came straight to you for help, knowing you would.' Her voice teasing, she said, 'You sure there's nothing between you two?'

He shook his head ruefully. 'There was a time, but . . . I think I missed the boat there.'

Ha. She knew it. 'Time to try again. Never too late. Look, I have to go. Scarlet will be up by now. Talk later.' She leaned over and kissed him, still marvelling how good it felt to hear her dad say he was proud of her. She'd missed that. She'd missed a lot.

And whose fault was that?

Chapter Nineteen

Charli

Charli presented herself at Scarlet's front door at seven-fifty and hesitated before she knocked. Was she too early?

'You must be Charli.'

Someone had walked up the path behind her. The woman's voice made Charli jump and she spun around, the backpack pulling her shoulder. She slid it off and dropped it to the ground. 'Yes. Hi! Are you Scarlet's cousin, Phoebe? She said you were visiting.'

The woman wore sneakers, cropped brown pants that showed how fit she was and a red short-sleeved top. Her hair was a lovely reddish-brown, not like Charli's straight black hair, long and beautiful. Charli wished her hair looked like that.

Phoebe reminded Charli of all the cool kids in school. The confident and smart ones, and she remembered Scarlet saying her cousin was a high-powered nurse in Adelaide.

She looked like a high-powered nurse: in fact, she looked a little bit scary. Charli swallowed, but then remembered Scarlet had looked scary too, when she'd first met her.

Phoebe stepped past and opened the front door. 'Come in. I need a word with my cousin and then I'll leave you two to your business.'

Charli's first day working for Scarlet flew by in a haze of whipping up, washing up and wonder.

As she watched her new employer scoot around the kitchen flinging orders over her shoulder, Charli smiled. She'd worked for fast chefs before but no one like Scarlet. This was no fade-out-and-daydream-as-you-work job. This was stay on the ball or else . . . Because Scarlet would take off your head with one of her enormous kitchen knives if you weren't paying attention.

Charli loved every minute of it. She even laughed a few times with her employer, who wanted to know where Charli had learned to move so fast.

By the end of the day they were both sweaty, dishevelled and delighted by how much they'd pre-cooked and slipped into the walk-in freezer room Scarlet had backed up to her kitchen door.

'Good work for a first day.' Scarlet clapped her on the back as she pushed Charli out the door. 'See you tomorrow and don't be late.'

'I won't,' she said over her shoulder as she slid her hand into her cleavage and pulled out her watch-locket – the one thing she owned of her mother's. She had an hour to get to her second job.

Charli rolled her shoulders as she walked away, and realised she was slightly weary. Something she hadn't really noticed before when she worked. Not surprising because she'd never seen anyone as focused and fast as her new employer. She still had time to get to the caravan park for a shower before she changed her clothes and headed to the pub.

The Birdsville Hotel had cars parked all the way up the side road, and when she pushed open the first door the sound of voices hit her in the face in a wave of words and accents from the bar that disappeared as the inside door shut.

Charli faltered at the crowd she could see through the gap before turning right and slipping into the dining room. Every table had a reserved sign on it, so it looked like they were going to be busy.

She suddenly wished she was back with Scarlet and just the two of them in the kitchen, but frowned at herself then pulled her face into a smile as she slipped behind the counter in the dining room and through into the kitchen.

The long apron was hanging where the boss had said it would be and she slipped it over her head and pulled on the rubber gloves.

Chef had his back to her, crumbing chicken, and a pile of dirty dishes on the long sink almost reached to her shoulder height. Good place to start right there.

She dived straight into the washing up – not literally, she thought with a smile to herself – but was up to her elbows in suds when Chef turned. 'You must be Charli?'

A tall, solid young man with dark hair and a web of scars up the side of his cheek. She'd seen him that first day. She'd liked his observant grey eyes then, and they were still kind despite the row of meal orders lined up above his shoulder on the wire. 'Yes, Chef.'

'Call me Kelvin. Good to meet you. I saw you in the bar with that fella the other day. Could've done with you an hour ago.'

His voice was gruff but she knew he wasn't cross. 'Still, you're here now. Don't suppose you can start an hour earlier tomorrow?'

He'd noticed her. Wow, and remembered seeing her. Well, she remembered him, too. The thought warmed her. But she couldn't help earlier. 'No, sorry. I'm working with Scarlet in the daytime and don't finish till four.'

Chef stopped what he was doing and turned to face her fully. 'Scarlet McFadden?'

'Yes. Do you know her?' Then wanted to slap herself in the forehead. Of course he did. This was Birdsville. Everybody knew everybody.

Chef laughed. 'If you survived today with her, you must be a good worker.'

She gave a small smile. 'It was fun.' It had been.

He laughed again. 'Yeah, right.' Then amusement washed away like the suds under her hands. 'Once you finish those dishes, I need another box of lettuce washed.'

'Yes, Chef,' Charli said placidly and placed a spotless pan in the rack.

By the time Charli let herself back into her little van her shoulders ached. And her feet were swollen. It had only been four hours but most of that had been spent at the sink washing up. She was in awe of the amount of food that had flowed out to the dining room – all made by Kelvin the chef, which was pretty impressive as well. Kelvin was nice.

The more she saw of Birdsville, the more she liked it. These people knew how to work. How to be kind. And she'd never felt so welcome.

Also, to her delight, they knew how to gently tease and laugh while they got the work done. She didn't think she'd ever been so happy in a place before. In fact, Kelvin was wonderful, and she thought he just might like her too. And not in a sleazy way. In a he'd-like-to-be-her-friend kind of way. Nice.

Except she hadn't had a chance to ask about the photo and suspected she wouldn't have time for that until after the races. Kelvin had said it was just gonna get busier for the next week and wouldn't slow until the Monday after. She could wait. She'd already waited eighteen years. As long as she sorted it before she flew out and the baby was born, she'd be happy.

Charli fell into bed as soon as she set the alarm on her phone and was asleep when her head hit the pillow.

Chapter Twenty

Gloria

From before she opened the clinic doors until morning tea – which she didn't expect to get – Gloria's morning had been hectic and unorganised because she couldn't do two jobs – meet and greet – and treat – and stay ahead.

At ten am on the dot, the front door opened, and Phoebe McFadden walked in, dressed corporate in blue trousers and a white shirt, looking spick, span and scarily efficient. 'I've come to be your admin,' she said. 'If you want me?'

Magic words. Gloria blinked and stared, not quite believing she'd heard correctly.

Before she could ask Phoebe said, 'Scarlet kicked me out because the new girl's working out so well. She doesn't need me in the kitchen. I think my skills will be put to better use here.'

Gloria stared at the gift horse, carefully not at her mouth, in case said gift horse turned away. 'Yes, please, my love. I accept with open arms. It's only going to get busier, and I didn't know how I'd cope until the race rush dies down.'

For Gloria, the day turned sensible from then.

Phoebe only needed the password to log onto the computer and away she went.

'How?' Gloria shook her head as she ushered her last patient out and her new one in. 'You seem to know how everything works.'

'Easy to grasp. I work in a tertiary hospital. I know this stuff. If I can run a hospital, I can manage the admin at the Birdsville Primary Health Centre.'

My word you can, Gloria murmured to herself. *Bless.*

By lunchtime, the place ran so smoothly Gloria could actually wait for patients to arrive. Huge difference when she didn't need to organise them before or after their visit.

Deep inside she felt bad. Phoebe should have been working beside her as a nurse practitioner, but her new admin had waved that away and put a cup of coffee into her hand. 'Take a break. You haven't had one.'

As she sipped, Gloria smiled to herself as she saw one of her frequent flyer patients walking away without getting past the foyer.

Was there a bit of triage at the front door?

She suspected Phoebe could be reminding malingerers that Gloria was a busy woman. The thought made her grin. And she didn't have to feel bad because Phoebe's experience meant her triage wouldn't miss a genuine, or even slightly worrying, reason for coming to see the nurse.

The best part of the day came when they were eating lunch together. Phoebe finally asked the question Gloria had been waiting for.

'Did you know about my mother?'

Gloria nodded. Swallowed her tea and put the cup down. Waited.

'And that Dad didn't gamble the money?'

She nodded again. Spiralling hope made her breath catch.

Phoebe reached over and cool fingers squeezed hers in reassurance. Tears stung Gloria's eyes at the lack of censure in the younger woman's gaze. 'I don't blame you for not telling me. It was Dad's story to tell. But I wish I'd known sooner.'

Gloria swallowed the tightness in her throat and let the words she'd been wanting to speak for years escape. 'I knew. Rusty had to tell someone about when she left. She just walked away. He needed someone to listen and I was the nurse.' She thought back. 'I think that was the start of our friendship.'

'Something good came out of it, then. But poor Dad. I've blamed him all these years and wasted so much time. We could have reconciled so much sooner if he'd told me.'

Exactly. Except one was as stubborn as the other. But Gloria didn't say that. 'It is what it is. I'm just glad he's told you, finally. And now both of you can move on.'

Phoebe shook her head. Her face clouded with what Gloria suspected was mega guilt. 'But I've blamed him for something he didn't do. Vilified him in my mind. I feel so bad.'

'He didn't tell you.' She shrugged, implying 'yes, but not your fault'. 'Of course, he thought you'd come home sooner but . . .' She shook her head. 'You're here now.'

'Thank goodness for Scarlet's wedding,' Phoebe said dryly, wordlessly imparting that she wouldn't have come without that.

Gloria smiled. 'Indeed.'

A bell rang from the locked front door. Phoebe stood before Gloria could move. 'I've got this. I'll come and get you once they're booked in.'

Gloria subsided and smiled at Phoebe's back as she strode away. They'd talk. And she'd tell Phoebe what she knew. And it was so good to have another woman to talk to who understood her work, Rusty, and possible futures. She could get used to this.

By closing time, they were running a slick unit. The place had been restored to immaculate. Records were completed. Computers up to date. One of the filing systems had been revamped for easier reference and medication had been restocked and re-ordered in date lines with a typed inventory and expiry dates. All things Gloria had been meaning to get to but hadn't had a chance to tackle.

Even the central resus room had been fully checked and notes taken on improvements needed.

'Oh. My. Goodness. Phoebe, you're my hero,' Gloria said as she turned slowly in the empty waiting room at one minute to four.

Phoebe laughed. 'No, dear, dear Gloria, you are my hero, working here doing what you do.' She shook her head and Gloria's throat grew tight at the unexpected and genuine admiration she saw in Phoebe's eyes.

'The respect these people have for you is greater than ten people's respect for one of us in Adelaide. You've met everyone's needs for so long and so well that I feel sorry for the people who replace you every fortnight.'

Gloria snorted. 'Don't be silly.'

'Seriously. You're a hard act to follow. You care and they know it. You're smart and on the ball and they know that too. Nothing is too much bother for you.' Here Phoebe pretended to frown at her. 'They certainly know that.'

'Oh, shoosh. You exaggerate. I just do my job.'

'A job that would exhaust three full-time employees and you do it all. Too late.' She held up her hand. 'Dad told me. Sixteen days in a row without a sleep-in, even if you've driven to Bedourie in the night.'

'Now, now. I get most weekends off.'

'Really?' Scepticism dripped.

Maybe a few. Gloria huffed. 'Sometimes. Disturbed nights don't happen that often.'

'It happens more often than it should.' Phoebe had her hands on her hips and funnily enough Gloria could see the skinny kid she'd been twenty years ago in the stance. 'Twice this week, I hear. No wonder you sleep most of your ten days off.'

Maybe there was some truth in that. 'You tell your dad to stop telling tales,' she said with faux affront. But she knew Rusty didn't like her workload.

Phoebe smiled. 'Who do you think worries the most about you?'

Dear Rusty. She knew that. The sweet man.

Phoebe broke into her thoughts. 'As long as Scarlet's still happy with her kitchen help, I'll be here tomorrow. And the next day and the next until the races are gone.'

Gloria's throat tightened until she could force away the big lump that had grown there. When she could speak again, she tried – and only because she should – to say no. 'It's your holidays, dear. You shouldn't be doing this.' Phoebe really shouldn't.

Her new admin's grin grew infectious. 'Come on. I enjoyed myself today. It's fun not to have the responsibility of being the clinician. I'm catching up with people I haven't seen for nearly twenty years. Being admin could be my new life goal.'

Gloria laughed. 'Nope, you'd get bored in no time.'

'Maybe.' Phoebe tilted her head. 'And if you haven't got any plans for dinner, Dad said you should come down and have dinner with us tonight. He's made a roast and invited Scarlet, so it will probably be a hoot. If politically incorrect.'

Gloria smiled but inside she froze. Was she ready for Phoebe to know that Gloria had more than a soft spot for Rusty? That she loved him with all her heart? She suspected Scarlet had cottoned on long ago. What if it showed on her face at the table? 'Are you sure?'

'Come on. Share the night. Have a laugh. I'll tell you about how I gave a couple of people their marching orders today.'

Did she want to know? Oh, yes, she did. 'I thought you might have.'

'Hope you don't mind.' Phoebe's expression showed anything but remorse.

Gloria bit her lip trying to be officious. 'As long as you're sure those clients are stable and they'll come back another time if their condition deteriorates, then I'm fine.'

'Oh, I'm sure they'll come back if something real pops up.' They both snickered.

Gloria said, 'But I'd really like to know how you got on with Atticus Bow?'

For a second there she thought Phoebe would blush. Instead, she lifted one shoulder. 'Just old friends. He was a kid when he left.'

'Really?'

Phoebe seemed to find whatever was happening out the nearest window very interesting. Gloria looked but couldn't see anything. She smiled to herself.

Phoebe lifted her chin. 'He's too young for me.'

'Uh huh. If you say so. From where I'm sitting, he's a fine-looking man who likes what he sees.'

'Hmmm. Interesting. See you tonight, Gloria.' Phoebe's voice sounded stern, and Gloria's smile grew wider as she watched her leave.

Dinner proved more fun than Gloria expected. Scarlet must have been on a high because she crowed that she'd achieved twice as much as she'd expected to with her new kitchen help.

Then there was the joy of watching Rusty and Phoebe interacting with such care after so many years of cold war – care on Phoebe's side anyway, and plain adoration on her father's.

Gloria could not have been happier for Rusty and in fact hadn't seen him this relaxed since before Phoebe left. She only wished those two hadn't wasted so much time with Phoebe's misconceptions of her father's mistake and Rusty's stubbornness in correcting them. As far as Gloria was concerned, the only mistake he'd ever made was marrying Phoebe's mother. But that was all Diamantina water under the wooden bridge out of town.

Rusty himself seemed to have found a funny bone she hadn't even known existed, regaling them all with fond tales of Phoebe's childhood with such amusing nuances that of course Scarlet added to the disclosures with relish.

By the end of the night, when the girls had gone across the road to bed, she and Rusty sat companionably together on the new sofa, and she sighed happily, if a bit wearily. She should go.

She leaned forwards to stand up to leave when Rusty laid a hand on her knee. 'Wait a sec. Please, Gloria. Something I want to say.'

'Must be the day for it,' she murmured, but her nerves twitched. She subsided back into the comfy lounge, turned her head and looked at the man she'd loved for twenty years. His hair was thinning and the lines at the corners of his eyes were scored by the sun, but he still made her heart thump.

'Yes?'

She heard him take a big breath and she narrowed her eyes. Had something happened? Had she done something wrong? Should she not have come tonight? Her throat went dry. She should have left earlier. Before the girls. 'What is it?' she asked, though it came out a bit hoarse.

Finally, he said, 'If you were to retire from your work – not that you should but just if you were thinking about it – you know you've got a home here. With me. If you'd like?'

Gloria's breath caught somewhere in her chest. And when she could breathe the trapped air came out in a little gasp. 'What do you mean?'

Rusty frowned at himself. Shook his head. 'That came out wrong. What I mean is I'd like it. I'd like it very much.' He turned more fully towards her and she saw that his face had grown softer, his eyes warmer, and his mouth curved in a tender smile. Suddenly her heart began to beat a little too fast and a little too hard and she lifted a hand to her chest to soothe it.

'I'm sorry. I'm so bad at this. This should have been said years ago.' He shook his head ruefully. 'I'm a fool for waiting so long.'

She actually heard roaring in her ears. Was she going to faint? Whispered, 'Waiting for what?'

'Hoping to sort out Phoebe's and my relationship before I spoke to you. And the years just got away.' He waved a hand at the departed years. 'No doubt about that. I've been a fool.'

'Rusty?' Now she was confused. And awkward. And way more nervous. 'What are you talking about?'

'I'm talking about the fact that you and I should have spent these years together. Here. Or at your house.' When she would have spoken he touched one work-roughened finger to her lips. 'You're my friend, my best friend. But that's not all you are.'

She shook her head. Fearful she wouldn't hear what she wanted to hear, wanting to put her hands up to stop him in case . . . but he went on.

'I see how hard you work. I feel your empathy for others. I see the good in you.' His turn to shake his head. 'The great in you.' His voice dropped. 'Too good for me, I always thought, too smart for me, but I love you, Gloria. I've loved you for years. And one day soon, if it's not too late, I want you to marry me.'

He gestured around at the house. 'It's not much but I want you to move in here with me. Soon. Maybe as soon as Phoebe goes if you're comfortable with that. Or even before.' He grinned. 'I think we could be happy living together. Happier than you going home to your house and me to mine. As husband and wife.'

She must have looked like one of those spangled perch from the billabong, blinking, spots of colour on her face and her mouth open. Gaping. She closed her lips and moistened them. 'You never said.'

'You never said either,' he copied gently. 'Both of us have not grabbed onto life when we could have. Should have. Years ago. And I'm sorry.'

'I never knew.' Her voice was a hoarse whisper.

Rusty gathered her closer until her head was on his shoulder, their bodies leaning inwards, side by side. 'I'm so sorry, love. I watched you tonight, loved having you a part of what I finally have again with Phoebe, and suddenly I knew I'd been a fool too long. You should have been a part of my life – of my family – for all of my life.'

Excitement bubbled and she tried to tamp it down. Broke in, 'It's very sudden.'

'No, that it isn't. It's well overdue,' he returned.

Her brain skittered and twisted, too overwhelmed to comprehend. 'I need to think.'

'Of course.' But he was looking at her with such a soft expression she could barely think at all.

She was too old for romance. 'What will everyone say?'

He barely shrugged, his eyes still on her face. 'Who cares?'

Oh my. Softly, 'I'm old.'

A firm shake of his head. 'You are a beautiful woman, wise in the world.'

Oh. Oh my goodness me, Gloria thought. Thought that might be the loveliest compliment she'd ever been given. 'What would Phoebe say? Scarlet . . .'

Rusty's gaze followed her panicked fluttering. 'Stop worrying about others. Think about us. Will you say yes?' He was the one worried now.

She touched his cheek. Smoothed his worry. Something she'd wanted to do for years. 'Yes. Of course, yes. Rusty. I've loved you for years.'

He sagged. Murmured, 'I've been such a fool not to do this sooner.' Then straightened and leaned towards her to kiss her.

She pulled back. 'Let's not mention this yet though. I don't want to overshadow Scarlet's glory for her wedding.'

He frowned at that. 'She wouldn't care. But you still say yes? You'll think about how and when?'

She looked at him, finally calming. Seeing his concern that she would push him away suddenly cleared her muddled head. And some of her nerves. 'Silly man.' She leaned in and kissed his lips. 'I don't think I'll be able to think about anything else for the next week.'

He stood and reached down to help her stand. Hanging onto her fingers when she was up. 'As soon as Scarlet's wedding is over, then we'll have a serious discussion about where you put your head at night. Every night.'

And after all these years she felt her cheeks flame in a crazy, adolescent-type blush. A blush she'd thought she lost decades ago. Because there was no doubting that Rusty McFadden had just propositioned her. Finally!

Chapter Twenty-one

Phoebe

On Phoebe's second morning working at the clinic, Atticus appeared unexpectedly. And yes, he did indeed present as a fine-looking man. Gloria's words came back to Phoebe, and she hid her smile.

The senior constable brought in a solo caravaner with a tooth-ache, the man moaning in extreme pain and Atticus steering him carefully towards the desk. His dark brows lifted in surprise to see Phoebe in the reception area.

'Hello there, Miss McFadden.'

'Senior Constable.'

'This gentleman has a toothache.' He handed her a driver's licence. 'He was weaving all over the road and gave me this when he couldn't talk.'

The man moaned holding his swollen jaw and Phoebe read the name. 'Mr Desley?' She didn't comment on his first name, Elvis, because she bet that caused him grief. 'Take a seat. Sister will be out in a moment. I'll just get you a cotton ball with clove oil until she can see you.'

She'd noticed the medicinal oil when she cleaned out the medication cupboard – they had used it many times in Adelaide for emergency relief. The wait for a real dentist in Birdsville would be a long one.

She returned quickly with the oil-soaked cotton ball in a gloved hand and helped Elvis place it gently over the painful area.

'Clamp down just a bit to hold it in place. Should bring you some relief while I create your file.' Once she had the man more comfortable, and the file started, they waited for Gloria to finish with the previous patient.

Atticus hovered. 'I'm going to the bakery. I could loop back? Did you want something special?'

'You sure?'

He spread his hands. 'Wouldn't offer otherwise.'

She smiled at that. 'A man after my own heart. I don't promise what I won't deliver.'

His eyes sparkled. 'Really.' Said very quietly. 'Good to know.' There was a world of meaning in that look and she resisted the urge to duck her head.

And why the heck had she said that? Cripes. 'Umm. A chocolate slice would be great. I know Gloria loves those.'

'And what do you love?'

She thought about that. She was a savoury girl. Too early for a pie. 'One of those savoury bread rolls with bacon and cheese on top?'

He grinned. That smile was doing things to her insides she didn't like to think about. 'Why am I not surprised? See you soon.'

The roll had long since been devoured when Atticus returned with another patient: this time a ringer he'd found at the side of the road, fallen from his horse.

Phoebe noted silently to herself that one of the bonuses of working at the clinic could be the increased opportunities to cross paths with Atticus Bow.

The first time had been a surprise, and the quirky smile the second time said he too was happy about meeting and greeting her as often as he could. Also lucky for the patients, if he was roaming the town looking for those in need of medical care. Phoebe huffed a quiet laugh at the thought.

Birdsville sprinted towards the races. The streets grew busier until finally the pub put up a fence between the verandah and the road because the traffic flowed so heavily.

On Tuesday, the stall holders began to set up.

The pub pulsed with happy seniors, ringers and slightly more inebriated younger folk. Tents, caravans and four-wheel drives parked everywhere. Rooftop tents and swags and motor-homes all across the free camping grounds between the houses at the end of Birdsville and the racecourse out of town.

Atticus wasn't the only copper in town now. Half-a-dozen colleagues had arrived and there'd be two dozen more by race day. The police barracks hosted officers sleeping on swags on the floor. The weather held. Not too hot. No rain. And as always, the dust never settled.

Gloria spoke about the year when it was forty-three degrees and the busloads of tourists were falling down with heat exhaustion. She barely had time for a sip of water herself that day and had begun to send them to sit in the cool of the Rex terminal air-conditioning. Thankfully not that hot this year.

Phoebe and Gloria had a routine going at the Birdsville Primary Health Centre and apart from call-outs for retrieval jobs, Gloria herself looked more relaxed and rested.

In fact, Phoebe decided, Gloria positively glowed.

Something had to be going on with her and Dad, Phoebe thought, because there were too many secret looks and whispers, and rendezvous between the two of them that fell silent when she came anywhere near them.

Phoebe had begun to think they were about to elope.

Go them. But Gloria wouldn't give any confirmation even when Phoebe asked outright if something was going on. So, she'd just have to wait.

Chapter Twenty-two

Charli

Tuesday before the races Charlene thought she just might be in heaven, making plenty of extra money working for Scarlet and then at the pub for four hours in the evening. But she *was* beginning to worry she'd have nowhere to sleep when her cabin booking ran out.

Over washing up she broached the subject. 'Scarlet. I might have miscalculated with the caravan park, and thinking I'd find somewhere to board.'

'Your booking running out?'

'Yes. And I can't rebook over the weekend. Do you know anyone with accommodation until after I finish my two weeks' work with you?'

Scarlet looked across at her with a frown. 'Not at this time of year.' She lifted a batch of pastries out of the oven. 'Everything's booked. You can't get rooms at the pub or the caravan parks for the four days over the races and I know their staff allocations are over-booked. Not even available for tourists.'

'What about all those tents in a row?'

'They're all booked months in advance.'

'I should have brought a swag. My friend Luke has one I could have borrowed.'

Scarlet looked at her over her shoulder. 'You can check out my parents' old caravan out the back. It's in the shed so it's out of the direct sun, but it still gets hot.'

Charli stopped what she was doing and looked into her boss's face. 'Really?'

Scarlet waved her back to the sink. 'Not now, later,' she cautioned, 'but after we've finished the last batch of pastry we can.'

The glimmer of hope had Charli grinning.

Scarlet added, 'Only until after the races and you can find a real place to live. There's a shower and toilet in the shed – no walls around it, mind you – but it would mean you didn't have to come into the house.'

Scarlet mixed butter and sugar while Charli began the washing up from the dough they'd just finished.

'Sounds perfect.' Charli could barely breathe with the excitement but Scarlet seemed very unconcerned.

'You can run the air-con, because we have the solar on and the power costs are covered.' Her boss stopped and turned to her. 'Just till after the races, though,' she said again. Making sure it was clear. 'It's not permanent.'

Of course it wasn't. But gosh. 'I understand that. I have to fly to Charleville after the races anyway. I've booked my flight for Tuesday, but I'll be back in a month or so and maybe something else will come up after all the tourists leave.'

Her boss looked relieved. 'Yeah. Well. If you do, I'll work on that for you. Maybe we could get you a job at the council. Sometimes they supply a house for staff.'

'What could I do for the council?' Charli didn't think they hired cooks.

Scarlet shrugged. 'You could work behind the counter in the tourist information centre. Or something with the library or council admin. People still have to register their dogs, you know.'

'They do that here?'

'Yeah. Like a normal town. And book plots in the cemetery. Plus there's taking the dingo scalps and pig snouts when the wild dog trappers come in for their money.'

'Dingo scalps? Pig snouts? That's gross. And cruel.' She'd seen Lazy Luke kill a pig once. It had been hit by a car and he'd put it out of its misery. But life wasn't always roses and she, as much as anyone, knew that. She could hold a dried dingo scalp at arm's length if she had to. But she didn't want to. 'I guess.'

Scarlet waved that away as if of course Charli would manage. 'Anyway, there's lots of jobs that council need people to do. Or maybe at the police station in the Q-Gap job.'

'I guess, but I'd rather be in a kitchen.'

Scarlet wasn't listening again. 'Might be a good job going at the airport working for the airport manager. Checking people in when they go on their flights. Running luggage on and off the plane with the ute.' She was nodding. 'They get other people working round town to do that so no reason you couldn't do it, too. Or you could clean at the health centre. Or the pub.'

The pub. Charli hadn't said she'd got that job at the pub and she guessed if her boss didn't already know, then she should be the one to tell her, though Scarlet had been the one to suggest it. She cleared her throat. 'I did get shifts at the pub in the kitchen. After I finish here. Five till nine.'

'So I heard.' A stare later her boss said, 'Wondered if you'd mention it.'

'I told them this was my main job. That I couldn't start any earlier because I was working for you.'

'Long hours you're doing.' There was more interest than censure in the comment and Charli relaxed a little. She did not want to get on the wrong side of Scarlet. Especially now there was accommodation in the offering.

'I like to work,' Charli said as she placed another bowl and spoon on the draining rack. 'I told you that.'

'You do, don't you? Gotta say, I'm impressed.'

Charli froze. Scarlet sounded sincere. Suddenly the words of Nana Kate came into her head with a jolt. *If someone compliments you, say thank you.*

'Thank you,' she said in a small voice, but she wasn't used to compliments and Scarlet's praise made her feel awkward. 'I like working for you, too,' she offered shyly.

'Do you?' Scarlet laughed. 'You'd be the first person in town to say that.'

Charli shook her head. No idea if that was true or whether Scarlet was just teasing. She shrugged. 'I'm happy.' And she was. Very, very happy.

Scarlet pushed the next batch into the oven and set the timer at the same time as Charli hung up the tea towel after the last dish was put away.

'Come on,' said the boss. 'Let's go out and have a look at your possible temporary home.'

Charli followed her out the back door, her heart thumping and her mouth dry. This is the start, she thought. Things were falling into place. This could be the next step.

Out of the air-conditioned kitchen, she felt the slam of heat from the day but she didn't even mind that. So, it was hot, and the flies greeted her like an old friend. Nothing could faze her today.

Across the sunburned stubble of dry grass sat the shed, and now she took it all in. Sturdy, dust-covered, but strong and secure. A big silver tin construction with a huge sliding door and a small side entry with a keyed handle. It wasn't locked.

Scarlet pushed open the door and Charli followed on her heels as they stepped into the gloom.

'It's hot in here,' Scarlet said as she switched on the light.

Charli didn't mind because in the corner sat a dusty, cute as a button, old-fashioned caravan half-covered by an even dustier tarpaulin.

'Maybe we should have done this after work,' Scarlet muttered, looking at the dust on her hands as she shifted the tarp to find the door of the van. 'Don't need to be covered in dirt if we're going back into the kitchen.'

'We could just pull it to one side,' Charli said quietly, terrified Scarlet would decide against the whole idea. 'I could just look?'

Scarlet glanced at Charli's despondent face and sighed. 'Okay.' She shifted the cover sheet and, true enough, with just a little edging of the tarpaulin, they could open the door enough to slide inside.

It was dim and dark but cleaner than outside. Charli could see a stripped island double bed, a little kitchen nook with a table and L-shaped lounge and even a half fridge and kitchen sink.

It was truly just a smaller version of where she was living at the moment.

'What do you think?' Scarlet had her hands on her hips, look-ing unimpressed. 'Is it worth pulling the cover off and cleaning it up?'

'I love it.' Charli scanned the small area, imagining her own space, no need to move until she went to have her baby. 'It's wonderful.'

A snort from the side. 'Your idea of wonderful and mine are a bit different. Still, I'm happy if you want to give it a go. No problem if it doesn't work, because it's only for a week.'

'It's perfect.'

'That it's not,' the boss said dryly. 'And while we're here in the dark, anything else you want to tell me?'

Charli's heart thumped. Apprehension filling her. 'Like?'

'Like the bulge under your shirt?'

'Oh.' Charli sucked in a breath, trying to pull her baby in, but the bulge stayed. 'That?'

'Yes, that.'

Terrified she was about to be kicked out after being so close to settled, she stuttered, 'W-w-what do you want to know?'

'Boy or girl?'

Charli's shoulders drooped. So, she really knew then. 'Don't know. Didn't ask.' She lifted her chin. 'But not due for five weeks yet and I can still work. I have to save money for the baby.'

'Why don't you go on the dole like everyone else?'

Charli gave her boss one of her own hard stares back. 'I like to work. I'll go mad if I have to sit at home all day just to get money.'

Scarlet pressed her lips together and after a long pause, finally said, 'You are different.'

Charli put her hand up to cover her lip.

'And I don't mean some tiny scar you cover too much. I mean you work hard. You're a good kid. That's different from the most common eighteen-year-old I see.'

'Nearly nineteen. And you won't tell the pub I'm pregnant?'

'I'm not lying for you. But, no, that's your job, but if they ask . . .' She shrugged.

Charli licked dry lips. 'I have to leave after the races – I have to be near the hospital from a month before. But I'm coming back, and I'll want my old jobs back.'

Scarlet's eyes were on her and they were intent. 'Why?'

Lots of reasons, but the main reason? That her mum could be from here and she might have family in town. She wasn't ready to put her dream out there yet. 'Can I tell you later?'

Scarlet narrowed her eyes – it should have been hard for Charli to see that in the dark but the boss used her whole face to scowl. No missing that. Finally, grudgingly, she muttered, 'I hate secrets. Turns out secrets hurt my family too much and I'd hate to see you start your own family with secrets that hurt them.'

Charli nodded. 'I promise. I'll tell you in a couple of days. I just need to check something first.'

'Okay.' Scarlet waved her hand. 'Seen enough?'

'Yes.' Charli nodded vigorously. Wanting to please.

'Back to work.'

Charli smiled. That sounded like a bark without a bite. 'Scarlet?'

'Yeah?' She didn't turn around.

So she spoke to her back. 'When can I move in?'

'Tomorrow morning.' Gruffly. 'Before work if you want.'

Chapter Twenty-three

Phoebe

When Phoebe walked into Scarlet's house after the clinic, her
cousin stood in the laundry with a spray bottle of cleaner and a
handful of cloths. 'Don't suppose you fancy helping me clean Mum
and Dad's van in the shed?'

Phoebe blinked. 'Umm. Sure. Why?'

'Because for the four days over the race period nobody can get
accommodation in Birdsville, unless you sleep in a tent, and my
little kitchen helper's lodging runs out tomorrow at the caravan
park.'

'Oh.' She couldn't help thinking Scarlet's helper had planned
poorly.

Scarlet rifled in a low cupboard for the dustpan and brush.
'I said she can move into the old van and use the shed's toilet and
shower for the next week.'

'Good idea. At least it's self-contained. Is the van connected to
the power in the shed?'

'Yep. Means the fridge works, and the extra garden hose is
snapped into the water so she can use the kitchen sink.'

'You're being very good.' Her cousin was not known for her charitable thoughts and only sometimes for her good deeds.

Scarlet snorted. 'That's me. A bloody philanthropist. Just been hiding it all these years.'

Phoebe's mouth twitched. 'You crack me up.' She put her empty lunchbox on the table. 'Let me change out of these clothes into something I can get dirty.'

Muffled from where she was bent. 'You're a champion.'

Phoebe huffed. 'Must take after my cousin.'

Nodding sagely without looking up, Scarlet murmured into the cupboard, 'Must be that.'

Fifteen minutes later Phoebe found herself wet-dusting walls and wiping out drawers in a retro caravan inside Scarlet's shed. The shed was a big one, so room enough for the kitchen van Scarlet took to the races plus this pull-along her parents had travelled around in.

It wasn't too hot inside the actual van because it had its own air-conditioning, go figure. She wasn't sure how that fitted with the whole 'we like to go back in the past' theme, but maybe that was just using your brains if you were going to caravan around central Queensland. Hence the air temp sat at a pleasant twenty-three degrees while, as Scarlet scrubbed the sink and wiped out the fridge, Phoebe buffed the windows clean on the inside.

Scarlet had done the outside glass, though the whole van could have done with pulling out of the shed and hosing down.

They were almost ready to make the bed up when Phoebe said, 'Tell me about your new friend. You must be very happy with her, doing all this to keep her for another week's work.'

'Like I said before. Something about her appeals.' Scarlet dropped the pile of clean sheets on the bed. Looked at Phoebe. 'She's had it tough, but she's upbeat. Works hard. Doesn't stop. A little too self-effacing for my liking, but I reckon I could fix that if I had enough time.'

'Time?' Sounded like her cousin was on a mission. 'How long is she staying?'

'Talking about settling in Birdsville. I hope she does. I think she needs a place to call home.'

'Didn't you say she was young?'

'Eighteen.' Scarlet grinned. 'No. Nearly nineteen.'

Phoebe squinted at her cousin. Was she mad? 'Your average young person doesn't fall in love with this place.' She thought about the rest of the absolutely stinking hot year out here and not just the glamorous and frantic week of the races or the Big Red Bash when it was all fun and lively activity.

Scarlet raised her face from her task. 'She says she loves it. I believe her. Has her reasons, apparently.'

Phoebe blinked at this further championing. 'Which are?'

'I'm hoping she'll tell me.'

Phoebe could see her cousin remained immovable on this and that was fine. Scarlet was a big girl and had great instincts, so she'd trust her. 'Okay. But you're not going to have extra work for her when the races are done. How will she live?'

'I'm thinking she could put in for something in the council if she comes back.'

'Comes back?' Now she was confused. 'I thought you said she was staying?'

'That's the kicker. She has to fly to Charleville next Tuesday.'

Phoebe stared. A bunch of thoughts jostled for pole position in her head. Because? Flights weren't cheap. Had there been trouble? A stalker? Was she going to court? 'Funny, the way I do not want to ask why . . .'

'She's pregnant.'

Phoebe stared. 'Pregnant? How pregnant?'

'Said she's got five weeks to go.'

Five?! And she hadn't noticed? Great midwife she was. Which meant right now Charli was a possible prem-labour working harder than she should. Something didn't add up. 'How long's she been in town?'

'Since the day you arrived.'

And came from where? But even she could hear the accusation in that question and left it unsaid. Calm down. 'I hope she's having antenatal care.'

'Said she's been seeing the antenatal clinic in Charleville. She's planning on having the baby there, then she's got an old foster mother who will put her up for the postnatal period in Roma.'

'Okay.' But it wasn't. Or maybe it was but it made Phoebe uneasy. 'Reckon you could get her to come down to the clinic at some stage? At least we can file some information in case something happens.'

Scarlet went back to poking the pillows into the pillowcases. 'Okay, I'll tell her to do that. She'll go, though I don't know when, since she's working for me during clinic hours.'

'If she comes after four, I'll wait for her.'

'She works at the pub from five till nine.'

'Cripes. What is she? A machine?'

'Told you she likes to work.'

'Good grief. I thought Gloria worked hard.'

'Charli's a tough little thing. When I realised she was pregnant, first day mind you, I almost flipped out, worrying she wouldn't cope. But kitchen isn't heavy work. Just on your feet all day. I felt I had to let her keep working because I wanted her to tell me. Or ask why she hadn't.'

'And the answer to that?'

'Oh, I gave myself that answer.' Scarlet huffed. 'I think she was worried I wouldn't have employed her if she'd told me. I just wouldn't have encouraged her to get a job at the pub as well. But today she said she's stashing the money for when the baby's born. Tells me she doesn't want to go on social services until she has to – for a short time only, she says, after the birth.'

'Good on her. But still, something's odd about moving to Birdsville with a new baby and no partner.'

'Says there's a secret.'

Phoebe winced. 'And don't I hate secrets.'

Scarlet snorted again. 'That's what I said. Apparently, she'll tell me in a couple of days. Wants to check something out.'

Phoebe didn't like it but that could just be because of her own disastrous surprises. 'Curiouser and curiouser.'

'True story.' They finished up in the van, and when they stood back, the new lightbulbs shone on the freshly made-up bed, and everything sparkled. The curtains were open even though the windows were closed for the heat.

'I left the top vent loose to let the hot air out. There's enough air leaking around the doors not to have to worry about windows. She should be comfortable.'

Phoebe raised her brows. 'It's like a perfect tiny house on one of those shows. I'd say she'll be in heaven.'

They'd ransacked Scarlet's kitchen and added basic condiments like salt, pepper, tea and coffee and a spray can of non-stick for cooking. Phoebe checked the smoke alarm, which needed a new battery, and they'd stuck a can of fly spray and containers of handwash and detergent on the sink edge.

They'd already cleaned the shower in the shed and now hung a curtain rod with two plastic curtains that surrounded the toilet, sink and shower. It was a makeshift room of privacy, so the girl didn't have to worry about someone coming in the door when she was in the shower or on the loo.

'This is a neat little set-up. When's she coming?'

Scarlet lifted one shoulder. 'She'll have to be out of the caravan park before she comes to work tomorrow, so I'd say in the morning. I'll give her an extra hour before she starts.' She looked around with satisfaction. 'I'm quite keen to see her face.'

So was Phoebe. And that wasn't all she wanted to look at. Her belly was next.

'Done then.' Scarlet dusted her hands at a job completed.

'How about a shower and then a glass of wine before tea?'

'Now that sounds like a plan.' She glanced at her watch. 'Because my dear heart arrives home Thursday, and we need to savour our free nights without a man in the house.'

'You're on,' Phoebe agreed and the two women smiled at each other.

Chapter Twenty-four

Atticus

On the Wednesday before the races, Atticus watched Brophy arrive and put up his boxing tent, the last legal boxing tent in the world, for the ring that takes all comers. His troop arrived every year to give the locals and tourists the chance to pit themselves against his professional boxers. Dressed in his signature red shirt and beating the drum that looked as old as he was, the man was a legend around Birdsville and all over outback Queensland.

Apart from Brophy, the market stalls were stocked up with memorabilia for the races. Books and paintings. Wood and ceramics. Hats and pins and stubby holders. T-shirts of all sizes and designs, which gave the town an outback Royal Easter Show feel, but without the show bags. The stalls on the town square made the flat oval area a different place from the open, dry paddock it had been last week.

He'd been told the music would start at the pub at four pm every day.

Vehicles streamed in from Jundah to the east, Coober Pedy to the west, Bedourie and Boulia to the north and Marree to the south. An invasion. A mostly grey invasion, with lots of smiles and happy people. He liked it.

Half-a-dozen more police had arrived this morning and would start work tomorrow. He was officially reinforced. And he had Thursday night off for the gala night and Phoebe would be there.

Sadly, Atticus found himself thwarted every time he tried for a trip down to the health clinic. Now the town had begun to fill, the other police officers surrounded him, and he had a buddy most times he went anywhere. Seemed he always had to go in the opposite direction to the Primary Health Clinic.

The tourists continued to be law abiding and, considering the fact that almost two thousand people had arrived in town three days before the races, everything stayed orderly and organised.

Still, he wanted to see Phoebe, and just had to come up with a decent excuse to walk into the clinic. No use asking her for a sunset drink at his place because the barracks and the station were now full of other officers, both men and women.

Salvation came when one of the junior officers tripped over a random dog: judging by his blood-curdling yell and the odd shape of his forearm, he'd snapped a bone. Guiltily hoping his wish hadn't granted his colleague a misfortune, Atticus made himself instantly available to usher him down to the health centre.

Worth it. He glanced guiltily at his colleague. The smile he received from the temporary receptionist as they went through the front doors was enough to make his day complete. Funny how much you could say with just a look, considering neither of them uttered words. Yep. A whole conversation right there, and he gathered she was glad to see him, too.

Naturally Phoebe dealt professionally with his colleague's details and discomfort in a speedy and efficient manner. Gloria arrived and towed the hapless bloke away and he had the pleasure of Phoebe's company while he waited. Couldn't leave the poor man without a lift back.

'Are you as busy here as we are in town?' he asked.

'Building every day. The patients tell me there's more police around town.'

'We'll have about thirty by race day.' He pretended to preen. 'But only one of me.'

'So modest.' She rolled her eyes. 'How are you handling the invasion at the station? Good to share the responsibility or too many cooks?'

'I like it. The change is nice. Short term. They're good company and I get a break from being on call. That's a bonus.' He glanced around the waiting room. Only two waiting. 'You?'

'I'm having all fun and no responsibility.'

He remembered on the trip back from Big Red she'd said she was worried how tired the nurse looked. 'Gloria looks relaxed.'

'She's amazing. Although I don't know how she would've done it all on her own.'

He did wonder. 'Maybe they would've sent someone from somewhere else?' But he didn't think so.

She didn't look convinced, either. 'Unless they'd hijacked a tourist, they wouldn't have had anyone else. But it's all worked out well. I've had a great week meeting locals. And being with Gloria I'm catching up on all that's happened in town since I left.'

He grinned at that. 'Ha. I knew it. At heart you're really a gossip.' But he knew she wasn't. He got a look for that comment, which made him smile wider. 'What about your cousin? Thought you were helping there?'

'Scarlet doesn't need me under her feet. She's found a kitchen hand, Charli, who's supposedly an angel. She's helping with the preparations for her catering for race day. I'm not really a fan of washing up and that's all she'd get me to do.'

'Is Charli the young woman who came in a week ago and is staying at the caravan park?'

Phoebe tilted her head. 'Really do know what's going on in your patch, don't you?'

'My job to know. And yep. I saw her and the bloke who brought her.'

'She's moving into a van at Scarlet's house for the next week.'

'Really. Must have made a good impression, then. I wasn't thrilled with the bloke she came with.' But that wasn't what he wanted to discuss. 'Listen, I finish work at five. What time are you done here?'

'We close at four. Usually out by four-thirty. Why?'

'Fancy a swim down the billabong?' Her face lit. He didn't know where it had sprung from but that there had been a stroke of genius.

'Actually, I'd love that,' she said. 'How about I bring a hamper and we have a bit of a picnic afterwards?'

'No alcohol.' He pretended to be stern and to his delight she laughed.

'Won't do that to you.'

'Okay if I pick you up from your cousin's house at five-thirty and we'll go down and do the sunset?'

'Sounds perfect. Won't have it to ourselves with everyone here but that's fine.'

The phone on the desk rang and Phoebe said, 'Hang on.' She listened. 'I have to help hold your friend's arm while we plaster.'

'Do you need a second person to hold him?'

'Might not be a bad idea. Come this way, sir.'

At five-thirty, Atticus rolled gently around the corner to Phoebe's cousin's house in his own car and she was already waiting on the front verandah. Pretty impressive considering the heat.

He pushed open the door and she slid in wearing a strappy little sundress that made his mouth water. This woman could turn him into a hormonal teen in two seconds flat.

'I brought home-made lemonade,' she said as she buckled her seat belt.

'Can't wait.' For lemonade. For nothing in particular. For everything. Just to spend some time with her, which was way crazy for someone he'd only reconnected with a week ago. Someone who lived twelve hundred kilometres away and thought he was a kid. But it didn't change the fact he'd been counting the minutes till now and hating the passing of the days till she was gone.

They drove past the Primary Health Centre and up the Eyre Development Road towards the racecourse and turned off onto the Pelican Point track. When they reached the gate, she jumped out.

Gotta love country girls, he thought, watching her, her hips swinging and her legs flashing in the sundress as she swung the gate open and stood back to wave him through. She shut it behind his vehicle and climbed back in so they could roll quietly down the track to the billabong.

To his surprise there weren't any other cars or even any walking traffic. In fact, no other people disturbed the quiet peace. A stroke of luck or maybe everyone was thinking about their stomach and dinner time. Suited him.

They climbed out and he put the cool bag and a couple of towels on the big table under the shelter beside the billabong.

Then remembered last time. 'I'm following you into the water. Since you know the short cut.'

She laughed over her shoulder, and the sound zinged through him like a current flipping his switch at the same time. She dropped her sundress, a wicked gleam in her eyes and he sucked in a breath. The bikini was tiny. 'Come this way, sir.'

He did. Fast. Then water closed over his head and his arms reached out for her but she slipped through his fingers like a wily fish.

Chapter Twenty-five

Gloria

Gloria decided this was the easiest lead-up to the races she'd had in the last ten years. Dangerous thoughts: she crossed her fingers to ward off bad luck. But having Phoebe around had been a godsend and a joy.

Except for the pesky new secret between them. Maybe she should have let Rusty tell everyone. So many times, she'd wanted to share Rusty's proposal of marriage. Each time she decided, no, it was up to Phoebe's father to tell her the news. But darn him. He should have overruled her. She was an idiot. Now she wanted to share her delight with Phoebe, and maybe Phoebe would settle her nerves about being too old for love.

Still, Phoebe had more things on her mind than antiquated lovers, she decided, since her soon-to-be daughter-in-law had looked mighty pleased when she left today with a plan to meet her admirer for a swim at Pelican Point.

'To be young again,' she'd murmured wistfully as the door shut after her, but then again, she doubted she could be bothered struggling into a swimming costume and walking barefoot into water you couldn't see the bottom of. Followed by the struggling out again. Then a gritty towel.

Her nice shower sounded much more relaxing.

Maybe it was time for her to retire. And with Rusty's proposal, there would be enough in her life – in fact, she had a whole new, wonderful life waiting for her. One she couldn't wait to begin.

The phone beside her rang and she compressed her lips. Looked like she wasn't going to get a shower, let alone time for a swim.

'Gloria speaking.'

'Is this Sister Revere?'

'Yes. Go ahead.'

'This is Constable Olsen. I'm working in Birdsville as support, and we've had a call for a rollover near Big Red. Senior Constable Bow said we had to contact you for liaison with the ambulance and all depart at the same time. He's not answering his phone at the moment.'

Gloria knew where Atticus was. Probably with his head under the water and out of earshot of his phone. Lucky him. 'I'll contact my usual driver and meet you outside the police station in ten minutes. Do you have confirmation how many people are involved in the accident?'

'Yes. Two. One apparently has a head injury, and the one who made the call claims to be unhurt.'

'Thank you. We should have the personnel for that without calling in extra help.'

Gloria said her goodbyes and speed-dialled Rusty, who picked up straight away.

'Hello, Gloria my love. Nice to hear from you.' And just like that she felt as if someone had rubbed a soft teddy-bear-of-caring all over her. Couldn't help the smile in her voice. 'Hello, Rusty dear. I wish it was a social call. Can you come down and drive the ambulance for me, please? We've had another rollover out at Big Red.'

'Sure. Be there in five.'

'Thank you.' And she meant it. She wasn't alone now, and she wouldn't be in the future. It took some getting used to. The call ended. Maybe she *had* stayed here too long because she was more nervous something would go wrong each time she went out.

'Get yourself organised,' she snapped out loud. Which wasn't a big ask because the ambulance was always ready to go. Always full of fuel. Always stocked with first aid equipment, replaced immediately on return to base after a retrieval.

Gloria contacted the flying doctor, told them what she knew, and promised to update them as soon as she had assessed the scene.

She looked in the fridge. Empty. She needed to shop. It wasn't that far out to Big Red, but sometimes it took a long time to sort out transfer of patients. Grabbing a small cool pack she added water and a bag of glucose sweets. By the time she left her house and walked the short distance to the clinic, Rusty had arrived and had already lifted the bonnet of the ambulance to check all was well. No vermin or animals had crawled in to sleep. Nothing unexpected had happened since last time.

'Everything's fine,' he said as he lowered the bonnet to stride over to her and smile down into her eyes.

She looked up at him. Such a lovely man. Her man. The thought swirled and curled inside her and she gave him a soft, uncertain smile. She cared such a lot for him.

'Any chance of a hug?'

She stepped closer and he pulled her into his arms. Patted her back as she sighed and relaxed into his lovely chest. She could get used to this. But not now. She stepped back. 'Thank you. I feel all recharged now.'

He laughed. 'That didn't take much. You're a wonder woman. But let me know any time you need a repeat. I'm always ready.'

She laughed, her world restored, and they climbed in. Rusty turned left towards town and past the pub to the police station at the next cross street. A four-wheel drive police vehicle waited for them at the edge of the road and they began the convoy out to Big Red.

Chapter Twenty-six

Charli

Charli's excitement about moving into Scarlet's caravan meant she had trouble dropping off to sleep after work that night.

She was tired, or her body was, but the pub shift had been great. She'd enjoyed her hours and already she and Chef – 'call me Kelvin' – were a team in the kitchen. He didn't say much but she caught his eye on her a couple of times and he seemed to be always smiling. A lot of the time she knew what he wanted before he even wanted it, and that made everything easy. And fun.

But Kelvin was more than nice. A big man, the gentle giant type, and he told her to sit down if she was doing something repetitive that could just as easily be done in a chair. People didn't say that to her but Kelvin did. When he had a break, he made sure she did too. If she didn't know better, she'd say he knew she was pregnant, but she didn't think so. Or offer the information. But from the second night he did seem worried she'd work too hard. As if.

There was something about Birdsville, the people and the place, that made her happy. Appreciated. And she hadn't realised how nice appreciation felt or how contented it would make her.

Of course, finding out about her mum was harder than she expected because she just didn't have the time. She probably wouldn't have a chance now until after the races, because, oh my goodness, the food that was going out of that kitchen. So many people eating at the pub. In the kitchen, she and Kelvin rarely stopped except for the breaks he made her take.

By the end of another shift she knew everyone, bringing out so many meals even the backpackers who worked the tables and served behind the bar were smiling at her, and remembered her name.

And now in her day job it felt good that Scarlet knew about the baby. It was good she hadn't been angry for Charli not mentioning her pregnancy earlier. Very, very good she hadn't fired her.

So, one minute she'd been lying in bed thinking about all these wonderful things that had happened today . . .

And the next it was Thursday, and her alarm was ringing.

Another busy day coming up and she had to make sure she left nothing behind in the cabin. She emptied the rubbish and wiped the sink. Stripped the sheets and folded them for the cleaners to take away. Checked under the bed – and suddenly she was packed and waiting.

She wondered how early she could turn up at Scarlet's house.

She made another cup of tea, and put the last of the long-life milk in it so as not to waste the protein for her baby. Sipped while she stared at her bulging backpack and the soft cool bag with the remains of her food. She needed to shop but keep in mind the small fridge. How lucky was she? She had a place with her own fridge, and it wasn't costing her anything.

She wondered fleetingly how Lazy Luke was going in Charleville, but the thought drifted away as baby stretched and rolled and pushed up under her ribs.

Charli slid a hand down and patted her round tummy, which seemed suddenly bigger. Excitement zinged through her – soon, baby, soon – but she didn't have time just yet to stop and enjoy. Not until Charleville. Her and baby would be a team.

'Morning, baby. Have you shifted your bottom? You feel heavier. We're moving into our new house today.'

She glanced at her watch. Still an hour till it was time for work but it would take a few minutes to hand back the key and walk the short distance to Scarlet's. And she wanted to unpack before she started, have everything ready for when she finished that afternoon – that thought gave her a jolt of pure joy.

Handy it was only around the corner from the caravan park and her bags weren't heavy. The backpack was easy to carry, anyway. She could walk slowly, take her time.

Charli finished the tea, washed the cup thoroughly, dried and put it back in the cupboard.

Charli saw Phoebe coming up the path. The other woman lifted her hand in a friendly way. Everyone was so nice.

'Scarlet said you're moving into the van today.' It was a statement but nothing negative.

'Yes. I'm looking forward to it.'

'She also said you're having a baby soon.'

Charli's gaze flew to hers. 'Yes. But not for five weeks.' Was Phoebe going to tell Scarlet to sack her?

Didn't look like it because she smiled. 'Congratulations. Where are you giving birth?'

Oh. That was okay. Nice, actually. 'Charleville. I did the antenatal visits there. My next one is in two weeks.'

'They have a great unit there. If it's okay with you, would you mind if the clinic here had some details from your antenatal card? Just in case you have any worries before your appointment. I'm a midwife so I should be able to help if you have questions.'

'I don't mind.' Charli shrugged. 'I'm feeling fine, but I can give it to you this morning when I unpack. Maybe you can photocopy it and give it back when you're done?'

'That sounds perfect.' Phoebe slid past. 'Come in.' She reached out. 'Here. Let me take one of the bags.'

Before Charli could stop her Phoebe had picked up the backpack from the ground and moved towards the door. 'Scarlet will be up. I think she's looking forward to you coming this morning.'

Scarlet was? Because she was moving in? That was nice.

There wasn't time to think more as Scarlet opened the front door before Phoebe could, and said, 'I thought you'd be early. I'll come out the front and we'll go around to the shed.'

The next few awkward moments of three women on a small verandah happened so fast she almost tripped as they turned, but Phoebe had her hand out and she steadied. 'Thanks.'

'Small space,' she said. 'And Scarlet moves quick.'

They smiled at each other as Phoebe's oblivious cousin scooted past and led the way.

Crikey. If she fell onto baby . . . Horrible thought and that would give Phoebe something to write to Charleville about. She didn't want that.

Scarlet led them around the side of the house to the shed. Phoebe carried the backpack and Charli the food bag, which left Scarlet free to open the side door. She waved with her other hand.

'In you go. See what we've done. Hope you like it.'

The first thing Charli saw in the shed, before she even reached the van, was that they'd sorted the one problem she'd worried about. 'You've put a curtain in the corner around the shower and toilet!' It hadn't been there yesterday. She'd actually been going to rig something herself – she wasn't sure what! – but this looked so much nicer than anything she could have managed. 'Oh. That's wonderful. Thank you.'

'Easy done. The rail was already there.' Scarlet had crossed the shed and opened the door to the van. She stood back. 'Well, come on, have a look.'

'Impatient much,' Phoebe whispered.

Charli smiled at her. They were making a fuss of her and she so wasn't used to it. By the expression on her boss's face, Scarlet really *had* been looking forward to this. She glanced at Phoebe and even she looked softer and less scary.

Charli hurried over and Scarlet took the food bag from her.

'Just go in and have a little look on your own. We'll hold these out here.'

So, she did. On her own first. Her heart beating with excitement.

She climbed the steps, which was a little bit harder than yesterday, and heaved herself inside.

'Ohhh,' she breathed. 'Oh my.' It was beautiful. The bed was made with floral sheets and a light comforter. Pillows plumped. The whole tiny room was so clean it sparkled.

'I put a shower curtain over the mattress. Just in case you did something disgusting like break your waters on my bed.'

Charli gasped out a laugh. 'You didn't?'

'I did. Turn on the lights. The electricity's connected.'

She turned back to the door, looked at Scarlet's smiling face, found the switch and turned on the lights. The little room lit up in a soft yellow glow.

'The air-con works,' Scarlet said as she poked her head in. 'The fridge is on. We put some bits and pieces in there, but you'll have to go shopping for real food.'

'I will. It's wonderful. I love it. Thank you, Scarlet.' The simple words seemed inadequate, but Charli had nothing else to offer. Maybe later she could think of something, some way to repay her boss, but right now she was having a hard time not bursting into tears.

Scarlet leaned further in without bringing the rest of her body and put the food bag on the floor. Phoebe did the same, though she swung the backpack up onto the seat beside the table, like they both thought the small space was too cramped for them. It wasn't small. It was perfect.

Scarlet stepped back. 'You've got a while if you want to come a bit later to work.'

'No, it won't take me long to put my things away and then I'll come in. I'll be ready to start work at eight.'

'Okay, but I don't want to see you before that, so have a fiddle. Make a cup of tea or something.'

'Thank you.'

They left. Just left her there, in her new place. And it was wonderful.

Chapter Twenty-seven

Phoebe

Phoebe followed Scarlet into the kitchen to make their own cup of tea.

'That went off well,' Scarlet said, switching on the kettle.

Understatement. 'It did and you're right. She is nice. I don't think she'll try to take advantage of your help.'

Scarlet shook her head as she pulled out the mugs. 'Not her style. The word from the pub is that they love her over there as well and Kelvin won't stop singing her praises.'

'She's only done a couple of shifts, hasn't she?'

'Three.'

'And she's already made her mark? That's impressive. Charli might yet find her home in town once she's had her baby. Which reminds me, I spoke to her about antenatal information.'

Scarlet glared at her. 'Don't you go hexing any disasters with my kitchenhand, cousin.' Scarlet looked ready to defend her kitten and Phoebe batted her off with a diversion.

'Last thing I want to do. How are your orders going for the races?'

Scarlet blinked and her gaze bounced to the big freezer. 'I'm almost done and will be after today. Best year of organisation I've had yet.'

'No thanks to me.'

'No, none. But I'm used to doing without you.'

'Spare me. Don't start. Not again.'

'Hmm. Anyway, there's a meeting this afternoon with the race committee for all the caterers. Was thinking I might ask Charli if she'd like to come with me, before she goes to the pub. It's a good chance to introduce her to the town's movers and shakers.'

'Great idea.' And it was. That's how it worked in Birdsville. Everybody knew everybody, and if you were new and sticking around, you'd be introduced to everyone. It was such an inclusive community: no barriers. If you did the right thing the town would look after you. Didn't matter if you were the person behind the desk in the information centre or the owner of one of the largest outback stations in Australia, everybody spoke to you. It was first names all the way.

She'd forgotten that. Phoebe felt like kicking herself. Why had she wasted so much time before coming back? Maybe she could blame it all on some Freudian thing about missing her mother and teenage hormones. But, if she was being real, she'd just been stubborn.

'What are you looking so serious about?' Scarlet had stopped pouring the tea.

'Thinking what an idiot I've been staying away for so long.'

'Oh, thank the Lord for that,' said Scarlet and pushed the tea across the table to her. 'Drink this and go. My man arrives at ten am and I'm so excited I want to have Charli set up with a string of jobs so I can go canoodle in peace.'

Phoebe slapped her hands over her ears. 'Too much information.' But she did love that dreamy expression on her cousin's face.

'He reckons our horse has a really good chance this year.'

Phoebe had been hearing about her dad and Scarlet's dream, a
broken-down racehorse named Just Finish, for a couple of years
now. She hadn't been interested because it all stank of the gambling
issues that had driven her away. But maybe she needed to let that
go, too – after all, Rusty had never been the gambler she'd thought
him. 'Well, that's exciting. I hope I get to the races. I'm not even
sure if the clinic is open on Saturday when the Cup's on.'

'The clinic's shut Saturdays. St John's do the first aid at the
races. Though I think your handsome copper will be on duty, so
you won't get to hold hands.'

'He's not my copper.' Her hands went to her hips uncon-
sciously. 'And I do not hold hands with boys. Especially old
schoolfriends.' Which was a very sad statement when she thought
about it – because she could imagine holding Atticus's hand while
they watched the races together, and she wasn't thinking of the ten-
year-old boy.

As if Scarlet had heard her thoughts she said, 'A *younger*
schoolfriend.' Teasing, but Phoebe winced.

Later, at work, Phoebe spoke to Gloria about Charli. The young
woman had handed over the antenatal card at eight, as promised.
Plenty of time for Phoebe before she left as the clinic didn't open
until nine.

Phoebe had entered the information on the card into the
computer and thankfully all the usual low-risk pregnancy markers

had been met. Nothing to worry about, except that statement about Charli not knowing of any health risks from either of her parents as she'd been a ward of the state until her majority.

Ward of the state. Did that mean she was never adopted? Poor Charli.

None of her business, and hopefully, they'd need none of this information. Though, if Charli was coming back to settle in town, information to put in birth records was always good for the new baby.

The clinic was surprisingly quiet considering the first race day, Friday, was tomorrow and the annual RFDS gala dinner was on tonight. Phoebe and Scarlet were dressing up for the event. She'd meant to ask Gloria if she and Dad were going, she assumed they were, but was sidetracked by the nurse's next comment.

'We might have our work cut out for us in the next couple of hours. The Fun Run finishes soon. Hopefully, we'll only get heat exhaustion, blisters and skinned knees to deal with.'

'That's new since I left. How far do they run?'

'Starts and finishes at the tourist park and goes out to the race-course and back. Just over five kilometres.'

Phoebe shook her head as if heartbroken. 'So sad. What a shame I couldn't be in it. Especially in pleasantly warm Birdsville.'

'Wuss.' Gloria waggled her brows and Phoebe thought again how much she enjoyed the older woman's company. 'It's not too hot at eight-thirty in the morning. They take walkers and funners as well as the serious runners.'

'Next year maybe . . .'

'You stick around you'll hear about it. There are upwardly mobile people on the race committee who'll grab you. It's a great thing. They promote it by saying if a hundred people raise one hundred dollars each, that's ten thousand dollars for the RFDS. Life changing for someone.'

Maybe she'd been too hasty and frivolous in her comments. 'Next year, if I come back at the right time, I'll reconsider. But today, I'll help you with the bandaids and the blisters.'

Gloria laughed. 'You're going to the gala dinner, though, aren't you?'

'Yes. Scarlet bought tickets.' And Atticus had said he was going.

Before she could ask about Rusty, Gloria supplied the answer. 'Excellent. Your dad and I go every year.'

And here was her opportunity. 'Is it my imagination or is there something going on between you and Dad? Something more?'

Gloria opened her mouth and closed it again. Finally, she said, 'You need to talk to your father about that. Rusty and I have been very good friends for many years.'

'More than friends?' Phoebe looked at Gloria, whose whole face and neck had gone pink. She pretended not to notice. Oh my. More intrigue than expected? Gloria looked away and clamped her lips shut.

'Well, I love you both.' She wanted to add, any happiness you find is a wonderful thing, but she wouldn't tease Gloria. Could see she was uncomfortable. Instead, she said, 'Speaking of romance, Scarlet's man comes home today.'

The strain round Gloria's mouth eased. 'Hot stuff.' Her eyes twinkled. 'Do you want to sleep at my place tonight?' Her laugh sounded tinged with relief at the change of subject.

Not that bad an idea. 'Thanks for the offer, but after the gala I thought I'd head over to Dad's and keep out of their way until they go to bed. Maybe stay a while after they go to bed. If what Scarlet says is true.'

Smiling, Gloria said, 'George is good people. He's worked stock on the stations as well as being a jockey. A bit like your dad, really, but very good with horses. One of those horse whisperer types. A master of many talents.'

Yes, his many talents were what she was afraid of. But she kept that to herself, though she was smiling when she said, 'Scarlet mentioned he helped their horse.'

'Absolutely. Word was Just Finish would never race again – he won his first two before his breakdown; he went down at his third race – but George nursed him back to health and got him galloping again.'

'Nice story.'

'Gets better. Saturday's race will be his second run since his comeback, and he had a good run at the Louth Races. It was all very exciting.'

'I did hear that.' She'd heard several times from Scarlet every day for a week. 'It's a nice dream.'

'He was fourth reserve for the Birdsville Cup, so we didn't think he had a chance for the draw, but a run of scratchings did it.'

Ah, she'd wondered how they got him in. 'I can't see him beating the expensive horses shipped out here nowadays.'

'We'll see. His dam won a major race. Be nice to have a horse owned by locals in the winner's yard.'

'Be nice to see Dad there, too?'

'There's that.'

*

George stood a half-head shorter than Phoebe – a slight man, as befitting a jockey – and he was sandy-haired with deceptively calm blue eyes that crinkled at the corners from the sun.

Phoebe discovered that his easy gaze was surprisingly perceptive. He also had a healthy sense of humour. He'd need it. If he hadn't been her cousin's fiancé, Phoebe jokingly told Scarlet, she could have been charmed by him herself.

She wasn't sure if it was his quiet voice or gentle kindness, or to do with the tender, yet lovingly amused looks he sent her cousin. Wow, these guys are really together, she thought, just a tiny bit wistfully.

On the face of it the pairing seemed odd, with Scarlet's acerbic, bossy sarcasm up against George's unassuming, easy-going persona, but over their early supper Phoebe came to see he was no pushover.

'No, my love. I'm not going to the gala.'

'You promised.'

'If I'd promised, then I'd be there. Was you who promised to take me, and I made no such commitment. Just Finish is nervous. I'll be settling him down every evening until the race on Saturday.'

Scarlet screwed up her face mutinously. 'I wanted to show you off.'

Unperturbed, he smiled at her. 'That's the reason I agreed to your fancy wedding, my love. I'll do all the prancing around you want then.'

Her face softened, like really soft, like besotted. Such a turn-around for someone used to getting her own way. 'Promise?'

He laughed. 'Maybe not all.'

Scarlet laughed too, and he picked up her wrist and kissed it. The kiss started out fun but when their eyes met, Phoebe felt the crackle in the air. Hooley dooley, the room was suddenly stifling. Time to go. She stood. 'Well, I'm off to Dad's. I forgot something. Be back to get dressed for the gala.'

Scarlet laughed. A sexy laugh.

Phoebe bolted.

Chapter Twenty-eight

Atticus

Atticus had seen it on the webpage. *The annual RFDS Birdsville Races Gala. The most glamorous event of race week. Live entertainment, special guests and charity auction. Numbers strictly limited so get in quick.*

His predecessor had warned he'd be expected to attend any social events in town, so he'd bought a ticket to the gala when they first became available. Now he felt particularly pleased with himself because he'd checked, and Phoebe had a ticket as well.

When he walked through the gate to the community centre his gaze found her unerringly. Like a laser beam. You couldn't miss her bold turquoise knee-length dress with spaghetti straps. The woman looked scorching. Trying hard not to mimic one of those dogs that dropped their tongues onto the ground, he kept his eyes above her chin.

She saw him at the same time and her eyes widened, which made him glad he'd taken the time to iron his new shirt.

'Senior Constable,' she said in greeting as they drifted together like two twitching magnets.

'Nope: off duty tonight,' he said. 'Atticus. How about you? Quiet day in the health centre?' She looked so lovely he wanted to steer her out of the throng and away.

'Nope.' She mimicked him. 'We had a big day with the Fun Run. I didn't see you in the line-up.'

'Ah, I was up at Bedourie this morning. Didn't get back till after lunch. You look beautiful, by the way. As always.'

'As always?' Her smile peeked out. 'Thank you. Very smooth, Atticus.'

'I can be.' Though not often around you, but he didn't say that out loud. 'You should spend more time with me and I could practise.'

'On me?' She laughed – which wasn't funny. 'Well, you look very handsome. Going to the races tomorrow?' She furrowed her brow. 'What I mean is, are you working there tomorrow?'

'On duty. Yes, all part of the job. I'll be there both days.'

'St John's cover the Saturday so I get to wear a frock and a fascinator then.' Her smile took his breath and held it. 'So lucky me.'

When he could speak, he said quietly, 'Can't wait to see the outfit.' Or you in it, anyway. And he couldn't. If the dress she had on now was anything to go by, he was in for a treat. 'Like a drink?'

She glanced around as a waiter – Bruce, someone she usually saw at the petrol bowser – drifted not too far away. 'Anything with bubbles would be lovely. Thanks.'

Atticus scooped a flute off the tray Bruce carried and a beer for himself, and they drifted towards the nibbles, saying hello to people as they went. They ended up standing beside her father and Gloria, who looked very pretty in flowing trousers and blouse, both in a soft shade of blue.

'Evening, Atticus,' Rusty said, his hair smoothed back and looking debonair in a jacket and open-necked cowboy shirt.

'Hello, Atticus.' Gloria gave him one of those pretty smiles of hers.

'Evening all. You look lovely, Gloria.'

Gloria blushed. 'Thank you.'

'I see you found Phoebe,' her father said, looking at him with maybe a hint of challenge.

Funny how that made him want to lift his chin but he restrained the action. 'Can't help myself.' And smiled just a little challenge back. Looked at Gloria pointedly and Rusty put up his hands.

They both laughed while the women furrowed their brows questioningly. 'I think we missed something, Gloria.' Phoebe swivelled her attention between the two men.

'I think we did. Men thoughts, I imagine.' She shrugged. 'You young people should go off and have a nice time, not hang with the oldies. I'm looking for somewhere to sit after today's exertions.'

Atticus nodded as Rusty led his date away and that left them alone again. Yes. Finally, he had her to himself.

Before he could say a word, they were crashed by her cousin. 'How come you get a date and I'm the one getting married?'

Atticus had met the unlucky George a few times. He seemed like a good bloke. Probably needed to rein in his preconceptions about Scarlet – there had to be a reason the man was besotted.

Phoebe turned to him and smiled, and he felt the earth tilt just a bit. She said confidingly, as if her cousin couldn't hear, 'He's with their horse. Babysitting him before the Cup.' She touched her cousin's shoulder. 'Poor Scarlet. His first night back. How's everything going? Did the catering meeting go well?'

'There's food here, isn't there?'

Yep, he disliked this woman. But Phoebe laughed. 'Grumpy Grinch Scarlet. And it all looks fab. Go get a drink and calm down. We're going to raise lots of money for the RFDS and have a great night.'

He hoped so. Scarlet flounced off and Phoebe took his arm. 'Quick, let's find somewhere private before she comes back.'

Her fingers were warm on his arm. Her eyes laughed up at him. Promising. He tugged her along, his feet silent and his eyes searching until he found a side path where he whisked her around the corner into a shadow. Now he folded her into him, against his chest, his arms around her. Warm and wonderful. 'Private enough?'

She laughed at him. Pretty obvious really, he wanted to kiss her in private, but he felt extremely happy she wasn't complaining. 'Taking advantage of a dark space where there's no cousins or fathers, or patients or criminals.'

'And?' she teased, her face amused, her eyes warm, and her mouth . . . Heaven above, her mouth was soft and curved and welcoming: he'd never seen her like this, but he'd certainly dreamed of it.

He rumbled quietly, 'What I really want to do is steal a kiss.'

'Theft?' She was mock serious. 'And you a man of the law?'

'You have me there. Don't really want to steal it – I want a freely given kiss from you. Any chance?'

Well, it was out there, and she searched his face with that odd, amused expression that drove him crazy, and though she didn't answer she rested in his arms and held on with her own. Moments stretched and the world receded. He could drink in the sight of her face all night.

Finally, he said, pretending to whinge, 'Aren't you even curious to know what it would be like to kiss me properly?'

He watched her mouth curve and her teeth glint in their shadowy world as she grinned up at him. 'Now that you mention it, I am curious. Kiss me, Atticus.'

He thought the four walls had shifted in on him or the ground had fallen away because suddenly space was different. The *world* was different as he leaned down and took his time, brushed his lips across hers in a gentle sweep, and then again, as if painting her velvet mouth with his. Just to feel. Just to breathe her in. And she stood still beneath his caress and breathed him in, too.

No rush. No anxiety. Both knowing the kiss was coming and that it would quite possibly change everything.

He leaned in and took her mouth gently but firmly, and the tingle of connecting was deeper than he'd expected. By her widening eyes, it was the same for her.

She tasted like honey, and wine and warmth and Phoebe, and that made his arms tighten as he stroked her open to ease in. His heart pounded and her fingers tightened on his neck, flattening her softness against his chest until she was jammed against him, asking for more. Moments turned to magic and magic to minutes. The world tilted. Both giving, taking, sharing. Dissolving into one in the dark.

'Phoebe? Phoebe? Has anyone seen Phoebe?' That woman's voice.

He eased away as the mouth beneath his trembled in a laugh. 'I fear she will be the death of me,' he growled.

'I'm sure you'll grow to love her.'

He stepped back, stroked her upturned face with his fingers and kissed her one more time. 'Your word on that?'

Chapter Twenty-nine

Phoebe

Phoebe stepped reluctantly back into the throng and bumped straight into her father holding two glasses. Her head was still swirling from the fact that Atticus Bow kissed like a master, oh my. The man had skills and the most wonderful mouth. 'Oops, sorry.' Thankfully nothing spilled on either of them.

'You're looking very flushed, my love,' Rusty observed, and his gaze lifted to stare over her shoulder as Atticus appeared beside her.

Good grief, her father was doing protection again. Sweet, but unnecessary. Still, she fanned her face. 'Hot, isn't it.'

Rusty's brows went up. 'Not really.'

'I'll get you a drink,' Atticus said from behind and she could hear the amusement in his voice. His fingers brushed the small of her back as he passed. Ever so slightly possessive. She liked it a little too much.

'Something going on between you and the copper?' Her father's question brought her mind back from the gentle caress.

She shot back, 'Something going on between you and Gloria?'

Rusty laughed. 'Touché.' The tension disappeared as if it had never been there between them. Two conspirators with their own little secrets.

Phoebe smiled at him. 'Gloria is an amazing woman.'

'She is that.' He tilted his head towards where Atticus had disappeared. 'And is Atticus an amazing guy?'

'Sadly, I'm coming to think so, but he lives in Birdsville.' Damn it. 'And I live in Adelaide.'

'Does that mean I might get to see more of you?'

She shrugged. 'I don't see how it could work. I don't even know if I want it to work. Reasons why it shouldn't. But I'm on holidays. It doesn't all have to be serious.' She looked at her dad. 'Does it?'

'No. No, it doesn't.' Rusty inclined his head in agreement. 'But this isn't Adelaide. Small town. It won't be private.'

He was right. If she had an affair with the town cop, oh yeah, it would be talked about for the next twenty years. She could hear it now, 'Remember the time Phoebe McFadden had that affair with . . .?' Yes. Worth thinking about. But then, so was the idea of disappearing into his house and not coming out for hours and hours. And maybe hours more. Oh my.

Atticus was back and she took the proffered glass of sparkling water. It caressed her fingers, cold and refreshing and wonderful, like the smile he just gave her. 'Thank you.'

Her dad was forgotten until he said, 'I'll take Gloria her drink. See you later.'

'Bye, Dad.'

When he'd left Atticus asked, 'Did you find your cousin?'

That amused her. 'I thought we didn't want to.'

'Peace comes at a price,' he said philosophically, and she took his arm. 'Come on. We'll see what she wants and then get something to eat.'

He put his hand over hers on the crook of his elbow and she realised what she'd done. Claimed him. Publicly. He said, 'People will talk.'

She was over it. 'So my dad says. Is that a problem?'

He shook his head. 'Absolutely no problem. Let them.'

Chapter Thirty

Gloria

Rusty had disappeared to find her a soft drink while Gloria sat at the edge of the well-dressed throng watching the Birdsville world drift by. Soon she could go home. Duty done.

People were so incredibly generous towards the RFDS, but then, living here so far from outside help, you never knew when you'd urgently need those angels from the sky to swoop in and save you.

Which made her think of mortality and time and suddenly she wished she hadn't stopped Rusty telling the world that they'd committed to each other – finally.

Why had she done that?

She'd short-changed herself and Rusty, as if she were ashamed of what they had. She needed to think about the years they'd lost already and the fact she and Rusty deserved happiness. ASAP.

Why did other people deserve more happiness than her? Such an odd frame of mind, and she wondered how she'd come to that place in her head. A place of back-seat positioning and non-decisions? She needed to stop that.

She thought about Scarlet, who grabbed what she wanted, and Phoebe, who made decisions, commitments – sometimes wrong decisions but at least she made them.

But Gloria . . .? Nooooo, she floated, pushed by the breeze like a leaf on the billabong. She trudged from one busy week to the next, caring for others.

She was tired of floating, trudging.

She wanted Rusty in her world. She wanted to sleep in his bed. She wanted to wake in the morning beside him. And she'd told him to wait. Said, 'Not yet.' Good grief. What was she waiting for? She was a fool.

Rusty handed over her drink and slid into the seat beside her.

She took the glass. 'Thank you.' The words were tight like her mouth.

His brow furrowed. 'You look worried, love?'

Rusty noticed her. She turned her head to study his dear face. 'Not worried. I think I'm cross.'

He laughed. Rusty laughed. At her. 'You never get cross.' He was teasing but, as he'd wanted, the tease drew a smile from her.

'I mean I'm cross with myself.'

He shook his head emphatically. 'I'm sorry. That's not allowed.' He whispered, 'Psst. Because Gloria is my fiancée.'

'And that's why I'm cross.'

He sat back, face falling, his brow creased in concern. 'You've changed your mind?'

'Never.' She reached out and touched his tanned and wrinkled cheek. 'Only about keeping it a secret. I want you to tell Phoebe so I can shout it from the rooftops. I don't know what I was thinking.'

'Ah, my love.' He reached and gathered her hand in his strong one and some of her tension eased away miraculously. 'You were thinking of others. Like you always do. But I agree. We need to think of us.'

Chapter Thirty-one

Phoebe

The town pulsed like a heart with palpitations for the Friday races, waiting for everything to begin. And this not even the Cup, which would be held the next day. Phoebe knew from experience once the gates to the races opened, the town's few streets would be almost empty again.

As she walked towards the Primary Health Centre, people passed her going the other way, gravitating to the bakery and then the pub for the Calcutta ticket sales.

Tickets went on sale at nine-thirty until the horses were drawn for the Calcutta. The ticket auction was held in front of Fred Brophy's Boxing Tent with proceeds to RFDS, Birdsville PHC and the Birdsville State School.

Shuttles would start not long after and run continuously out to the racecourse from eleven when the gates would open – both express and 'stopping all stations' across the town common for the campers. They'd run all through the day until night.

The ticketed OBE tent, sponsored by the far-sighted pastoral farmers, opened at twelve for the trackside hospitality packages, but the first race on Friday's meeting wouldn't start until just before one-thirty.

While she walked, she heard an aircraft land noisily. Every few minutes another approached from a far-flung station or distant town. The airstrip behind the pub would be filling up.

She guessed she and Gloria would have a busy day in the clinic before shutting for the weekend, but she'd found a rhythm and satisfaction in this provision of service that helped her understand why Gloria had stayed so long. She was almost over being secretary though – must be an adrenalin junkie. She laughed at herself.

Last night Atticus had asked if she wanted to stroll around after work to check out the entertainment with him tonight, and she'd said yes, but it wasn't the stalls she was keen to see. She'd been thinking about the opportunity to kiss the man again. Not wander in crowds. She wasn't sure where all her reasons for not getting involved with him had gone.

By the time Atticus appeared at Scarlet's house after work, she'd been watching for him to arrive and her skin tingled as he took her hand at the door.

Scarlet and her parents had gone out to the stables to talk to George so she had the house to herself. Even Charli wasn't in her van because she'd gone to work at the pub.

She tugged his fingers to pull him inside and his brows went up. 'Nobody home,' she whispered, her lips curving with the mischief she couldn't help bubbling inside her.

'Ah,' he said, and his eyes darkened as he stepped in and pushed the door closed behind him, not letting go of her hand. 'I've been thinking about kissing you all day,' he rumbled, the words sending goosebumps up her arm as he leaned against the door and drew her back towards him.

'Didn't cross my mind,' she lied.

He laughed. 'You fib. Come here and fulfil my fantasies.'

'And doesn't that sound amazing,' she murmured a little too audibly as her arms slid around his waist and she looked up into his beautiful face.

His mouth curved as his face came down. 'Mmmhmm.'

Fifteen minutes later Atticus pulled her out of the house and Phoebe sulked over the need to return to civilisation. Though it had been a little too civilised for her taste inside the house too, because she had hoped this might progress further than it had. She was turning into Scarlet.

They wandered around the stalls with the returned racegoers and listened to the live music at the pub. There was a big crowd outside Fred Brophy's Boxing Tent but they kept going until Atticus took her home and left her at the door. Darn it.

Saturday morning held the first hint of the heat to come with a six am breath of warmth on her cheek. Race day but she had time for a quick stroll out to Pelican Point and back.

A good thing Atticus had said he wouldn't make it, because she needed to think about last night. About the way he'd kissed her, the way she'd kissed him back, and the way she'd lost herself in his embrace.

Yup. Phoebe needed to think about the way she'd wanted to do more than kiss this Queensland cop because a relationship involving a man living out here wasn't on her agenda.

She suspected Atticus wasn't looking for a one-night stand either. Darn the man – he wasn't helping her stay focused on leaving. Once she was on her own on the road she said it out loud. 'Falling for someone in Birdsville doesn't fit Adelaide or your career.'

Where was her 'Don't get involved in Birdsville' mantra? Now she felt connected in an unexpectedly wonderful way with Gloria, with her dad and Scarlet, and even with the health centre.

But Atticus. She wanted more of Atticus. Because she enjoyed his company. Driving with him in the desert. Sitting and talking. He made her laugh and feel special, and he filled her with the warm and fuzzies when so far in her boring life, sexy younger men had not been her thing. And he had other skills. My word he did. And she was leaving.

Being kissed by Atticus had altered her perception of herself: that was the kicker. He made her feel desirable, wanton, and just as frustrated by him making her leave Scarlet's house as he'd been at the gala when Scarlet had called her name. His body language and expression made no bones about saying she was incredibly special to him. Amazing.

Sensual? Good grief. She hadn't been sexy, ever. She'd been Phoebe, that nurse from ER or maternity or the supervisor's office. The one who couldn't hold down a relationship because none of the men she dated were on the same wavelength as her. Did she really have a *Birdsville* wavelength?

Yep, she needed to walk on her own and think about this.

Because after Scarlet's wedding she was going to walk away and go back to Adelaide and be a career spinster. And despite the bells and whistles going off when she was with Constable Bow, she couldn't see Atticus doing anything big to change her mind in the next ten days.

By the time she turned around and strode back towards Scarlet's house, Phoebe hadn't made any decisions, but at least she'd been imbued with the peace of the birds on the track and the brightening of the world with the sun.

Until she returned to the mayhem of the road, where the busy traffic from the campers jarred her back to reality. Almost like Adelaide.

She hadn't taken much notice on the walk out, but looking now she was shocked by the sheer number of tents, cars and swags that spread right across the creek and paddocks as far as the eye could see.

Birdsville Races had grown exponentially since the time she lived here.

She did like the fact that the campground out of town was still free. Portable toilets supplied but no showers. Showers were situated in town, which could explain why, even this early, streams of tourists were heading the same way as her, some walking, some in cars, and she could just imagine the line-up for coffee at the bakery when it opened at seven-thirty.

Maybe her cousin should invest in a coffee van for next year. Maybe young Charli could. Charli?

Now she was doing it. Feeling protective of and invested in

the young woman neither she nor Scarlet had much knowledge of. Birdsville did that to you. Made you notice other people because, except for race time and, she imagined, the Big Red Bash desert music festival, there were so few people here, and they all needed to look out for each other.

Scarlet sent her to the pub at nine-thirty to try for some Saturday tickets in the Calcutta for the races, because both of them had missed the same scenario yesterday when they'd been working, but she didn't expect success.

The street stood packed with tourists and mad racing fans, hungover young bloods, stockmen and ringers from the surrounding stations. Yep, a scrum. She caught sight of police uniforms but not the one she wanted to see and stifled the disappointment. Disappointment? This was getting ridiculous.

At eleven forty-five she was back at Scarlet's house, still without a sighting of Atticus, but she now clutched three Calcutta tickets. They were dressed for the races and ready to go, though Scarlet had an apron in her hand.

Phoebe checked her hem in the mirror. Scarlet stood beside her and twitched her collar. 'Reckon we look pretty good,' she said as George appeared from the kitchen.

He leaned his shoulder against the door frame and a slow smile crept across his face and up to his eyes. 'You both look more than good. Especially the one in green.'

Since Scarlet wore mint and Phoebe's dress shone plain emerald, he was being cheeky. Blue eyes twinkled as he reached out and took Scarlet's hand and twirled her. 'You look gorgeous, my love.' Their faces drew closer as if neither could look away: they were going to kiss. Extensively. Phoebe just knew it.

Now would be a good time to disappear back into her room to collect her phone and find enough cash to pay the bookies if she wanted to put a bet on.

Ha – even to *think* she'd be punting was a change. Something she hadn't been able to stomach even on Melbourne Cup Day since she was old enough to bet. She'd hated the whole idea of gambling so much after her childhood, but maybe she needed to prove she was moving on. At least show herself how far she'd come. She could add one bet on the big race, for Just Finish, with George riding. She'd be an unsupportive wowser if she didn't.

Two weeks ago, she wouldn't have considered it.

Phoebe scooped up her floppy-brimmed emerald hat, bought with the emerald dress and swirled with black concentric circles. The wide brim looked great with her wavy hair, and it kept off the sun. Bonus.

She'd chosen low-heeled black sandals because the red dust would kill anything pale.

They were catching the shuttle bus, the gold coin ride between town and the racetrack. The police would be vigilant with the breathalysers today, though they rarely had to charge anyone. They were so obviously checking every car that people who planned to drink caught the bus, or walked. It was a good system.

She'd counted to fifty. Tapped her foot. Couldn't hear if they were still kissing. 'You ready, Scarlet?' she called out, pausing before she left the room. Were they finished? Was it safe to venture out? There was a shuffle. A laugh. And some footsteps.

'Yeah, I'm ready to go. Sadly.'

When Phoebe inched out of the safety of the room her cousin's cheeks were rosy and George looked more than happy. Her menace of a cousin winked at her fiancé. 'I'll see you out there, Hot Stuff.'

'I'll make myself scarce if you're going to share my secrets with everyone,' he murmured.

'Okay. I'll call you George and save Hot Stuff for the bedroom.'

Phoebe didn't like to say that she had heard that name, but she did seriously think of moving in with her dad. She had a room over there and even if he was in some form of relationship with Gloria, something she still needed to ask him, no way would he make her embarrassed like Scarlet did over here.

She'd talk to him about it after the races were over.

All the food had been finished off and decorated as much as they could except for cream. Charli had been here since four am and was coming with them on the bus.

Scarlet and Charli would be decorating the last of the lunch desserts later in the morning at the racetrack, working out of the refrigerated truck so at least they'd be cool – George had towed Scarlet's big kitchen refrigerator on wheels back out to the race-track that morning.

Chapter Thirty-two

Charli

Charli had never been to the races.

She guessed today didn't really count, because working and not wearing one of those posh hats meant she wasn't a racegoer. She'd just be decorating cakes for the big tent.

She'd struggled just a bit getting up at four am. They'd been flat strap all day at yesterday's races, and it had been sooo busy in the pub last night that her back ached, but she'd made it here to help prepare sandwiches and decorate cakes with Scarlet in the early morning hours. They were done now and it was cup day. Finally.

It was nice of Scarlet and Phoebe to wait for her to shower and put on her clean baggy dress so they could get the bus together. Now she followed them through the gate with her eyes wide.

Stalls, trailers and so many people everywhere. Laughing faces, pretty dresses, pretty hats, and strange outfits.

She stared at a group of men dressed up as Bananas in Pyjamas. Yellow tubes over their heads and just their faces peering out. They must be so hot! It was thirty-five degrees already.

Over there she could see four girls in grass hula skirts with leis around their necks – at least they were cooler. Oh, they must be with those men in Hawaiian shirts. That made sense. There were four of each, so a group of people had come all dressed up just for fun on the day.

She thought that was pretty special. Couldn't think of anyone she knew who'd do that. Lazy Luke wouldn't play – that was for sure. She wondered if Kelvin would.

Two tall slim young women swayed past, talking about Fashions on the Field. One held a pretty pink bag that matched her shoes and the other had orange accessories. Such high heels.

Charli had never owned a pair of high heels and reckoned she'd have to learn to walk in them, but the dresses were swish with the shoes. No good for working in a kitchen, she thought, as she glanced down at her sneakers. Even those were getting tight with her ankles swelling.

Scarlet had disappeared while she'd been gawking but thankfully she caught sight of Phoebe's bright green dress through a crowd of people. She hurried in that direction until she caught up.

Phoebe turned and smiled. 'She went through there, Charli: there's the corner of the kitchen trailer.'

Phew, she could see it now. She waved her thanks and knocked on the door of the small van.

Scarlet had her mobile phone to her ear and waved her in. 'Yep, got that. Will send the first trays over soon.' She ended the call and turned to Charli. 'Let's go, girlfriend. We're on.'

And that was the start of the busiest afternoon Charli had ever had. The best thing was that she saw so many now-familiar faces from town as she scurried, laden with trays, between van and tent.

And they saw her. Really saw her. Some even said, 'Hi, Charli,' and smiled. Seemed like most people did at least one other job at the races before they had their fun and all of them were friendly.

She loved this place.

Inside the big marquee, tables had white cloths and pretty flowers in vases, shiny cutlery and wine glasses engraved with *Birdsville Race Club Inc.*, a picture of two horses and one of the pub. Mrs Carter, the main hostess, had promised Charli two glasses to take home after it was over.

Thirty minutes before the actual Birdsville Cup, Scarlet pulled off her apron, re-applied makeup and pinned on a hat. She cast her eye over Charli and tilted her head.

'How about you brush your hair and wash your face? I've got my makeup with me, so we'll polish you up a bit.'

No. 'I'm fine.'

'Nope. Got a headband with a blue rose that will go with your shirt. I threw in half-a-dozen bits and pieces this morning before we left because I didn't know what colour you'd wear.'

Since she only had two dresses and both of them were blue, Charli guessed Scarlet had seen all of her wardrobe. Obediently she washed her face and flattened her hair. One thing about the kitchen truck was it was cool inside, and she wasn't sweaty at least.

She brushed her fringe back and stood still, just a little scared of what Scarlet might do to her face with makeup.

'Get that terrified look off your mug. I'll be subtle.'

Charli stifled a laugh. She knew what subtle meant. Delicate. Quiet. Subdued. 'Scarlet' and 'subtle' didn't go in the same sentence.

'Okay.' She guessed it didn't matter but she knew lots of people here now and didn't want to look silly.

'Trust me.'

Did she trust Scarlet? She blew out a breath. Yes. She guessed she did, so she closed her eyes and let Scarlet paint her face.

It wasn't as long as she thought it would be before Scarlet stood back. Nodded. Rummaged in her huge handbag and pulled out a skinny plastic headband with the cutest blue rose on top. She slid it into Charli's hair and just a bit into her scalp. Charli winced at the stab of pain.

'Oops. Sorry. You have nice hair. Dark like Phoebe's mother's was. Pretty.'

Charli couldn't help it. Her hand went up to cover her lip.

Scarlet glowered at her. 'Why do you do that? It's such a small mark. And until you point it out nobody sees it.'

Not true. She'd seen people staring at her mouth.

'For goodness' sake. You're a pretty girl. Put your head up and look people in the eye. You like Kelvin, don't you? Do you stare at his scars?'

Charli blinked. How had Scarlet known that? And she never even thought about Kelvin's scars. Except maybe a brief flash of empathy when she'd first seen them because people would stare at him, too.

Scarlet wasn't finished. 'Of course not. So stop worrying about yours. Put your head up, woman.'

So, just a little scared of her boss, Charli did. And the first person she saw when she stepped out of the refrigerated truck was indeed dear, safe Kelvin. It almost looked like he was waiting for her.

'Hello, Charli,' he said. 'You finished work?'

'Umm, yes.' Charli could barely speak. Her cheeks felt hot. A strange buzzing delight scooted around inside her brain. Had Kelvin actually been waiting for her?

'You look pretty.'

Charli froze. What? He just said . . .

But Kelvin was going on. 'I like the headband,' he said. Scarlet appeared beside them. 'Mind if I steal her, Scarlet?'

'Not at all. I'm busy. Looking for my man.'

'Come on, Charli. Let's go get a drink.'

She dropped her head and then forced it back up. No. She needed to hold her head up, like Scarlet said. 'I'd like that,' though her voice cracked a little and came out so soft that she wasn't sure he heard.

He must have because he tucked her arm in his and she almost stumbled at the unexpected joy of it. Her arm felt warm, safe, linked into his.

He smiled down at her, his scarred face crinkling in some places and not moving at all in others. 'Bet you're tired.' He looked down at her sneakers and swollen feet. 'Think I better get you a chair. Give you a bit of spoiling for a change.'

He steered her over to a clear patch of rail. It was a fair way from the winning post, but it caught the tiny breeze that still flowed across the racecourse. Now she was able to see the track, where the horses raced, and Kelvin produced a stool from somewhere – she had no idea how he'd managed that – but she sat gratefully. The instant relief made her sigh.

He shook his head at her. 'Never met a woman who works as hard as you. You want a lemon squash?'

She moistened her dry lips. 'Love one, yes please.' He nodded and strode away, to look after her, and Charli realised her mouth had dropped open in shock. She snapped it shut.

She liked Kelvin. A lot. In a different way from the American bull rider. Not a dangerous attraction, but a warm friendship that had grown over the last week of working together into a comfortable and delightful ease. A rapport she'd never had with a man, not even Lazy Luke, who was more of an erratic brother. No, she respected Kelvin, and she hoped that Kelvin respected her.

One of the girls from the pub, Abby, dressed in a baby-doll dress and looking gorgeous, waved. Surprised, and with a quick surreptitious glance behind to make sure it wasn't anyone else she meant, Charli waved back.

Okay. Kelvin had even said she was pretty. She didn't believe that but maybe she had made a few friends. Either way this had to rank as one of the best days she'd had so far.

Kelvin returned with their glasses. In fact, he held a tray with two squashes and two beers. She could hear the ice in her glass chinking as he approached, and her mouth did that shrivel thing in anticipation. She couldn't wait.

'There you go. The bar's a bit of a scrum so I bought us two. You want to put anything on the main race?'

She guessed he meant bets and she'd thought she might if she had a chance. 'I'd like to. Yes. But I've never bet on a horse before.'

'Sensible girl.' Kelvin smiled. 'Should be proud not embarrassed about that one.'

'Scarlet said I should put twenty on the nose for Just Finish in the Cup. Twenty dollars is a lot, but I've made money here. And it's not like I'm ever gonna do it again.'

'Then you should.' Kelvin didn't look shocked.

Which was a relief. 'No idea how to do it, though.'

He glanced at her swollen feet. 'Want me to put it on at the bookies for you while you stay here?'

'Would you? I'd like that. Please.' Oh, yes. She sagged with relief at the thought of not struggling through the crowd she could see around the bookmakers – darkly dressed men with tall spinning boards. People calling out. It looked intense.

'Sure. We're running out of time before the race. I'll dash across and do it now.'

Except she didn't want him to go. 'What about your beer?'

He grinned at her. 'I'll take one with me. You relax here. Back as soon as I can.'

She almost told him not to worry about it. She'd rather have his company than any fictional winnings that would take him away for another ten minutes, but he looked pretty happy to be doing it, so she watched his broad back disappear.

She could just sit, and relax, and watch everyone while she waited for him to come back. Which she did, until someone tapped her shoulder and she spun around. 'Lazy Luke!' She smiled and then, weirdly, she felt disloyal to Kelvin. 'What are you doing here?' A little too sharply.

He screwed his face up at her. 'What sort of greeting is that?'

'Sorry.' And she was. Luke was her friend. She reached out and touched his arm in apology. 'You surprised me, that's all. I didn't expect you to be here.' She glanced away to where Kelvin had disappeared into the crowd.

Lazy Luke raised his brows at the round tray on the ground beside her. A beer and a lemon squash. And one in her hand. 'You here with a bloke?'

Well, yes, she was. And at the thought she smiled. 'Yes, I am.'

'Hope he's better than the last one.'

'He is.' Thanks for that, Lazy, she thought, rueful at her friend's lack of faith in her taste. Remembering Scarlet, she lifted her chin and looked into his eyes. 'He's gone to put a bet on for me.'

Lazy's eyes lit up. 'You got a tip?'

She nodded. 'Just Finish in the Cup.' She spoke as if she knew what she was talking about. Pretty funny really.

Lazy glanced hopefully towards the bookies. 'You got ten bucks?'

She sighed, opened her wallet, and gave him the note. 'You know, Lazy, I like this guy and really don't want you to be here when he comes back. But when he is back, come over and meet him. Okay?'

'Sure.' He grinned at her and took off.

'Who was that?'

So much for getting the first word in, she thought. 'That's Lazy Luke. He's going to come back over and meet you in a minute. He's gone to put ten dollars, which he scabbed off me, on our horse.' She lifted her chin and looked in Kelvin's eyes. 'He's never been my boyfriend and never will be. But we shared some foster homes when we were growing up.'

Kelvin smiled at her. That odd shifting of skin she was growing to appreciate very much. 'I like you,' he said gently. 'And you don't lie, do you?'

'Never,' she said. 'Too many times I've been lied to.'

'Me, too,' said Kelvin, and he leaned down and kissed her cheek. 'Good luck to us with the next race.' They chinked glasses and smiled at each other.

*

The loudspeaker heralded the fifth race, the Birdsville Cup, and Charli stood with Kelvin at the rails, her pulse pounding in a fizz with excitement. She had her hand on his arm and it felt wonderful. He'd lifted it there and patted her fingers gently as he helped her to stand. Her first race and she even had money on a horse. Lazy Luke had come over, shaken Kelvin's hand, and disappeared into the throng again.

The sun beat down on the track as Kelvin stood beside her at the rails, his big frame casting a shadow she stood in. It felt exciting, and grown up, something new she'd never done before. The fact that Kelvin's arm was hooked through hers was causing lots of raised eyebrows with the people who knew them.

'So, when's the baby due?' Kelvin's question stopped her happy thoughts, and she frowned. So, he'd guessed too.

'Not for a few weeks. I'm flying to Charleville on Tuesday to stay there until afterwards.'

Kelvin nodded. Not meeting her eyes. 'Where's your baby daddy?'

'Gone.' Another good time to lift her chin. 'I thought he was a nice man, but he wasn't, and he's never coming back.'

Kelvin glanced at her in surprise. 'I'm sorry he hurt you.'

'Thank you, Kelvin, but I was the silly one. I thought there was more there than there was. Baby was an accident but I'm happy, now.'

Kelvin nodded again. Opened and shut his mouth a couple of times. Ran his finger under his collar. 'So, you coming back after the baby's born? Back to Birdsville?'

'Yes.' It came out a bit too loud. Embarrassed, she added, 'I really want to.' Even more now after today. But she wasn't getting ahead of herself. 'Scarlet said she'll help me find a job.'

'Good.' He looked down at her. His face, the parts that could shift, melding into a gentle look that made her insides flip over and curl. 'You could work with me in the kitchen.'

Except there'd be no races. Few tourists. 'I'd love to, of course, though they might not want two people when everyone goes. I imagine there's not much work after the races are over. If they don't need me, I'll find somewhere else to work. I love it here.'

'Good,' he said again. But his brows furrowed and he looked undecided, as if he wasn't sure he wanted to say what was coming. 'It gets hot. And empty. And it's a long way from anywhere.'

So, just a warning. Sounded like one he hadn't wanted to give. The thought made her smile. Keeping her chin up she said, 'People are the important ones. The rest is the price. I'm happy to pay that if I find a real home.'

His expression eased. Relief? Or she thought that's what that grimace was. Then he said, 'When you come back . . .' he shuffled his feet '. . . I think we could be good together. I really like you, Charli.'

Awww. She smiled up at him. And remembered her baby's daddy. Her smile fell away. 'Early days yet, Kelvin. But yes, being with you feels good for me, too.' She kept her head up like Scarlet said she should and pretended she didn't have a scar on her lip. 'Everybody's very nice to me here.'

'And why wouldn't they be?' Kelvin's head snapped up. As if offended. For her?

'I'm unknown.' Why would they? She shrugged. 'I'm a nobody.'

Kelvin sucked in a breath and he frowned at her. 'That sort of talk needs to stop.'

Goodness. He meant it. She filed that away for later mulling. But they were announcing on the loudspeaker. 'The race is starting. And I want to watch every bit and cheer our horse home.'

She turned her face, and her lip, to the track and smiled.

Chapter Thirty-three

Phoebe

Phoebe stood beside Scarlet in the sun, thankful for her shady hat, and smiling at Rusty as he leaned against a wall with his arm crooked through Gloria's.

Bodies stood three deep behind the rail, everywhere packed with excited racegoers like budgerigars flocking down to a creek. Further along the rail she thought she could see Charli and Kelvin, but maybe not.

Most of the horses were at the gates now – or so the race caller said. The heat shimmered off the red dirt and they were too far away to see clearly.

Simultaneously, the crowd lifted their hands to shade their eyes and stare at the far straight where horses and their brightly coloured jockeys milled around.

'I think I can see him,' Scarlet said.

Better eyes than me, Phoebe thought as she smiled, though she didn't really believe her cousin. Too hard to distinguish from this far away with the haze. Wasn't game to say it, though.

They'd know soon enough.

The crowd chattered excitedly, Scarlet grew more agitated, and Phoebe took her cousin's hand in hers and squeezed.

The waiting was over. They were off. The crowd erupted, cheering and hooting. Scarlet stood still and her nails dug painfully into Phoebe's hand as she barely breathed in and out.

The race caller went through the line of horses that had come into view, name after name not the one they wanted to hear, as their group listened breathlessly.

'And sixth on the outside, Just Finish. A thousand to go. Behind that horse . . .'

Scarlet had begun to hyperventilate, as Phoebe watched them, these people she loved, her dad concentrating, Gloria jumping up and down, around them the cheering crowd working themselves up to a roar. She smiled and shook her head. It was fun but not fascinating. And stressful! She doubted she'd ever get the racing bug.

The thunder of hooves was drowned out by the crowd, but the cloud of dust, the swirling, never-settling Birdsville dust following the horses grew closer as they rounded the home stretch. Spectators jumped and called out.

And then Phoebe saw the colours, red and black, saw the jockey, George, low over his horse's neck, urging with his hands on the reins. Saw the horse leap forwards, pass one, then two in front, until there was only one between Just Finish and the winning post.

'Neck and neck,' the race caller shouted above the din. 'Beef Jerky and Just Finish two lengths ahead of the rest. Beef Jerky. Just Finish. Beef Jerky. Beef Jerky. It's gonna be close.'

Scarlet dropped her hand and took off for the winning post.

Phoebe glanced at her dad, a smile on her face.

She never saw the finish.

Rusty paled to ashen, a sheen of sweat appeared on his brow and, suddenly, limply, he slid sideways to crumple on the ground, pulling Gloria to her knees.

Phoebe hurled herself to the ground and felt for his pulse. Easy to find. Slow, so slow, but steady. Unquestionably there. Thank God.

She let out the breath she hadn't known she was holding. 'It's okay. He's got a pulse. Slow but strong,' she told Gloria. 'He must have fainted. Probably dehydrated and hypotensive with the heat.'

'I told him,' Gloria snapped, relief turning to out-of-character fury for the ever-calm clinic nurse. 'I told him to drink more water.' Tears sparked at the bottom of her eyes. 'Why can't he listen . . .?' Her voice broke on the last word.

'I know.' Soothingly. 'He's lying flat now. His blood pressure will come up. Just a faint.' Phoebe settled her own galloping pulse and tried to do the same for Gloria. The woman's borderline hysteria was heartbreaking.

At that moment Rusty opened his eyes. Slowly focused. Focused on Gloria with tears on her face. Blinked at his daughter leaning over him. His brow furrowed. 'Wh-what happened?'

'You fainted, you fool man,' Gloria snapped, and then slapped her hand over her mouth. Sobbed into her palm. 'Sorry.' Waved her hand as if to scrub out her words.

Phoebe laughed, though she did sound a little hysterical too, so she shut it off. 'You're fine, Dad. Just the heat. Go slow as you sit up. I'll get you some water.'

When she returned with a bottle of water, she found Rusty sitting against the wall with Gloria beside him. Shoulder to shoulder and holding hands. Definitely putting it out there now. 'How are you feeling?'

'Better. And foolish.'

'No truer word,' muttered Gloria, who still had spots of colour on her cheeks. Even ten minutes after the excitement.

'So, when are you two getting married?' she asked her father. Maybe it was best to get him while he was vague and because Gloria had been terrified she was going to lose him.

'Straight after Scarlet's wedding,' he said, looking at the woman beside him, who flushed even more. 'That okay with you, Gloria?'

'Fine.'

'Totally fine,' said Phoebe, just a little bit shocked. 'Congratulations.'

Rusty shook his head. 'Did our horse win?'

'Apparently by a head. I didn't see it.'

Chapter Thirty-four

Gloria

For a few moments there Gloria's heart had felt like a tyre blow-out at a hundred kilometres an hour.

She'd thought she was going to lose Rusty – when she'd finally found happiness – and the fear and panic had immobilised her. Made her freeze when she should have jumped into action. That had never happened before. But she'd been practically useless until Rusty woke up. Maybe it really was time to retire?

Or was that an excuse to grab onto as she slowly forgave herself?

It wasn't that she regretted any of the years of sleepless nights, or the people she'd saved – it was what she'd done for twenty years. And she'd been appreciated. She had a sudden clarity that she didn't want to be that person now.

She did regret not being brave enough to reach for what she really wanted years earlier. She could've worked all those times and still been with Rusty. Why hadn't she demanded his attention sooner?

But Rusty was okay. It didn't matter that she'd frozen. Today, she could only be grateful that Phoebe had been with them, calm and solid. Phoebe, who must've been just as terrified as Gloria, but Rusty's daughter hadn't been a stunned statue. Nope. Gloria had.

She thought about how amazing it would be to have Phoebe here all the time. Phoebe, who could have Gloria's job in a heartbeat and Gloria could possibly do the fortnightly relief and have the rest of the month off. That sounded like a nice way of edging into retirement.

The idea firmed. If it wasn't Phoebe, then she'd just have to find someone else. It was time.

She imagined, for a few more dreamy moments, Phoebe coming back to Birdsville to stay. Such a shame she carried on about the lovely Atticus being younger than her. As far as Gloria could see, a hunky younger man would be a bonus and the boy looked smitten. Rusty was two years younger than her, and he was a bit of a hunk himself – when he wasn't fainting and terrifying the life out of her.

Before she could relive those horrible moments again, Scarlet appeared, rushing, jumping out of her skin to share her excitement with Rusty.

'What's going on? We have to get to the winners' enclosure.' Scarlet frowned down at the couple on the ground. 'Why are you sitting in the dirt?'

Ah yes, Just Finish had won the Birdsville Cup, though they'd all missed it. Now she could hear the loudspeaker announcing the presentation.

Rusty wasn't up to that, and she just hoped he wouldn't try. To her relief he said, 'You go, Scarlet. Lex will be there. Accept it with him and George,' he said. 'I had a bit of a turn with the heat. We'll get to hold the Cup later.'

Nice way to put it, Gloria thought, as Scarlet looked concerned for a moment, until Phoebe shooed her off and she hurried away.

Gloria closed her eyes. 'We'll stay here,' she agreed. She doubted her legs would hold her just yet, either. But her heart was settling.

Later that evening the McFaddens came together for an impromptu engagement party – Scarlet's idea, after being informed by Phoebe that another wedding was in the forecast.

Gloria had been secretly pleased by the fuss and even Rusty smiled mistily at his daughter and niece as they brought in a cake, finger food, and a bottle of sparkling wine.

Gloria had never had an engagement party, or been engaged, and to her shocked delight Rusty produced an enormous sapphire he'd mined up at Rubyvale years back, already made into a ring the exact size of Gloria's finger.

'Just how long have you had this ring, Rusty McFadden?' she asked quietly.

His gaze soft on her and filled with tenderness, he said, 'About ten years, my love.'

Tears prickled her eyes at the swell of emotion that swamped her. 'We are both fools.'

'Not now, we're not,' he said smugly and slid the ring onto her finger. Then he kissed her and everyone applauded. She, Gloria, was swamped by hugs all around from her new family.

Gloria wiped her eyes. 'I'm too old for all this excitement.'

'What did you say?' Phoebe whispered as she hugged her. 'You're not old. You're a champion and my new stepmama. Welcome to the family. I can't wait for the wedding.'

'You'll have to come back to Birdsville.'

'I can do that.' Phoebe took another look at her face and turned Gloria around so her back faced the others as if they were sharing a secret.

Gloria sniffed and tried not to cry. 'It's been such an emotional roller-coaster of a day.' She shook her head, hearing the wobble in her voice. 'From the worst moment when Rusty collapsed to having you say you're happy for us.'

'Huge. But I know you don't want to cry on your party night. Take a breath.'

'Thank you, darling, Phoebe.' Phoebe knew her well. 'I don't.' She stopped and closed her eyes. Breathed in and out and let out the last of the fear from earlier. She did feel better now. She'd needed that minute to settle her emotions.

Phoebe nodded her head in satisfaction. 'I'm so very happy for you.' Her dear face crinkled with amusement as she crossed her arms over her chest and pretended a petulant expression. 'But I'm not calling you Mum.'

Gloria laughed shakily and hugged her again.

Chapter Thirty-five

Charli

Charli sat down on her little caravan bed after the biggest day in her life. Or at least it felt like it. Not just hard work from four am but the excitement of the races, of Kelvin cosseting her, 'cause that's what he'd been doing, and she'd never ever been cosseted before. Plus, she'd won two hundred dollars on her first ever bet.

Kelvin had laughed and kissed her when the horse had won, his mouth firm and excited, and they'd both stilled, and slowed, and it had turned into a very nice kiss like none she'd ever had before. It made her thoughtful. And Kelvin thoughtful, though he'd apologised and looked a bit embarrassed afterwards, avoiding her eyes, but he'd reached for her fingers and taken her hand in his and barely let it go.

She liked holding Kelvin's hand. But she'd take it slow. She'd been a fool once, trusting a man. But there was something about Kelvin, and it wasn't only the fact they both understood about not being perfect . . .

The ten days here had been huge, with her new jobs, meeting Kelvin, and her little van. Even Scarlet caring enough to help her look almost pretty was a milestone in her life.

But it had been hectic with a capital H. Not surprising she looked forward to a relaxing day tomorrow. Maybe even sleeping in to seven. Imagine. She didn't think she'd slept in for years. Really, she didn't want to waste a minute of being here. Sadly, it was just three more sleeps until she flew out.

Kelvin had invited her to breakfast, at his own house, before he started work at nine – it was almost their first real date.

In the morning when Charli woke, the backache had returned, but apart from that she'd slept the sleep of the truly exhausted. Curled on her side, fingers splayed over her rounded stomach, she could feel her baby shifting and rolling beneath her fingers as she opened her eyes.

'Good morning, baby.' Then she grinned as she remembered. 'We're having breakfast with Kelvin this morning.' And she couldn't help the nervous excitement as she lay on her pillow and stared at the corner of the little van where a tiny windchime had been hung by someone. Probably Scarlet's mum. She really liked that windchime.

She'd miss this van when she left on Tuesday, but right now she needed to get up and shower, and get herself down to Kelvin's before eight am.

Kelvin's tiny house sat three doors down from the pub, fronting the main road – so tiny it must only have two rooms. It was hard to see properly because the slatted wooden fence cut the footpath off from his front garden, and tall bushes in the garden hid the corners of the shack.

She pushed open the dark wooden gate. It wasn't really a garden, she saw now. More like a meander through a native bush patch with hardy desert plants and lots of coloured gravel and rock.

She'd noticed this place but hadn't realised how wonderful it was or that it was Kelvin's house.

Up the gravel path she could see so many interesting things. A tiny windmill made from bolts and steel. A pretty birdbath created from a ceramic plate on a piece of quartz, and an interesting piece of driftwood that looked like a bird leaning back – quirky and requiring a second look as she passed. Three steps led to the tiny stained-wood verandah and Kelvin opened the door before she'd even knocked.

'Good morning, Charli.' His stretched smile welcomed her like he'd been waiting impatiently for her to arrive.

She resisted the impulse to check her watch because if anything she was early. 'Morning, Kelvin. I love your front garden.'

He ducked his head, but his smile tried to grow more. 'I'm glad. Welcome to my home. I've set the table inside where it's cool,' he said, and his warm gaze made her pulse jump a little in her chest.

'You're spoiling me, Kelvin.'

'About time somebody did,' he said gruffly, and held the door wide.

She passed him and huffed a little gasp of surprise at the clever simplicity of the main room. There may not have been much furniture but what was there had been lovingly polished so the warm honey of the old wood glowed against neutral-coloured rugs and mustard walls. Two beautiful photographs of the desert, one in the morning and one in the night, hung opposite each other.

'Oh, Kelvin, this room's beautiful.'

'It's not finished yet,' he said.

'I love it. Did you take those photos?' When he nodded shyly, she tilted her head and studied him again. 'You're an artistic guy, aren't you?' He looked away but she knew he was pleased with the compliment.

'You should have noticed that from my cooking,' he said, but he was teasing.

'I should have,' she teased back and it was so nice to be here and feel so welcome that she leaned up and kissed his cheek. 'Thank you for inviting me.'

He froze and turned away to lift up a sheaf of brown paper and thrust it at her. 'Here. I picked you some flowers. First date, after all.'

She took them. Looked down and then back at him, her eyes wide. 'So, this really is a date?'

'A short one. I leave in an hour for work. I work a lot this time of year so there's not much time otherwise.'

She knew that. She'd agreed to work tonight and tomorrow night at the pub for her usual hours but then she'd be gone.

Kelvin was saying, 'You leave on Tuesday so I'll get in what I can. When we work together it doesn't count as a date because we're working. So, breakfast it is.'

She smiled shyly. Recognising the flowers. They were the white daisy-like ones with a yellow centre – she'd seen them among the red dirt at the side of the road when she'd driven from Charleville, with Lazy Luke. It felt like months ago, but it was less than two weeks.

She'd liked the flowers then, growing in the desert, white against the harsh red of the sand, and she loved them now.

She pushed her face into the small bunch but pulled away because they didn't smell great. Sort of herby and dungy.

Kelvin laughed. 'You don't smell them. They're Minnie Daisies, and I picked them from the side of the road. But they always make me smile.' He swallowed and said bravely, 'Like you do. You make me feel good when you're around. Always.'

That was a compliment. A big one. She remembered Nana Kate. 'Thank you, Kelvin.' She hugged the brown-paper-wrapped bouquet.

He shrugged awkwardly. 'It's not just that you never stare at my burns – you never did even on the first time I met you. You make me forget that my face is a mess.'

She frowned at him. 'Your face isn't a mess. It's my friend Kelvin's face.'

Suddenly she remembered Scarlet saying Charli's scarred lip wasn't as bad as she thought it was. Even Nana Kate had said that. Maybe it was true, because she didn't think there was anything wrong with the way Kelvin looked. But now she thought about it she understood why he'd say that.

'I think you're wonderful, Kelvin. I don't even see your scars because they're yours. I see you. And I like you the way you are.'

They were silent for a few moments, the words falling around them like a shower of leaves, but judging by Kelvin's face she thought he might see gold in them.

Finally, he said simply, 'Thank you.' Then he chewed his lip and waved the heaviness away. 'Let's eat.'

He gestured her to the little white-cloth-covered table with more flowers in a small jar in the middle. Two places were set with bone-handled cutlery and shiny glass tumblers of orange juice.

'I made frittata and Turkish bread. If you like it, I thought you might like to come again tomorrow, and maybe Tuesday, before you fly out. Same time?'

'That sounds wonderful.' It did.

Chapter Thirty-six

Atticus

Early on Monday morning the final relief police officers drove away to return to their own stations and Atticus waved off his first Birdsville Cup experience.

More than six thousand people, not one person ticketed for driving under the influence, not one fight except for the gazetted ones in Brophy's tent.

The whole weekend had been a huge, law-abiding success, though of course the vast majority of the racegoers had always been law abiding. The young and reckless people were definitely in the minority.

Still, it had been big. Bigger than anything he'd been involved in, but the high-profile and consistent presence of the law, and the mature demographic, had created goodwill and bonhomie.

While the usual suspects for trouble – those who drank too much – had still been around, a mere word from the law had been enough for them to be taken home and put to bed by their mates.

He went back inside the police station and through to his living quarters, opened the fridge and stared. It was full of fancy cheese, unopened dips in plastic tubs and exotic jars of olives, colourful pickled onions, and something dark he didn't like the look of. On the bench were unopened packets of savoury biscuits, potato chips, and nuts. His colleagues had stocked him up. Looked like Christmas.

Certainly enough for a party. Or a date with a curvaceous nurse for sunset nibbles. At the thought he glanced at the clock.

He'd open the station, wait half an hour to make sure there weren't any urgent matters, go for a drive around the town common to see the campers were all happy, and then drop into the Primary Health Centre on the way back. Just in case they had trouble there. Of course.

When Atticus opened the door to the PHC, Phoebe sat at the reception desk looking calm, confident and so captivating his chest hurt. Funny how the smile she gave him took away some of the darkness he'd held since Dali's death. Things had certainly heated up since the night of the gala.

'Good morning, Constable Bow.'

'Good morning, Sister McFadden. I've come to invite you to barbecue and drinks for two at my finally silent police station and barracks.'

She pretended to look around in case they were overheard, though there was no one else in sight, and whispered, 'Are you going to lock me up, officer?'

He fought not to smile. Sternly he whispered back, 'Only if you want me to.'

'Good to know.' She grinned at him. 'Even without the lock-up I'd . . . love to.'

Those two words flew straight to the centre of him. 'The sun sets at six-thirty tonight, and I finish at five,' he managed to get out.

'Then I'll see you at five-thirty.'

Too long to wait. 'Five past five would be fine.'

She laughed. 'I'll be there.' God, he loved that sound. 'What can I bring?'

'Just yourself. The troops left more than enough for both of us. I'll be sending you home with a basket.'

She gestured him closer, and he leaned down. Very quietly she said, 'I might not want to go home.'

He needed to leave before he reached across that desk and kissed her. At work. In public. Straightened. 'I'm hoping you'll feel like that.' Raised two fingers in a salute and forced himself out the door.

The day dragged. He pulled the clock off the wall twice to make sure the battery was in properly. The station itself had been quiet all day – surprising, considering how many people were still in town.

He'd had a few lost articles handed in and retrieved. Several requests for information on road conditions. So far, nobody had broken down. There'd been no accidents. And apparently everyone was happy.

Especially him.

Five pm arrived and he shut the door to the office with a finality he hoped the gods would listen to. He wondered briefly if Phoebe knew where the door to the residence was, but such an intelligent, assertive woman would soon let him know if she didn't.

He had four minutes to shower and don the clothes he had waiting on the freshly made bed. Maybe they could do the men and women in uniform fantasy another day. He smiled at the dreaming. Bolted to the bathroom.

Five minutes later a knock sounded at his front door. On fast, still damp bare feet he ran to pull open the door and stepped back. Draped in that little sundress that he loved, yep, she made his heart thump. 'Welcome to my home, Phoebe.'

He wanted to pick her up and carry her into his room and unwrap her like a present but instead he pointed the way inside and gave her a smile that probably said what he was thinking anyway.

She grinned at him. Yep. She suspected. 'Hello, Atticus,' she said as she went past and kept on walking. 'I'm feeling very welcome.'

Chapter Thirty-seven

Charli

It was Charli's last night in Birdsville and she wished she didn't have to leave.

It had been a little quieter tonight in the pub – still busy but not as frantic as last night had been. She'd actually had a surprising amount of energy at work until Kelvin had finally said, 'Stop cleaning.'

He'd made her sit down to a tiny pot pie he'd made especially for her and even cut the pastry in a letter C on top of it for Charli. When it came out of the oven the C was browner than everything else. She'd enjoyed that.

She enjoyed everything about Kelvin.

Tomorrow would be the last of her three breakfast dates with him. And she'd miss their conversations while she was away in Charleville waiting. Waiting. Waiting until after baby and she could come back. Though he'd said he'd phone.

*

The first contraction came as she cleaned her teeth at her little sink. Her belly went tight as it had been doing for a few days now, but this time accompanied by a niggling discomfort like a bad period pain a few inches lower than her belly button.

She frowned as she breathed through it. Ouch. Finally the nasty tightness eased and she forced the frown away.

The pains would stop. The back pain had. She had to pack tonight, not that it would take long, but she wanted to leave the van immaculate for Scarlet.

She was still in her work trousers when the next contraction grabbed low in her pelvis and ground through her like a bulldozer pushing barbed wire. This wasn't normal.

No. Oh, no. She cupped her belly with both hands and whispered, 'Not now, baby, Mummy is going tomorrow. It's our last night in the van. Wait.'

The next contraction arrived not long after the last had finished. Her legs felt wobbly and she sat on the bed and wondered where Phoebe was. She should have asked for her number, though she did have Scarlet's – who had mentioned this afternoon she was going to bed early tonight with her man, so she wasn't going to be happy if Charli interrupted them.

She should ring Gloria, the nurse at the clinic, but she didn't have her number and she didn't want to call triple zero. Did she? She just wanted advice.

Why did this have to happen now? Just one more day. That was all she needed. Everyone had been so busy and she didn't want to bother any of them.

The next pain twisted, and suddenly she felt a pop, hot dampness gushed, and she was sitting in a puddle that grew fast on the wet bed. Oh, noooo, her beautiful bed. Scarlet's beautiful bed. That upset her more than anything. Scarlet's sheets and quilt. Saturated. Horribly messy. Everything was wet.

She had to ring Scarlet. Now. Had to.

Charli dialled the number but it rang, and rang, and rang. She hung up and tried again; again it rang, but nobody answered.

She thought about triple zero and couldn't bring herself to do it. Finally, she phoned Kelvin's number, one he'd pressed on her that day at the races after asking when the baby was due. Just in case. As if he'd known she'd need someone. Well, Kelvin . . . she did.

He answered. 'Kelvin. Hello? Who's this?'

And of course, a contraction started, and she couldn't speak. Could only breathe. Gasp. Struggle and reach for a word that didn't come.

He'd think she was a spam caller. Hang up. But he didn't. 'Charli? Charli? Is that you?'

How had he known? What sort of man recognised heavy breathing? She knew that answer. The best sort. She whispered through gritted teeth, 'My waters broke. Contractions. It's too early.'

'Charli.' Her name came out with a sigh. 'Oh, Charli. I'm coming.' He lived close so he wouldn't be long. It was just a street away. She needed to change. Fast.

Five minutes later he was there. 'Charli. Babe. Have you rung Gloria?'

She shook her head. Horribly embarrassed by the wet bed. She'd pulled on a fresh pair of underpants and two pads from the drawer and bundled up the damp clothes, then pulled her nightie on because her trousers were wet. Like the bed.

'You have to ring Gloria,' he said quietly but firmly, and she nodded.

She couldn't speak as another one rolled over her. Finally, she gasped, 'Can you do it?'

He pulled his phone from his pocket. 'Of course.'

And right at that moment, she thought she might love him, this big, wonderful man, who had come to help because he cared.

Chapter Thirty-eight

Phoebe

Phoebe was lost in the divine sensation of Atticus pressing firm lips to her throat, desperately wondering where his bedroom was so she could have her wicked way with him, when her phone vibrated in her pocket.

She'd been so patient, eating his cheese and crackers, watching the sunset, talking and talking, the whole slow evening drawing closer to this moment, till they were both ready to make the step that would change everything.

The phone vibrated again. She wanted to throw it across the room, but you never knew. And she felt a foreboding she didn't like to ignore. She pushed her hand against his chest. 'I have to look at this call.'

He stopped. Instantly. And she shivered as the air hit her heated skin. Their eyes met and the understanding in his said they would resume when able.

She smiled at that and finally glanced at the phone. Yep. 'Gloria,' she said to Atticus before she answered.

'Gloria?'

'Phoebe, thank goodness. Scarlet's young charge has broken her waters. I'd appreciate your midwifery back-up down at the clinic if you could. Your dad's just picked her up in the ambulance and she's labouring at thirty-five weeks. Flying doctor's unable to come for at least three hours.'

Her eyes met his. And that would be that. 'Charli's in labour.' At least they had her antenatal records. The poor kid would be exhausted after the week she'd had. 'On my way.'

When Phoebe arrived, she could hear the moans. Ouch. That didn't sound good.

And then she heard the grunt and picked up speed. Yikes. She hoped the air-con was on warm because tiny babies went hypothermic fast.

She needn't have worried.

Gloria had this. The room felt very warm. And calm.

Gloria stood placidly beside the bed with Charli in it, a white hospital gown, unopen side, tucked over her patient, ties undone. Phoebe suspected that Gloria expected the baby to come, and planned to whip the gown away for skin to skin if that was what Charli wanted.

A folded-back sheet covered Charli's naked thighs and hid her feet but was untucked, and the small ultrasound doppler was pressed into Charli's low abdomen: the sound of a speeding baby's heart, galloping along like it should, filled the room.

In a soothing undertone, Gloria said, 'See, baby's happy.'

Phoebe was almost happy too at that reassuring sound. Tension she hadn't realised she'd collected, eased away.

Even Gloria looked almost happy.

To Phoebe's surprise there was a man there too, holding Charli's hand. She recognised him from the pub. Maybe the kitchen? Keith or Callum or something? Scarlet had said his name.

'Thanks for coming, Phoebe.' Gloria's calm voice broke into her thoughts.

'No problem.' She washed her hands and went straight to the little bed made up under the well-lit bench. Nope, of course there was no baby resuscitation trolley in Birdsville. People didn't have babies in Birdsville. Except today.

She checked the infant airway bag for lung inflation and it puffed out a breath smoothly when she squeezed. Puffed it a few times. Checked the size of the attached mask. Cast her eyes over the array of tiny Guedel airways she really didn't want to need. Right size for a thirty-five-week newborn. Checked the connection of tubing for the oxygen, which she also didn't want to use. So much better to resuscitate with air. So much better not to have to resuscitate at all.

She'd have to see about reallocating those purpose-built infant resus trolleys at work in Adelaide. The ones that had been replaced with later models, ones she was pretty sure were just standing shrouded under sheets in an empty office.

One of the Neopuffs would be good, too: an automated air delivery system for inflating an infant's lungs – less chance of over-inflation and less tiring for a place like this where hours of inflation could be needed and staff were thin on the ground.

But not the thought for now.

Quietly, trying not to disturb Charli while she breathed and moaned, she said in a low voice to Gloria, 'If we have this baby . . .'

she glanced at Charli sitting up on the high pillows squeezing the man's fingers in a death grip; the young woman hadn't even seen Phoebe arrive '. . . which looks likely, would you like to catch the baby or do the resus?'

Dryly, Gloria said softly back, 'How about you catch the baby and take it to the resus? I'll worry about mum after the event. I can deal with third stage.'

Phoebe smiled. 'That's fine with me. At almost thirty-six weeks, baby should be fine. Just prone to issues maintaining body temperature and maybe slow with feeds. And the flying doctor will manage all that when they arrive. They'll have a humidicrib.'

Charli fell silent and sagged back in the pillows. She opened her eyes and stared at Phoebe. 'Oh. You're here. I'm sorry, Phoebe.'

'What for, sweetheart?'

'I didn't mean to cause trouble.'

'You and your baby are not trouble. You were doing the right thing. Planned to leave at the right time. You didn't know you'd go into labour early.'

That wasn't what she'd been thinking earlier as she sprinted down the road to the PHC, but she knew, in her heart, and looking at Charli's face, it was true.

She crossed to Charli and touched her free hand. 'Everything will be fine. If your baby doesn't wait for the flying doctor, we can keep him or her safe until they do arrive. You'll be doing the cuddling and keeping him or her warm against your skin.'

The relief was real on the young woman's face. 'Oh, good.' Her face pinched. 'Because I don't think I can hold on much longer.'

RFDS would probably be happier if Charli birthed before their arrival anyway, Phoebe thought wryly. If she birthed while in the air and amniotic fluid spilled onto the floor, the whole aircraft would be grounded until it was stripped down and assessed for damage by the engineers. Perfect fluid for babies and toxic to aircraft. One of those bizarre facts Phoebe had never understood but knew to be true.

A moot point as Charli groaned, grunted and pushed.

Then she wailed.

Loudly.

With speed Phoebe washed her hands again, pulled on a disposable plastic apron, and donned sterile gloves.

Gloria had set a small trolley with a kidney dish for the placenta, two long-handled clamps and a pair of scissors. She even had one open plastic disposable cord clamp and two spares unopened.

Phoebe smiled sideways at her. 'You thought of everything.'

'It's been a few years.' Gloria's smiled looked undeniably tinged with relief. 'Phew.'

Charli groaned and Gloria folded the sheet back to just below her hips, allowing Phoebe to see the pink fluid, a small amount of blood, and a gaping introitus. No need to examine for cervical dilation: this baby was on its way.

'You're fine, sweetheart, just listen to your body. Nothing to be afraid of. Baby is running this show.'

Phoebe glanced at the man beside Charli, studiously watching Charli's face and nothing below, and noted his cheeks wouldn't be able to fade any whiter. Possibly he was going to float to the floor like a printer sheet, too. 'Might need a chair here, Gloria. Before we end up with a male head injury.'

Gloria scooted a chair across and bumped it into the back of Kelvin's legs. That was his name. Kelvin. The tall man folded at the knees and wobbled down into it, heroically never losing purchase on Charli's fingers or shifting his gaze.

Gloria slid an injection tray onto the table beside the bed so Phoebe could twist her neck and read the ampoule. Syntocinon for after the birth. Excellent.

'Looks like baby's almost here.' She touched Charli's hand to get her attention. 'Gloria will give you an injection in your leg as soon as baby is born. It may sting for a second. You're allowed to jump. It lessens the chance of bleeding after the birth.'

Charli nodded that she understood.

'You're not allowed to bleed in Birdsville. Okay?'

Suddenly Charli's eyes went wild. 'Now. Right now. Can't help it. Have to go to the toilet.' She struggled to sit higher. Jerking her hand free out of Kelvin's to grab the edge of the bed to pull herself out.

Phoebe soothed, 'No. It's the baby, Charli. Feels like the head is pushing everything out of the way down there. We're ready. Let it go.'

'I'm gonna make a mess,' she panted, and with a horrified look at Kelvin, she wailed.

'No. You're gonna have a baby.' He took her hand back and said, 'It's okay. You're amazing. Everyone's here.'

Under the sheet, Phoebe could see the first mound of head. 'Baby is coming. No fear now. You're a star. Doing a wonderful job. Just breathe and let your body do it.'

Charli stared hard at Phoebe, narrowed her eyes and Phoebe recognised the moment she understood. Charli's head leaned back, she blew out a big sigh, sank back and groaned.

Charli's knees flopped out, making a sheet tent with the top half of her under and the bottom uncovered. Her shoulders slumped.

She groaned again and the round dome of her baby's sparsely haired head slid free. Such a tiny dome.

'Ohhhh,' Charli said, 'oohhhhh,' and the rest of the head eased so, so gently into the world until the little face slowly rotated to free the shoulder.

'That's perfect. Gentle like that. Perfect.'

Charli's eyes remained unfocused. As if she were reading instructions on a wall only she could see. She blew out a long noisy breath and sighed deeper into the bed.

One baby shoulder eased free.

Phoebe loved this moment. Her midwife's hands not touching anything except a brief scrutiny to check no cord lay around the baby's neck. The total absorption of the birthing woman as she obeyed the unspoken wisdom of her body. Wisdom that had been inherited through her genes and lain dormant for this moment in time as she became an instinctive mother.

In the silence, Kelvin closed his eyes and a big fat tear slid down his cheek.

Phoebe felt her own eyes mist and she blinked the moisture away. 'Exactly like that, Charli,' she whispered. 'Keep going.'

The second shoulder jerked free and suddenly the body was coming. Phoebe gathered the skinny torso as back, hips and legs tumbled with a splash and coil of purple cord into her hands. Safe.

'Ohhhh.' Charli blew out a big breath and shuddered. Kelvin sobbed once.

The room hung silent in that one moment between birth and life and then the baby squealed.

Charli's eyes flew open. Gloria choked out a strangled laugh. Kelvin sobbed again.

Phoebe wiped the baby with the warmed towel Gloria handed her, drying the damp skin, careful not to touch the cord, allowing the ebb and flow of the blood inside to find its own balance between placenta and baby. She swept away the sheet and carefully lifted baby onto Charli's chest under her white robe as far up as she could with the cord still attached.

'Take the gown off,' Charli growled, as her eyes latched onto the squirming tiny human she'd just delivered herself. Her hands reaching, reaching . . .

Gloria slid the needle away with the tray. Seemed Charli hadn't even felt the injection, and Gloria helped the mum drag her arms out of the wide sleeves until she was naked, except for an old-fashioned watch-locket on a silver chain, under the sheet. Phoebe's eyes caught on it and then slid away as she assessed Charli's condition.

'It's okay, baby.' Finally, Charli scooped the baby onto her chest between her breasts and soft squeals quieted as her mother rubbed her back and soothed. 'Mummy is here. I'm here. I'll always be here.'

'Boy or girl? Charli?' Gloria asked, her eyes alight with delight and relief.

Everyone waited for Charli to see. She lifted a tiny leg and peered. Her glowing face split in delight. 'A girl! My Brianna. My little lioness.'

Phoebe turned away. Her eyes filled and she closed them to hold back her stupid emotion. Charli would be there for her baby. Charli had missed out on so much. Charli hadn't had her mother. Like Phoebe.

But Charli hadn't had a dad either.

Chapter Thirty-nine

Phoebe

The next morning, Phoebe sat sipping tea with Scarlet. 'You should have seen Kelvin, Scarlet. Like a soft rock. A pale monolith, immovable. He wanted to go in the aircraft with her but there wasn't room. They had another patient.'

'Bet he was glad he didn't when he woke up this morning at home, not wondering how to get here,' Scarlet said sleepily.

'Probably true,' Phoebe agreed. 'Charli will be back in a few days they think, anyway. But Charli was . . . she was amazing. The type of birth you dream of when you're a midwife. Fast. Controlled. With mum and bub driving it all. The baby cried not long after birth. A tiny little thing, she is. Always such a relief when they're vigorous.'

She had a memory of Charli reaching, naked, for the baby. The silver watch-locket between her breasts. Charli pushing the silver disc over her shoulder out of the way. It looked heavy, old, ornate . . .

Had she seen one like that somewhere? She had. Suddenly, unexpectedly, she had a crazy thought. She needed to see her dad. 'I have to go. Something I've thought of. Back in a while.'

Scarlet stared sleepily up at her. 'What? Go? Go where?'

'To see my dad.' Surely not. How could . . .? Or was it just one like it?

Phoebe dashed across the road and Gloria opened the door. Ooohhh, Gloria stayed the night? No time for that. 'Sorry to barge in, Gloria – is Dad here?'

Gloria, flushing just a bit, pointed, and Phoebe slid past. Her father was standing at the stove cooking bacon and eggs. Phoebe's stomach rumbled.

'Hello, love.' He smiled past her at Gloria: definitely a wicked twinkle in his eye. 'Have you come for breakfast, too?'

'Morning, Dad. No, but yes, please, and . . .' She turned and checked the room again. No, the photo wasn't there. 'Have you still got that photo of my mother that used to be on the side table?'

'Of course, love. I wouldn't throw it out. It's yours.' His face clouded at the memory. 'I put it away the day you left.'

He bent to the bottom kitchen drawer and pulled it open. Rummaged. Finally lifted out an old tea towel wrapped around a square object. He straightened and unwrapped it. His mouth turned down as he stared at the face behind the glass for a moment and then he gave it to her.

Her mother's eyes were the same as Phoebe's. Her hair straight black. There it was. A silver watch-locket. Ornate. Old. On a silver chain the same as Charli's. She stared at it. 'What's the story with the watch?'

His brow furrowed. 'The watch?'

'The watch-locket.'

Gloria had come across to look at the photo, too. 'I remember that,' she said. 'She always wore it.'

Rusty frowned. Remembering. 'Said her mother gave it to her. Put it on every morning and tucked it under her shirt. Her most precious thing.'

'Do you think there's a lot of watches like it? Would it have been common in those days?'

'No.' He shook his head. 'Well, not like that. It was heavy. And very old. It had a winder not a battery. On a silver chain. Though she probably pawned it after she left. She was always broke. Which is why I sent money and we were poor.' He studied her face. 'What's all this about?'

Or she didn't pawn it and left it for her own daughter. Phoebe's thoughts twirled, her brain shifting it all together like a puzzle with pieces missing.

'So, she died having a baby. When I was seventeen?'

'Yes.'

'And I'm thirty-five now.'

'Yes.' He laughed. 'I know how old you are.'

'So, if her baby lived when my mother died, the baby would be eighteen, nearly nineteen, now?'

The laughter died in his eyes. 'But the baby died.'

Hmmm. 'How do you know the baby died?'

'The police were notified here because I was still legally married to her.' His voice trailed away and horror crossed his face. 'Or maybe they didn't mention the baby, and I just assumed.' He searched Phoebe's face. 'What are you saying?'

'Nothing yet. I'm not sure. I'll explain it all later.'

'You should explain right now.' There was a sternness in her dad's voice she'd so rarely heard, and Gloria put her hand on his arm.

'Rusty. She'll tell you as soon as she knows.'

Phoebe flashed Gloria a grateful look.

To her dad she shook her head. 'I can't. I might be wrong.' Kissed his cheek and turned for the door. 'I don't know all the facts. But I will come back as soon as I can.'

Before she could get out the door, he said, 'Phoebe, are you saying that your mother's baby has been alive all this time?'

'Possibly. Maybe. She could have been made a ward of the state.'

'She?'

Gloria gasped. 'You don't mean . . .?' Of course: she'd seen the locket and it looked as though things were coming together in her mind, too.

'It was the watch that made me wonder, but we'll have to wait till she comes back to town.'

'She?' Rusty's voice rose. 'Gloria, what do you know about this?'

'I know Phoebe needs to get all the facts before she tells everybody what she thinks.' Gloria held her finger up at Rusty. 'I'll explain in a minute.'

Phoebe looked gratefully at the older woman. 'Thanks, Gloria. I'll see you in a bit. Don't eat it all. I'll come back for a bacon sandwich.'

*

Phoebe stepped out of her father's house and the world looked different from when she went in. And in a bizarre way the only person she wanted to talk to was Atticus.

As she walked towards the police station, it was still only seven, and she thought about the way her father had put the photo away the day she left.

The day she hurt him so badly by believing he had broken her trust. How he had taken that blame on board because he *had* taken her money – only not for him. He didn't gamble, he said. Just liked horses. In fact, it had been her mother who'd been the real gambler. And she'd died having a baby.

So had Charli's mother.

What if this crazy idea turned out to be true rather than a series of wild coincidences? There was a chance that Charli could be Phoebe's half-sister. Imagine if she had a sister . . .

Her gaze focused on Atticus up ahead, talking to three similarly built men, holding his bike, as if he'd just got home. He must have been out for a ride. Funny how she could pick him out even when others were around his height.

Must be the way he carried himself. His broad shoulders, the tilt of his head. As if he could feel her gaze he turned and glanced up the road and spotted her.

Instantly he spoke to the men and then with long strides came to meet her.

Phoebe had only wanted to walk for a few minutes to clear her head, and seeing Atticus had seemed like a good idea. The reality was even better.

When he reached her side he searched her face, his direct and questioning. 'What's wrong?'

'And you can tell something's wrong just by looking at me?'

He smiled. 'I've been looking at you a lot over the last fort-night. I should be able to tell when there's something not right. You haven't come to report a crime, have you?'

She smiled. 'No.'

'So, why?'

And that was the kicker. 'I don't know. I just wanted to see you.' After a pause. 'Something happened.'

'What happened?' When she didn't answer, he said, 'Apart from the first baby in Birdsville in a very long time.'

'News travels fast.'

'News said you did a great job.'

'Thank you. Gloria had it all under control. Charli was great, but something happened, and . . .' She blurted, 'I suspect Charli could be my half-sister.'

He stilled and studied her. Lifted one hand and touched her hair. His gaze travelled her face and he frowned at her hair. 'Possible. There are similarities. But not the hair. Eyes are different.' He looked more thoughtful. 'I wouldn't be surprised.'

She half-laughed. 'Well, I'm surprised. I didn't know I had a half-sister. My father didn't know she was alive. He kinda assumed the baby died with my mother.'

He tilted his head to watch her. 'So, how do you feel about this development?' Looking down with a calmness and kindness she was coming to expect from this man. And that was why she was here, borrowing some of that composure. He didn't seem younger than her now. In fact, she felt the junior.

With Atticus she could say what was in her mind because he cleared her head. 'We might share a mother. My dad's not her dad.

But she's family. She's a not-really-a-cousin to Scarlet, but she'll become one.'

'Poor Charli,' he murmured.

Phoebe laughed. 'You will see the amazing side of my cousin one day.'

'Her amazing relatives?'

'Of course. But other reasons, too.' She did feel better. Quieter. More focused. And ready to get on with her day.

He smiled at her. 'I have to go back and sort out these guys waiting for me. It'll be over by lunch time. Why don't I meet you at the marvellous Scarlet's when I'm finished?'

He touched her shoulder. 'We could discuss that next sunset date.'

She nodded and watched him go. Tall, broad, striding away. Wonderful eye candy to carry in her mind back to Scarlet's.

Thoughts began to spin again. Half about the fact that she might have a sister. And half about how this guy she'd met less than a fortnight earlier understood her so well.

The fact she'd actually taken herself down to see him, not so much for advice and reassurance, but just to see him while her world rocked and rolled around her. Yes, that bore even more thought.

Chapter Forty

Charli

Charli lay in her bed in the busy regional hospital and still couldn't believe the events of the last twenty-four hours. When she'd first been admitted, Brianna was whisked away while she'd been checked over and had showered, but they'd brought her baby back quickly and she hadn't left Charli's sight since.

Right now, Charli was feeding her again at the breast as she snuggled her carefully. Crazy how empty she felt when she didn't have her in her arms.

The midwife was saying, 'The paediatrician said she looks great. You just have to keep her warm and feed her any time she's awake.'

Didn't sound too hard. She loved feeding her. 'Okay. I can do that.'

'She'll keep you on your toes, I think.' The midwife laughed. 'I've never seen such a ravenous thirty-five-week baby. She's wonderful.'

'She is.' Charli felt a glow of pride. 'So that's good?'

'Yes. Because the more she drinks, the faster she's going to grow strong and keep herself warm.'

'Lots of feeds then.' She could do that. Back in Birdsville, Phoebe had explained about making sure she understood not to damage her nipples when feeding.

Phoebe had been adamant. 'You'll need them.' She meant Charli would need her boobs. Which had made Charli laugh, but she'd been careful to attach Brianna exactly as she'd been shown. Luckily she had small boobs, because Brianna's mouth was so tiny.

She couldn't help asking. Knew it wasn't the first time she had. 'When can we go back to Birdsville?'

'You'll both be here at least a couple of days. But as long as she does all the right things, shouldn't be longer than that.' The midwife wrote the current feed on the chart at the end of the bed.

'What's the wrong things?' Charli hungered to understand so she could avoid them.

The midwife smiled. 'Not wrong exactly. Just an added job her body must do. Because she's early, she'll probably become jaundiced. Her liver is immature and now she's breathing air, all those extra oxygen-carrying red cells she didn't need while she was living inside you have to break down and leave her body. With an immature liver to deal with them, it's hard work for her to process. Which makes jaundice.'

'I read about babies getting their oxygen through the cord. And the extra red cells needed for that.'

'Wonderful. Well, normally that removal of the unneeded cells after birth happens in the baby's liver and then they get flushed out of her system in the waste. The more she drinks the more you help her liver. Otherwise, the yellow by-product, bilirubin, stains her skin, floats around in her bloodstream all the way to her brain and makes her sleepy. If she's sleepy she might not drink enough. And then the flushing is even less efficient.'

Ah, so that's how it worked. 'And then she gets more sleepy?'

The midwife beamed at her. 'Correct.'

'Right.' Charli nodded. Imprinting the information. 'Feeds. Warmth. And she stays with me, here, all the time? Is that right?'

'Absolutely, Charli.' The midwife nodded.

Charli felt warmed by the approval she could see in the midwife's eyes. 'Can you show me how to take her temperature, please?'

She laughed. 'You are an excellent mother.'

At the end of that first day a big basket of colourful flowers arrived from Gloria, Phoebe and Scarlet, the first real florist flowers Charli had ever received. Though Kelvin's hand-picked ones from their first breakfast still remained special.

The note said, *Congratulations on Brianna's safe arrival. We'll see you both when you come back. Your van is waiting.* Those words, let alone the wonderful flowers, were so beautiful she'd cried.

Kelvin phoned her that first night and she'd got such a shock when she heard his voice.

'Charli? You there? That you?'

'Kelvin.' Oh, how wonderful. 'Thank you for ringing. It's so good to hear your voice.' She'd been feeling a little lost and alone even with Brianna sleeping beside her.

'Good to hear yours, too.'

She'd been wanting to talk to him, thank him, had been going to write a letter tomorrow, but this was so much better. 'Thank you, Kelvin. For being there. For everything.'

There was a pause. A cleared throat. 'I didn't do anything.' Gruffly.

'You were there. For me. It meant a lot.' It really had. His hand had been a lifeline when she'd thought she'd lose control.

'You're welcome.' He paused. 'Umm. Charli?'

'Yes?' He sounded worried. Why? Was something wrong? She didn't want Kelvin worried.

'Umm,' his voice dropped until she had to strain to hear, 'I hope you didn't mind I stayed.'

'No! Of course not.' And now she understood. 'You were very brave to stay, Kelvin. I wanted you there to hold my hand. And you did. You stayed when I needed you. A lot of men would have run. But you didn't. You're my hero.'

'Thank goodness.' The relief in his voice clear. 'Don't know about a hero but I'm glad it's okay.' He cleared his throat. 'Just didn't seem right to leave you.'

'And Kelvin?'

'Yeah.'

'She's Brianna Kelly Bryce. I'll never forget you were there for me at her birth.'

There was a long silence on the phone. 'Oh. Okay.' But she could tell he was touched, by the thickness in the words.

Enough awkwardness. 'You should see her, Kelvin. She's amazing.' And suddenly it was easy again and he even laughed when she told him about the midwife saying Brianna was ravenous. They talked for half an hour.

He spoke about the goings-on in town. How all the extra police had gone. How Brophy's tent was down and the marketplace dismantled and all the stallholders had left.

Most of the tourists had departed on Tuesday but there were still a few living in the rooms at the hotel and camped at the caravan park. He missed her in the kitchen and they'd run out of some ingredients because the races had been so successful.

She could almost imagine she was standing in the kitchen beside him.

On the second day, pink roses arrived from Kelvin. This time she blushed when the midwives teased her about a man sending her roses. 'No, he isn't the father,' she wished he was, 'but he's a very nice man.'

She'd phoned Nana Kate and told her Brianna was here, but that she wanted to go back to Birdsville instead of coming to her in Roma, as she'd made friends. The idea that she'd made friends who cared, sat wonderfully. Nana Kate had been thrilled for her and promised to send a bundle of baby things in the mail to the PHC because Charli would be seeing the nurse there and she didn't have a real address yet.

Charli had never felt so special in her life.

But most of all she loved Brianna. And Brianna loved her. Those dark eyes would seek out Charli's face every time she latched on to feed, or when her mother passed by her cot: she'd stare seriously and unwaveringly and Charli would stare back. Talking softly. Explaining that Brianna had to drink lots, wee lots, and they'd go home to Birdsville soon.

Though how they were going to get there she hadn't worked out yet. All she knew was she wasn't going via Roma and a stay at Nana Kate's.

Scarlet phoned on the second night to say she had most things sorted for her wedding on Saturday and Phoebe had had to help her because Charli had left.

Charli was pretty sure she was teasing and said shyly, 'Sorry.'

Scarlet laughed. 'You always were a bonus and Phoebe was supposed to help when she came anyway.'

'Oh,' she said, but she was thinking, she was a bonus? That sounded like a good thing.

She needed to say the next bit, though it made her squirm. 'Scarlet. I'm sorry about the bed.'

'Nah. All good. Lucky I had that shower curtain on it. All washed and sorted. Ready for you to come back to until you find a place.'

Tears prickled her eyes. She was so lucky. 'Thank you.'

'Anyway, I rang to say we'd like you and Brianna to come to my wedding if you're home?'

Home. Charli couldn't stop the tears falling. And Brianna was invited? 'I've never been invited to a wedding before.'

'Well, you're both invited to this one.'

Charli and Brianna's first wedding. 'Thank you. If Brianna is allowed to leave, we'll be there as soon as we sort out how to travel.' And as soon as she sorted out how to get a few baby supplies she hadn't bought yet. 'I hope to be back by Friday but if Brianna isn't well enough then we'll stay as long as we have to.'

'Of course. Just to think about. That's all.' She hung up.

*

On the third day, Lazy Luke came to see her: no flowers, but his cheerful face brightened her afternoon. She'd texted him and asked if he'd take her into town for some supplies when he got off work, and here he was. So again, he'd proved a friend.

When he arrived, he peered at Brianna, and nodded. 'Looks good. For a baby. You need something?'

'I found a lady selling baby things online on the Charleville marketplace site. Could you run me to her house to pick things up, please? We don't need much.'

'Do we take the baby?' He looked a bit concerned about that – as he should, since he had a utility.

'The midwife said I could leave Brianna after the feed and go out for a little while and sort things.' His face cleared and she smiled. 'It's so much easier than in Birdsville. I might even buy the woman's pram.'

He frowned. 'Aren't you going to buy a new one?'

She'd decided not. Sensibly. 'Thought about it, but there's lots of things I need, and it's going to be rolling over dirt so won't stay new for long. The lady says this one's in perfect condition.'

He shrugged. 'Makes sense.'

In the end, Charli was allowed to go back to Birdsville early on the Friday because Phoebe had said she'd check her and Brianna every day. Although Brianna didn't need any treatment, she had become jaundiced. The good thing was that after four days Charli understood about temperatures, bathing, breastfeeding hints, and the changes in the dirty nappies that meant her milk was changing too.

She also learned to ensure Brianna made enough wet nappies to prove she was drinking enough.

Like a sponge Charli soaked it all in and loved everything about the experience.

Kelvin had offered to come for them Thursday night. He'd arrive too late to visit, but would be there early in the morning to pick them up.

When he came to take her home his eyes widened when he saw the pile of things she'd collected. The flowers he'd sent her were wilting but she wasn't leaving them behind.

'Hello, Charli.' His voice sounded gruff but his smile cracked wide and happy. 'How are you? How's Brianna? You look pretty.'

Oh. She blushed. 'We're both great. Thanks, Kelvin. We really appreciate you picking us up.'

'Nah, it was easy.' He waved his hand. Then, more shyly, 'I wanted to.'

She hoped so, because it wasn't a simple drive. He would have had to leave yesterday after work to get here in the early hours, and he'd clearly taken tonight off, otherwise he would have to make it back in time for the dinner run. Exhausting return trip, which was why she'd had no visitors from Birdsville. Even Nana Kate was a three-hundred-kilometre drive away at Roma.

'It's a big favour, but I'll find a way to repay you.'

He looked down and shuffled his feet. Brushed off the praise. Raised his brows at the pile. 'You got some stuff to take with you?'

'Yep. And there's a baby seat we have to fit in your car. You reckon you could do that?'

He looked more confident than Charli felt about the installation. 'How about I take it now, then come back and get you once it's in?'

His offer sounded so wonderful. 'Perfect. I'll feed her again so she's full and we'll see how far we get before she needs to feed again. I hope we don't make too slow a trip for you.'

'Be nice to have the company,' he said, and Charli smiled shyly up at him.

'Thanks, Kelvin.'

When Charli arrived back at Birdsville, the last of the daylight had drained away an hour earlier and Kelvin had driven more slowly and carefully to avoid the wildlife as soon as dusk approached.

But she was home – at least it was home until she found something permanent. Finally, she could breathe a sigh of exhausted relief.

It was such a long way from Charleville, more than eleven hours with stops, and though Brianna had slept most of it, she'd cried every now and then and Charli had worried she'd annoy Kelvin, so she hadn't ever relaxed.

Of course he'd laughed, and said he'd been there when Brianna-Kelly was born and that her baby could never annoy him, which was sweet, but she still worried.

Scarlet wasn't home when she arrived. It felt strange going past the house to the shed, as it was after eight pm, and she was glad Kelvin insisted on carrying the bags in while she took Brianna.

When she opened the door to her little van, thinking she'd have to make up the pram so Brianna could sleep, she found the most gorgeous white wicker cradle sitting on the dining room table waiting for them. A propped note said, *Welcome home, Charli and Brianna. From Scarlet, Phoebe and Gloria.*

She sucked in a startled breath. 'Oh, look, Kelvin.' Tears prickled behind her tired eyes and her shoulders slumped as emotion overwhelmed her. They'd been so kind. Such wonderful caring people. Palest green sheets and a small cotton blanket were folded back just like they folded the sheets back in the hospital.

Still standing outside, Kelvin poked his head around hers. 'Nice.'

'Gorgeous.' And with relief she unwrapped Brianna and slipped her into the bed so she could get herself organised after the trip. It felt surreal to tuck her own baby into her new bed. It was momentous, so of course her emotions swelled.

Kelvin took one look at her face and backed out. 'I won't come in. You're tired. You need your space with your daughter.'

She blinked at this kind, kind man. 'Oh, Kelvin. You're my hero again. You saved me from all the difficulties of getting Brianna back here myself.'

The tears spilled over as she tried to hold them back. He looked terrified and she snuffed a laugh. 'Just silly baby hormones. Thank you. Can I come and see you tomorrow? To thank you properly.'

'You know my hours. Know you're welcome any time.' He looked worried for a moment. 'Unless you want me to do something for you now?'

'No, you go. Have a sleep. Thank you and I'll see you tomorrow.'

He nodded and glanced at the baby. Smiled softly. 'Hope she lets you sleep too.'

Chapter Forty-one

Phoebe

Phoebe woke on Saturday, the day of the wedding, with her brain still crazy with the implications of Charli possibly being her sister.

She wished Scarlet had put the wedding back another week but she'd been the one with the holidays she couldn't move and there had been that cruise Scarlet wanted as her honeymoon that left on Wednesday from Brisbane.

But Charli? A sister? Dad refused to discuss it until Charli came back and he saw the pendant. Didn't think the photos proved it enough but he had admitted that Charli did look a little like Celine.

Gloria had shaken her head and said he wouldn't shift on that stance. Maybe Phoebe had got her stubborn streak from her dad.

For Phoebe, the whole idea of having a sister was strangely exciting, and a little daunting, because although she liked Charli, she really only knew her as the young woman who'd worked so hard for Scarlet. She didn't 'know' her. Yes, she'd been there for Brianna's birth, so she did know her very well in some ways – she smiled at that thought. But not as someone who shared a birth mother. What if they didn't get on?

Now that was crazy. She threw back the sheets in disgust at herself and went off to shower and find Scarlet for advice on how to broach the subject with Charli.

When Charli knocked on Scarlet's back door, Scarlet took the initiative and threw open the door and drew her lodger in for a hug. Phoebe watched Charli stiffen and struggle not to drop her phone, but she was glad to see she shyly hugged her boss back.

Phoebe's mouth pulled up in a smile and her nerves settled. Charli smiled at her, too, and Phoebe could see the very warm welcome hadn't been expected but was appreciated by the young mum.

'What's this for?'

'Congratulations on Brianna.' Phoebe added softly, 'Go easy on squashing her boobs, Scarlet, they'll be tender from feeding.'

She'd seen the wince. Obviously, Charli hadn't liked to say but Scarlet stepped back immediately and grumbled, 'Well, I wouldn't know, would I? Not having had a baby.'

Charli's eyes met Phoebe's and they both smiled. Probably thinking the same thing. The way Scarlet and her fiancé spent so much time in the bedroom, she might have one soon.

'May I hug you, too?' Phoebe asked, and she saw Charli's eyes mist. Poor kid. Hormones and emotion. A sure recipe for tears. Phoebe didn't have that excuse, but darn if she didn't feel like crying too.

After she'd also very gently hugged Charli, Phoebe steered her to the kitchen table to sit. 'Is Brianna asleep?'

Charli's face transformed. Phoebe couldn't help her grin. Here sat a mother in love. Charli glowed.

'Yes, I've just fed her. There's a camera near her bed.' She lifted the phone and the screen showed Brianna's bassinet and the sleeping baby. 'I can check her on my phone if I'm across here. Otherwise, I'll have her with me in the pram. It came with a bunch of stuff I got from a lady in Charleville selling all her baby things.'

She looked up and her smile lit the room. 'And thank you, both, and Gloria too, of course, for the beautiful bassinet. It was just what I needed last night after the drive. She went straight to sleep.'

'So pleased you're happy with it.' Poor kid. 'You've had a massive week, I'll bet you're exhausted. I thought you might stay in Charleville a little longer to rest.'

She shrugged. 'I'm fine. I wanted to come back here and Scarlet said I could use the van until I find a place.' Charli looked down at her hands. 'I think Kelvin must have been more tired than me. Such a big thing for him to do for us.'

Phoebe loved the way she said 'us'. Brianna and her. A team according to Charli, and what a lovely thought. Phoebe realised she hoped she could become a part of that team, too, if what she suspected was true.

But where to start? 'I have a question for you, Charli.'

Charli straightened. A line of worry creased her forehead and Phoebe wondered how many times people had pried into her past. 'You don't have to answer if you don't want to. It's just . . . that locket that you're wearing? Is there a story behind it?'

Charli's hand crept up to cover it, but her eyes were big. And maybe a little excited? 'The locket? Yes.' Her gaze travelled between Phoebe and Scarlet and back to Phoebe. 'I've always been told they didn't know who my mum was, because she left me outside the hospital when I was born, before she died of complications. But in the box with me was the locket.'

Phoebe's heart thumped. 'Go on.'

'When I was in Roma with my last foster mother, Nana Kate, she tried to get more information for me, but all they had was what was in the box they found me in. There was an address label on the box that said "Birdsville". Nothing else.'

'What does that mean?' Phoebe asked, excitement building. 'That she was born here? Or came from here? What?'

Charli shook her head. 'I asked that. There was no other information. So, I started to save up to come here and ask.'

'And the locket?'

'I've had it with me all my life.' Her gaze searched Phoebe's. 'Do you know something about it? Have you seen it before?'

Phoebe's mouth felt dry but she was also aware that she needed to be careful not to raise hopes that could be dashed. 'I might have.'

Charli looked at Scarlet and then Phoebe. 'I wanted to find if I had any family in case something happened to me like to my mum. For Brianna. Before she was born. So she wouldn't be alone.'

Scarlet nodded, encouraging her to go on.

'So, I asked Luke, who'd been in foster care with me, to drive me here.'

Phoebe's heart squeezed for the young woman who had had so little. Been so alone. The opposite to her, Phoebe McFadden, who had a dad who loved her and Scarlet's family too. She'd thrown it all away for eighteen years for what? Hurt pride and anger with her dad for something he hadn't even done. She didn't deserve her family, not like Charli did. She would make it up to them, she would. But she'd faded out on the conversation and pulled herself back.

Charli was saying, 'The first day I came, we went to the pub. When I was leaving the bar, I saw a photo on the way out. On the wall. This lady had a locket just like mine. I saw the locket in the picture. And I've just been waiting to see who I could ask.'

Charli scrolled through her photos on her phone. Phoebe could see there were lots of Brianna already. Her finger stopped on one further back. 'Do you know who this is?'

Phoebe's breath caught. She looked and there she was. Her mother. She nodded.

But Charli had rushed on. 'I saw the photo and then the locket. I thought the locket looked like my locket and I thought . . .' She swallowed. 'I thought I might look a bit like the lady in the picture.'

Phoebe struggled for words. It seemed easier and also harder than she thought it would be. There was her own mother as a young woman, more than thirty years ago. Her mother really *did* look like Charli.

Phoebe had always taken more after her father, but Charli was all Celine. She leaned over and pulled the picture frame from the counter where she'd put it face down. She turned it to Charli so she could see.

It wasn't the same photo, but it was the same woman and the same locket. Or it looked like the same locket. The one her mother's mother had passed on.

Charli's eyes turned huge. She whispered, 'Do you know who she is?'

'Yes. That's Celine McFadden.'

'McFadden? Like you and Scarlet?' Her eyes opened wider. 'What are you saying? Are we related?'

Phoebe glanced at Scarlet, who watched them both, her face softer than Phoebe had ever seen it. She turned back and didn't quite answer Charli's question. Instead, she said, 'I was told my mother died when I was five in a car accident on the way to Charleville.' She shrugged. 'This time home I found out that she'd just left, instead of dying, left my dad and me for another life, and asked my dad to lie to me.'

Charli opened her mouth, but Phoebe held up her hand. 'One sec. But my dad discovered she did die later in childbirth, when I was seventeen, which I also found out recently. My dad thought the baby died too.'

Charli sniffed and whispered, 'Maybe she didn't. The baby, I mean.'

Phoebe smiled at her, tears in her own eyes. 'My mother asked my dad for money for gambling debts. And maybe for the baby. Which I guess could have been you. What do you think?'

Charli rubbed her eyes, barely breathing. Her hand was tight against her chest with the locket squeezed in her fist. 'You think we could be half-sisters?'

Very gently Phoebe said, 'It's possible.'

'You two.' Scarlet rolled her eyes. 'Not possible.' She shook her head at them both. 'Probable. It's probable. Idiots. You look the bloody same. We need to talk to Rusty. We'll get a DNA test when we can arrange it, but that's for the future if you want it. Let's go wake your baby, Charli, and we'll all go across to ask Phoebe's dad. I want this settled before my wedding.'

Phoebe and Charli looked at her in surprise. Phoebe spluttered, half-laughing, but also happy with the release of the terrible tension that had built up. 'This is not about you, Bridezilla.'

'Yes, it is.' Scarlet didn't look abashed. 'I need my new cousin and her daughter at the wedding. And it's this afternoon.'

Chapter Forty-two

Gloria

Gloria opened the door to three young women and a baby. There were similarities between all of them.

Gloria had been studying photos that Phoebe had of Celine and she could see a lot of Celine in Charli. And some in Phoebe as well.

She smiled at the young women and stepped back, knowing what this was all about. Somehow, no idea how, Rusty hadn't been introduced to Charli, and she suspected he was in for a surprise.

She watched his face intently as he first set eyes on the girl. Saw him breathe in deeply in shock. Even heard the whispered, 'Oh, my.' And her heart ached for him because she just knew he'd end up feeling guilty he hadn't known about Charli, which wasn't his fault.

'Dad,' Phoebe said into the suddenly quiet room, 'this is Charli.'

Charli stood stiffly, shy and uncomfortable, with her head down. After a poke from Scarlet she lifted her chin. 'Hello, Mr McFadden.'

'You better call me Rusty.' His smile was tentative and awkward as well, and his voice soft. 'You certainly have the look of Celine.'

Charli reached up and lifted the silver chain over her neck and handed it to him. 'The locket they said was my mother's.'

He took it carefully in his work-roughened hand and looked at her eyes, looked at the locket. Looked at her eyes again then put his other hand over the top of the watch casing to rub them together. Then he pressed his thumb in a certain place.

It popped open to the clock. 'It's the same,' he said. 'Same watch. See this little bit here?' He pointed with the tip of one finger. 'I had to solder that on when it broke. Welcome to the family, Charli.'

He shook his head in amazement and looked at Phoebe. 'Looks like you've got a sister.' Looked at Scarlet. 'And you another cousin.'

'I don't suppose you'd be my stepdad?' Charli said, and Rusty's face flushed with delight. 'I'd be honoured.'

He looked back at Charli and held out his arms. 'Welcome to the family, little one,' and there were tears in his eyes. Gloria blinked back her own tears. 'And we get to be step-grandparents too.' Everyone laughed.

'Right then, excellent,' said Scarlet. 'Now we need to find you a dress for the wedding.'

Chapter Forty-three

Phoebe

Phoebe, Scarlet and two girls from the pub finished decorating the community centre for the wedding later that morning. Charli had wanted to come but Brianna had been fussing and she had only made it right at the end. The baby had slept through the walk down in her pram.

The area was still hung with fairy lights from the previous Thursday, which were ready to shine in the warm night air, but today they'd pinned paper flowers everywhere they could to make it bridal. A host of paper daisies caught the sunlight as they ran up and down every standing structure. Large quantities of real flowers were problematic in Birdsville, unless flown in, but the paper ones looked lovely, and the few fresh ones were a community effort – kindly donated from now denuded gardens. And there were pots of Minnie Daisies from the desert, which Charli seemed particularly fond of.

Kelvin as caterer had been a worry, depending on which day Charli's release from hospital fell on, but with the three safely back in Birdsville yesterday, the chef was on.

The girls from the pub had lined the white plastic chairs up in two rows ready for the ceremony, with a borrowed carpet runner down the centre and a small table with flowers to the side with the register ready to sign.

At five o'clock Phoebe stepped out of her room, draped in a Grecian style gown of sapphire blue, the hue of an outback sky: Scarlet's chosen bridesmaid colour. The warm breeze brushed her free shoulder and promised at least a zephyr of coolness for the late afternoon of Scarlet's long-anticipated wedding.

Now all Phoebe had to do was ensure the bride arrived on time, though since Scarlet's parents had landed and were also in the house, that task would be easier.

She'd checked and the flying priest had also landed safely.

Charli had whispered shyly that she'd already emailed him about Brianna's christening, which made Phoebe smile. Seemed her shy half-sister could make things happen when she wanted them to. Just like Scarlet.

The only two matching vehicles in town were both red four-wheel drives polished to within an inch of their lives and belonging to Phoebe. Now, both sported white ribbons from windshields to front bumpers and Rusty stood waiting by the Desert Lizard to drive the bridesmaid's vehicle.

Scarlet's dad, Neville, waited by the later model cruiser with his daughter and wife in the back seat. Once everyone was settled, they drove around town twice, to absorb the value of all the work that had been put into preparing the vehicles, as the venue sat only one street away from the houses.

While they drove, Phoebe experienced a rush of gratitude that she'd had the time to settle into the world of her childhood before the event. In fact, she couldn't bear to think about what she would have missed out on if she'd decided not to come home. So much had happened and none of it expected.

Reuniting with her dad.

Working with Gloria.

Meeting Charli – she had a sister, for goodness' sake.

Even the races and watching Dad's horse win – though they'd missed the end – had been a highlight.

Dear Scarlet's wedding had given her so much that was wonderful.

And of course, if she hadn't come for this celebration today, she would never have run into Atticus again. But she tamped down the burbling excitement left over from the last few evenings in Atticus's police residence. The man made her feel like a princess in a fairy tale, except he hadn't taken her to bed – but she'd get him there before she left. And she didn't want to think about leaving on this happy day.

Everything had been brilliant, though she hadn't had a chance to talk to Atticus about Charli's birth and the identity resolution at her dad's this morning. And she really wanted to share that with him. Weird how important that was. But again, for later.

Finally, the two-car cavalcade stopped outside the community centre, greeted by the applause of the guests waiting for them to arrive.

The white ribbons fluttered in the warm afternoon breeze, the red paint gleamed, and Phoebe glanced at her tiny dress watch as her dad held the door open for her. They were fashionably late, but they were here.

Uncle Neville helped Scarlet from the car and she looked amazing in her long white off-the-shoulder gown, her tiny veil framing her face, and her red hair falling in sun-burnished ringlets.

Through the gate Phoebe could see George as he stood at the end of the carpet, strong and wiry, waiting calmly for his bride, his eyes alight with anticipation.

Beside him stood his employer and friend, Lex McKay. Lex was a quiet powerhouse of a man but also a loyal friend to many and handy with his helicopter as well, Phoebe thought, remembering her first and second days back in Birdsville, when Lex's helicopter had brought medical help. More people to be grateful for.

Lex and his mother were such a part of the community, even though they didn't live in town – though Blanche, a force who championed the women in the outback, had taken a step back since Lex had married his darling Eve. Blanche only stayed part-time at Diamantina Downs now, one of their biggest stations, out near Red Sand and Windorah.

The music swelled and Phoebe began the procession, catching the eye of the handsome local constable as he watched her from among the waiting friends and family. Their eyes met and held, and she felt her cheeks warm. She hoped she knew where she'd be sleeping tonight.

The service was over in twenty minutes; the crowd cheered, George picked Scarlet up in his arms and kissed her thoroughly, and carried her up the aisle to the applause of the gathering.

When he put her down Scarlet's cheeks shone flushed and delighted, and Phoebe had never seen her cousin so beamingly joyful.

Most of the guests moved inside for the refreshments while the bridal party photos were taken, but that part was finally over. Thank goodness. Now Phoebe really wanted to find Atticus.

There. Leaning against the wall, right where they'd disappeared down that path the other night for their first kiss, and there was no doubt he was waiting for her.

As she moved towards him Blanche McKay touched her shoulder. 'Phoebe McFadden. Good to see you back.'

Phoebe stopped. Smiled politely. 'Blanche. I saw you there. Lex looked very fine in his best man clothes. How is Eve?'

'Due very soon. Twins, you know. We're very excited.'

Phoebe smiled. Imagined that. Busy times. 'Congratulations.'

Blanche nodded politely and got to the point. 'Lex said you did an excellent job at that crash site a couple of weeks ago. I understand you're an experienced midwife and emergency nurse now?'

Nothing to do with the twins then. 'Ah, yes.'

'Administration duties in Adelaide. Big hospital, is it?'

Good grief. It sounded like Blanche was conducting a job interview. 'Adelaide Central. I'm the evening and night nursing supervisor.'

'Thought so.' Blanche nodded decisively. 'We'll need you here in town, soon: any chance of moving back?'

'I'm not sure.' Phoebe blinked. Now why had she said that. She'd always been nervous around Blanche but she hadn't seen the woman since she was a kid. 'What I mean is I wasn't thinking of it.'

Blanche nodded as if she could accept that. For now. 'At least it's not a definite no.'

Lex stepped up to them and put an arm on his mother's arm. 'Hello, Phoebe. Nice to see you again. Mother. Phoebe doesn't need the third degree here. She's bridesmaid.'

Blanche's brow furrowed. 'I can see that. Just sounding her out, Lex. Opportunities and all that.'

Lex smiled and gently suggested he had someone for her to meet but before they moved away, she added, 'Do consider coming back. Gloria is an amazing woman, but she deserves a break.'

Lex kept walking. Blanche looked over her shoulder. 'I understand she and your father have plans.' A stern look. 'They deserve time, and this town deserves skilled medical care.' Then she was gone.

Phoebe stared after her. At her side Atticus was laughing. He must have overheard Blanche's – what was it? – job proposal? Entreaty? Coercion?

'You can laugh. You weren't held in her thousand-yard stare. She makes me nervous.'

Atticus took her hand and kissed it. 'I can see I've been going about this all wrong. Discussions aren't needed. I should have just told you we're meant to be together.'

She turned to look at him and saw the amusement in his gaze. Plus warmth and something deeper, hotter, more serious. Something that made her breath catch and her heart pound.

But he just smiled and tucked her hand into the crook of his elbow and turned her towards the festivities. 'Let's go enjoy the wedding until you can leave without offending anyone.' And more quietly, 'Then we can go back to my place and continue this discussion, because it's only five days until you are supposed to depart.'

Chapter Forty-four

Atticus

Atticus unlocked the door to his house and pushed it open for Phoebe to go in front of him. He knew she'd hoped they would've slept together by now, but he wanted to make sure he could make her happy, be everything she needed, before he broke his own heart afterwards in case she drove away.

He wanted her. He'd decided that the first day. She was the one. But he wanted her to be happy. That was it. End of story.

And this was her town so he wasn't having anyone talking about his Phoebe unless they had concrete plans for a shared future.

He'd just been too gutless to ask her for commitment. But tonight. He'd ask tonight.

Of course, if she knew that was his reasoning for the sex drought she'd tell him she'd look after her own reputation, thank you. He knew that, but he couldn't risk falling even further into love without knowing what was in store. Though she'd certainly made holding out challenging. He smiled at that thought.

These last four evenings they'd discussed dreams, pet loves, pet hates, even future kids: she wanted two; he wanted six. She'd laughed. He'd been serious.

He'd listened to how she enjoyed her job, its trials and benefits; and he'd told her about his life as a police officer. His family. His great childhood until things went wrong. And even the way that load seemed lighter with Phoebe in his life.

He was in this for the long haul, and he wasn't blowing it by jumping into sex before she knew who he was and what he was offering.

But he didn't think he could wait much longer, especially with her glued to his side like she was now, pulling him into the house.

He spun her and she flattened against him, lifting her mouth in an undeniable invitation. God, he loved kissing her. He loved everything about her.

He loved this woman so much, so fast. So overwhelmingly. He needed to do it tonight. Talk before . . .

His mouth met hers and the world disappeared for a while.

In the end all he said was, 'You leave on Tuesday. Three nights . . .' And somehow, they'd ended up sprawled on his big bed and it was as if they both were filled with such urgency and impending loss that any semblance of restraint had been swept away.

That night, Phoebe didn't leave.

It was a long, glorious night of insatiable activity and when Atticus finally woke the next morning it was to the feeling of Phoebe's fingertips spidering up his belly.

He was dreaming. Fabulous dream. And then he wasn't dreaming. 'Good morning.' His voice sounded deep even to him, filled with memories and satisfaction, and maybe a little male pride that he'd satisfied his woman so much and so loudly he was glad the police station was on its own block. 'Great morning.' He reached down to cover her fingers. 'What are you doing?'

She crawled up his side and smiled sleepily into his face. 'Substituting. You know I like to go for a walk in the morning.'

He laughed, scooped her up and rolled her over and on top of him. He loved this woman. He just needed to say it. But nothing was said at all for a very long time.

Later, they showered together, then had to shower again, taking a very long time cleaning each other very thoroughly, and by the time Phoebe let herself out of his house to walk home they both knew it would be all over town.

Somehow, neither of them cared about that. But he still hadn't asked her.

By lunchtime he was a mess. He hadn't spoken of the future. What if Phoebe McFadden left Birdsville without a commitment to him? It would be like before and he'd lose her for another two decades.

Sadly, he still had no idea what Phoebe thought about the idea of settling down – because that's what he wanted. And yes, he knew there was only one way to find out, but what if she said no?

He assumed she liked sharing space with him: she'd come over every night that week, and on his side, he'd missed her as soon as she left. So the dilemma was: act or wait. The choice being to sit in his lonely police station and tell himself, but not her, that two weeks wasn't enough – and watch her go. Or put himself out there.

The first inkling of support came from Gloria; he'd been invited to lunch with her and Rusty on Sunday to meet Charli properly and be introduced to her as Phoebe's stepsister. He met Phoebe there, and the two of them studiously avoided physical contact so soon after their incredible night together.

Phoebe took Charli out to have a proper look at the Desert Lizard, still wearing white ribbons from the day before, with the idea of giving the vehicle to Charli and Brianna as a safe vehicle for them and a loving home for the second car Phoebe didn't really need. While they were gone Gloria took Atticus aside and whispered, 'You love Phoebe.' It wasn't a question.

'Absolutely.'

'If you're that sure – and take it from someone who has procrastinated – don't waste the years. Make a stand and ask her for the commitment.' Then she slipped away.

She must have said something to Phoebe's dad because the older man came next, prevaricated a bit about the weather and then muttered, 'I should have asked Gloria to marry me the day I knew my wife had died. Almost missed the boat, nearly twenty years later.'

Atticus took the olive branch as he assumed it was intended. 'So . . . I have your permission to court your daughter?'

The older man laughed. 'Why do you policemen always end up in court?'

He hadn't meant it as a pun, and really it wasn't funny the way he was feeling right now, but Rusty was amused. Goes to show how far his sense of humour had departed. 'I want to marry her.'

'I know. You got my blessing, not that you need it.' Rusty grinned at him. 'The worst she can say is no, and you can always try again later.'

Surprised, Atticus wished he could smile back at that idea, but Rusty went on. 'I reckon you and Phoebe are a good match. Great. And to be selfish, while you stay in Birdsville, I like to think she's got a future here, too.' He shrugged. 'I'd get to see more of her.'

Back-handed compliment much. 'Um. Thanks?'

Phoebe's dad shrugged. 'She's been happy here the last few weeks and part of that is you. Time's ticking away for Phoebe as well, and I'd like more grandkids.'

Atticus smiled at that odd addition until he got it – he was impressed by the 'more'. 'Charli's baby is your grandchild?'

'My word she is.'

That afternoon at the pub, when he was called away to talk to the proprietor about a tourist's delayed arrival, Kelvin pulled him aside. 'You gonna try to hold onto Phoebe?'

Did everyone know? Of course they did. It was Birdsville. 'That's my plan.'

'You got one?' Kelvin's brows went up. 'A plan?' His hands went out. Eyebrows waggled. 'You know?'

Atticus could feel the stress building just talking about it. 'Not really.' Though he knew what he wanted. Unexpectedly the words formed. 'I want to take her out to dinner, wine her and dine her, then propose before she leaves.'

'Ballsy.' Kelvin inclined his head in respect. Thinking. 'Maybe I could help?'

Atticus wished he would. He'd take any help he could get.

Kelvin leaned in. 'When I worked in an Italian restaurant, I knew this couple.' He sighed beatifically at the memory. Went on reminiscing. 'Liam and Lisa. The bloke took her out for dinner. They used to go there a lot, so she didn't suspect it was special.'

Kelvin raised an eyebrow and Atticus got it. Okay. A surprise. It would be that.

'Anyway, he got the staff to play a special song of theirs once they'd eaten, and suddenly the waitress brings out some flowers and two glasses of Champagne.'

He could organise that.

'Course,' Kelvin said ruminatively, 'they'd been going together a lot longer than you two.'

Yeah, yeah. Anyone had been together longer than he and Phoebe, but still, he'd known her for years . . . It was their two-week reuniting anniversary coming up tomorrow night. The night before she left. His stomach sank.

Kelvin was on a roll. 'Anyway, this bloke – Liam – once the flowers and Champagne were there, he gets up, goes down on one knee, and pulls out a box with a ring in it. Even had a cheat sheet stuck on the back of the box so he got the words right.' He sighed romantically. 'Went over like a lark, it did. Don't remember all the words but it ended with, "Will you marry me?"'

Well, of course. But . . . He waited for the punchline. 'What did she say?'

Kelvin flicked his fingers out theatrically. 'She loved it. She was crying.' He thought for a minute. 'Actually I think the first thing she said was, "Are you kidding me?" Which got a laugh. But then she said, "Yes."'

Atticus could picture that. There was something brave and romantic, and beautiful, about that story and he knew, without a doubt, he wanted something like it. Something ballsy. And here . . . here certainly was a plan.

He wanted Phoebe to remember his declaration for the rest of her life. Hopefully while spending said life with him.

It was ballsy. Kelvin had it right about that. If he did put himself out there, it may as well be in a big way. Hell, the occasion called for a big statement. Phoebe deserved big.

'You reckon you could help me with that at the pub dining room tomorrow night? We have a song.' He had sung her that Piña Colada one. He could croon a little. No idea about flowers before tomorrow night. 'The Champagne?'

'No problem,' Kelvin said. 'Totally on board. Give me the name of the music and I can arrange that.'

'Sure. Book it in. Flowers?'

'Scarlet could arrange flowers in a desert.' Kelvin looked thoughtful at that. They were in a desert. 'Anyway, she can. And the boss has Champagne.'

It felt almost feasible and some of the panic that had dogged him since the morning settled. 'I need a ring. Or at least a token ring she could wear when she goes back.' Crikey, he was going to do this. 'If she says yes.'

Kelvin patted his shoulder. 'She'll say yes.' Nice to know he felt positive.

'Know anywhere in town I could buy jewellery?'

'Rusty has rings in his opal collection. Doesn't usually sell them, but for his daughter . . .' Kelvin shrugged with a twinkle in his eye. 'Reckon you'd get a beauty at the right price.'

*

The next night, when he ushered Phoebe to the table for two he'd booked at the pub's restaurant – he knew it was his table because they'd written his name on a big sign with a whiteboard marker – and he winced at the way every other table was packed. With locals. All looking his way. Smirking.

Oh yeah, word had got around. He'd wanted splashy; he hadn't wanted notoriety. But apparently the two went together in Birdsville. Chin up. He'd have to grin and bear it. And so would Phoebe. That had better not be a problem.

They sat, ordered. Phoebe talked, smiled at the other people, who all seemed to find an excuse to come over and chat, and dinner took forever.

Oblivious to his plans, Phoebe sparkled like the stone he had in his pocket. She looked far too beautiful, and far too happy, for somebody leaving him the next day. Although she had pressed his hand a couple of times during the no-doubt delicious meal he couldn't remember – he'd had to wipe his palm because he was sweating bullets.

Funny how uncomfortably over-warm it felt in the air-conditioned room. He couldn't recall the topics they'd covered, should have been paying more attention, but his heart thumped along as he mentally rehearsed what he planned to say.

Finally, she put down her knife and fork and sat back. Replete. With a quizzical smile, she raised her brows at their empty glasses and said, 'Did you want another drink?'

He looked up and caught Kelvin's eye. The music faded out then quickly faded in again. New song. The Piña Colada one she'd changed the words to.

She smiled. He hummed until the last of the backpackers, Emily, a gorgeous Pom who thankfully hadn't left town yet after the end of the tourist season, crossed the room with a wrapped bouquet of flowers in one hand and a tray with two glasses of Champagne balanced perfectly in the other.

She looked so much classier than if Kelvin had done the job.

Phoebe took her glass. 'What's the occasion?' she asked, and that was his cue. Showtime.

Atticus sucked in a breath and, pretty sure there was a little more colour than usual in his face, he launched into his carefully prepared words. 'Tonight is our anniversary.'

Phoebe stared, and laughed. 'Heading for three weeks? Yes. I do believe you're right.'

'Two, nearly three *amazing* weeks,' he clarified. 'Incredible weeks.'

Now Phoebe had colour in her cheeks, too.

He went on. 'Soon you'll be gone. And a long way away. I just want to make sure you don't forget me.'

'I don't think I'll be doing that,' she murmured.

'I'd like to make sure.' He stood up. Cleared his throat. The room went silent. Crickets even. 'In front of all these,' he added dryly, 'very nosy people, I have something to say.'

The uninvited audience laughed. Some clapped. Phoebe's beautiful violet eyes widened. Her hand came up to cover her mouth.

Gently he pulled her fingers away so he could see her face and cleared his throat again. 'Dearest Phoebe. From the first moment I saw you on the Birdsville Track saving lives, you stole my breath.' Even now he could capture that memory so clearly in his mind. His Phoebe 'vision splendid': so unexpectedly striking, her eyes so intense and direct. Yep, he'd fallen.

He smiled. 'The second time we were driving out to Poeppel Corner for a rescue, and the trip never felt so short. You told me you were leaving as soon as the wedding was over, and even then, I knew I didn't want you to go. Ever.'

'It was a fun trip,' she said quietly, watching him warily, glancing surreptitiously at the crowd of unashamed eavesdroppers.

He really wasn't sure if this was going well or not. Still. Too late to back out now.

Pushed on. 'The third time, when we powered up Big Red in your Desert Lizard, I fell deeper.' The song played and the words inspired him, so he added, 'Even though we haven't made love in the dunes at midnight like in the song . . .' a few hoots came from the corner of the room – Scarlet, of course – but he finished clearly '. . . you stole my heart.'

Her gaze had locked on his and suddenly it was easier. Just her and him. Reading each other in perfect honesty. The room faded away and there was only Phoebe.

He pulled the hastily borrowed ring box holding the newly purchased ring from his pocket, crouched in front of her and went down on one knee.

She gasped.

'Phoebe McFadden.' He smiled at her wide eyes. 'With your father's permission, and just so you know I'm not rushing you . . .'

That got a few laughs from the peanut gallery.

'. . . I'm offering a longer engagement than our courtship . . .' He opened the box and flashed the glorious green and blue opal ring her way. 'But in the not-too-distant future, Phoebe, my love, will you marry me?'

She stared at him, down at the ring and then back at him. Then to his immense relief she held out her hand for him to slide the ring on. 'Yes! Please. Absolutely.' Then Phoebe threw herself at him and he almost fell over.

Later that night, after a pretty amazing impromptu engagement party enjoyed by what felt like all of Birdsville's reduced population, they were back in his bed in the police residence.

'So, how long were you thinking of making this extended engagement you promised me?'

'At least a month,' he said lazily as he stroked her neck. 'It takes thirty days to sort the paperwork.'

'A whole month? Lengthy. You have been planning.'

'There's more.' He leaned in and kissed her. 'I was thinking a celebrant, and Big Red at sunrise. Wedding breakfast at the pub.'

She laughed softly. 'After all the organisation of Scarlet's wedding that sounds perfect.'

They took a small break for athletic exercise, and then Phoebe said, 'I'll go to Adelaide as planned tomorrow and put in my notice. When I pack up my flat, I'll be back.'

'I can get leave. Would you like a hand?' He rested his fingers on her hip. 'I could borrow a trailer.'

Her fingers trailed. 'Where would you get a trailer?'

He smiled and the words were soft as he nuzzled her neck. 'Lex McKay phoned and offered it tonight. It's a lovely Gooseneck he left behind in town after the races.'

She stretched her throat, giving him access. 'Now that's an offer I can't refuse.'

'Mmhmm,' he purred against her satin skin. 'I'm planning on making a lot of those.'

She pulled back until she could see him and her nose rubbed his. 'Including the one you made so heroically tonight?'

He laughed. 'Can't take full credit. I had coaching.'

He watched her mentally scan the people of her acquaintance. 'I don't believe it. Who in town could possibly give you coaching?'

It was funny. 'Kelvin. I'm having him as my best man.'

She laughed out loud. 'Kelvin the cook? Charli's Kelvin? This whole day has been crazy.'

He had never been happier. 'I'm crazy for you. That first day you backed out of the wreck with the best backside ever.' His hand slid over said backside.

She stopped his hand. 'I'm serious. Do you know what you're getting into? I can be headstrong. Stubborn. What if we fight?'

'Your dad wants more grandchildren. Make-up sex.'

She laughed and he kissed her, and said seriously, 'I have no doubt there will be fights, arguments, door slamming.' He grinned at her. 'My wilful, wonderful, Birdsville Bride. I also have no doubt that the making up will be worth everything.'

Chapter Forty-five

Phoebe

Two years later . . .

Birdsville has its first twin play group, Phoebe thought.

Technically, it was really a lunch to welcome Charli home after the birth of her and Kelvin's baby boys and a chance for the three couples to compare notes. There's a lot of room for sharing experience with twins, Phoebe thought, with a smile. If it hadn't been for Eve . . .

Lex McKay's wife, Eve, had often come across for the lunch with their two-year-old sons, Thomas and Toby, blond bruisers, both good-natured and calm like their mother, and the eldest child, at four a mischievous replica of his father.

Phoebe couldn't be grateful enough for her friendship with the other midwife, and their comradery had grown into a warm and wonderful relationship from the moment she'd been diagnosed with a twin pregnancy herself and asked for advice.

The two women spoke on the phone often when they couldn't get together because of the distances. Eve had learned to fly Lex's helicopter and she dropped in when she could. Phoebe was thinking about getting her pilot's licence too, but she might have to wait now.

Phoebe and Atticus's darling twins, Patrick and Yasmin, had just celebrated their first birthday, and she could hear her love saying to Kelvin, 'I did say three lots of twins was fine instead of six pregnancies, but I think we might go a little slower. Ask for help, is all I can say.'

Lex laughed. 'True story. Wait till they start to walk.'

The corner of the pub dining room had acquired a play pen, with five little people currently inside. Phoebe's two were still fascinated by new toys while the McKay twins and Brianna were throwing said toys out. Charli and Kelvin had flown back in last week and this was their first outing with Brianna and the twins. 'She is so proud of her babies,' Charli was saying, watching her eldest daughter with pride.

Phoebe felt so proud of her sister. Charli looked remarkably unworried as she rocked the same pram she'd had with Brianna with two little bodies sleeping inside. There was enough room on the tiny mattress for the moment. Kelvin had added extensions to their house.

The three fathers carried ice-clinking lemon squash in tall glasses to their lady loves and Phoebe appreciated that each man's expression held a very similar, adoring serenity as he admired his family.

She smiled at Atticus.

'You look beautiful,' he said quietly into her ear. He was such a romantic. 'As always,' he added, and she put her hand up and touched his fingers.

'Thank you. And there's something I need to tell you about that second set of twins.'

Book Club Notes

1. Phoebe hasn't gone home to Birdsville for nearly twenty years and has barely spoken with her father. What do you think she lost in not making an effort to address the conflict with Rusty?

2. Have you ever lived or visited somewhere as remote as Birdsville? What was that like?

3. Do you think financial pressures or internal expectations are driving Gloria to keep working? What challenges does she face in retirement?

4. Why do you think Charli is so driven to find out about her mother?

5. Do you think Rusty did the right thing in keeping the truth about the money from Phoebe? Why or why not?

6. Phoebe worries about the age difference between her and Atticus. Discuss whether or not you think this is important and how it might affect their relationship.

7. 'Charli didn't believe in luck.' Discuss whether you think luck plays a role in Charli's search for family and the events that unfold when she arrives in Birdsville.

8. How do you think Phoebe's and Atticus's respective pasts affect how they approach their blossoming relationship? What differences do you see between them?

9. What are your favourite romance tropes in *Back to Birdsville*?

10. Scarlet's manner is no-nonsense and she is quite abrupt at times. How does she show her softer side throughout the story?

11. Do you think Charli and Kelvin are a good match? Why or why not?

12. Who would you cast in a film version of this story as Phoebe, Atticus, Charli and Gloria?

Acknowledgements

Thank you so much, dear reader, for choosing my book. I've wanted to write this novel for two years, ever since I read a fascinating article about the Mailman of the Birdsville Track. Intrigued, I followed that up with the full audiobook story and then *Back of Beyond*, the 1954 movie starring the real Tom Kruse mailman. I read the wonderful memoir by Neale McShane, *The Birdsville Cop*, and *Birdsville* by Evan McHugh. Yep, I was inspired. Now I wanted to see the town for myself. Plus, I could see Phoebe's story there.

Geographically, Birdsville is in the middle of Australia. I live midway between Sydney and Brisbane, and it's still over twenty-two non-stop hours' drive from me. Of course, then I would have to decide how long I want to drive each day, and therefore if it's going to take three or five sleeps to get there – and that's one way. You can see why I decided to fly.

Once there, you can be forgiven for thinking there's nothing in Birdsville apart from a pub, a couple of hot streets, the September Birdsville Races, and the Big Red Bash music festival in July. You'd be mistaken.

ACKNOWLEDGEMENTS

I flew in with my trusty travel buddy and indie editor, Bronwyn Jameson, to see the Birdsville Races on a two-day tour in and out, spending a grand total of six hours in town in thirty-eight-degree heat. Four of those were spent on the racetrack for the Birdsville Cup – which was definitely fun and amusing with all the costumes we saw – and two hours wandering around town and sitting in the cool of the pub.

Yet, when I sat down to write this book, I found it difficult to authentically describe what I'd read, taken note of, and seen so briefly.

Me to long-suffering husband: 'I have to go back to Birdsville.'

Ian: 'You said you didn't have to go back.' Incredulity. I know. The town is remote.

Me: 'It's not authentic. I can't feel it. I need to talk to people without the races.'

So, I drove to Brisbane, which took five hours, and flew 'Back to Birdsville' again. You've read about the trip through Gloria's eyes, and it's six hours with five landings with, if you're lucky, the wonderful Vanessa the flight attendant – her real name – looking after you.

I stayed on my own for four days at the pub, where I fell in love with Birdsville and the people, just like my character Phoebe did when she came home. I talked to Tom at the bakery, went on the Big Red Tour with Alex to hear about the history of the town and the late Dusty Miller and his camel pies (mentioned in the book) and saw the sandhills and the sunset.

I talked to laconic Senior Constable Stephan Pursell, Birdsville policeman, who helpfully assisted in correcting my logistical mistakes; the men and women working the pub bar; and

Thiwi Rowlands, who makes fabulous coffee at Karrawa Wirinya Coffee. Thiwi drove me out to the Waddi trees on the Birdsville-Bedourie Road. In the book, I repositioned the Waddi trees onto the Birdsville Track at the first accident in the book – my apologies – but I wanted to mention them because I loved the fact they are so rare and ancient. I also didn't wish to distress the traditional custodians of the land by imagining damage to these ancient trees. Plus, Phoebe needed to come from Adelaide via Marree, like the Mailman of the Birdsville Track.

When Thiwi showed me the Waddi, she told me they'd stood there for between five hundred and a thousand years. She called them the old men of the desert. I love that title.

In the book I've also mentioned Rob, inspired by Thiwi's father, Don Rowlands, the Park Ranger, a respected elder of the Wangkangurru people, whom I was lucky enough to meet briefly, but I used the facts from *The Birdsville Cop* to acknowledge him in my own book as one of the real experts on the area.

Of course, I visited the Birdsville Primary Health Centre and was blessed to meet Sue Wilkes, RN.RM. The all-around amazing, wonderful nurse who, while way younger than Gloria, was my inspiration for both Phoebe and Gloria and is a champion of the sick and injured in such a remote setting. I don't think she has any idea how remarkable she is. She also gave me the hint about the sports bra for corrugated roads, which made me laugh.

Sue has read the first draft, helped me with plausibility and mistakes in the book, and any new mistakes are absolutely all mine. She introduced me to RFDS nurse Jo and pilot Ben when they came the next day, and we chatted about possible scenarios, past retrieval logistics and all sorts of fun stuff. Sue also facilitated me being introduced to the wonderful Nell Brook, matriarch of the Brook family, who invited me to morning tea. There I met her entrepreneur daughter, Jenna, Nell's husband, David, and several inspiring managers of the huge stations in the Brook holdings.

To me, the Brook family and their station managers are all outback heroes. They hold these enormous cattle stations in their capable and caring hands and yet are so aware of the pulse and needs of the community. Very much like my fictional Blanche McKay, but kinder, more welcoming and with way better social skills!

My Birdsville visit was a huge success for me. And I hope to make it back there one day – but I'll fly in, not drive.

Finally, I need to mention Atticus and his proposal. I was stumped about how I could make it as memorable as it deserved to be for two such lovely people as Atticus and Phoebe, when along came the true story of my friend Marg's son, Liam, and his heroically romantic restaurant proposal. That was it! Huge thanks and congrats to Liam and Lisa on their engagement and wedding plans for Melbourne Cup Day this year.

As always, I would love to thank the team at Penguin Random House. My awesome publisher, Ali Watts, my wonderful editor, Amanda Martin, who follows up all my questions, designer Louisa Maggio, Veronica Eze in audio and Anna Tidswell in publicity, who works so hard to let readers know my book is out in the world and waiting to be found. Thanks also to Kate O'Donnell and Vanessa Lanaway for your insight and polish.

Special appreciation to my travel buddy, first reader and super-savvy writer friend Bronwyn Jameson for your amazing input with that first draft. I do love your sense of humour in dealing with me. You are a great mate.

ACKNOWLEDGEMENTS

To all the reviewers who do such an amazing job of sharing their thoughts on my fiction, I thank you. Writers know the best chance of their work being read is through word-of-mouth recommendations and you share those words so beautifully.

I also would like to thank my so-savvy agent, Clare Forster, who is never too busy for me and is the person I turn to for career advice and as my sounding board. Thanks, Clare.

Thank you to my writing friends in RWAus and RWNZ, where I found our lovely Maytone group – special mention to Trish Morey, who always provides forward motion when I lose my way. To Jaye Ford/Janette Paul for being my sounding board when we're at retreat, and all the WWOW writers at lunches for motivation. And Annie Seaton who always says, 'You can do it,' when I'm running for a deadline.

Then there's my hero: my husband. No acknowledgement would be complete without the man who brings me back to earth and makes me laugh every day. Dearest Ian, my love, my best friend and my biggest fan – I am *your* biggest fan. Thank you.

All these people to write a book. That's what I love about writing – we give, we learn and we share so that we can create books that touch our readers, experience magic moments, and inspire the joy and satisfaction that comes from creating a story we love. I hope, dear reader, that you'll love *Back to Birdsville* and want to visit this amazing small town with the biggest heart. Our outback towns need you. Thank you for your wonderful support.
xx Fi

Powered by Penguin

Looking for more great reads, exclusive content and book giveaways?

Subscribe to our weekly newsletter.

Scan the QR code or visit penguin.com.au/signup